LIBRARY OF THE DAMNED

NOVELS BY JERI WESTERSON

Paranormal

BOOKE OF THE HIDDEN SERIES

Booke of the Hidden

Deadly Rising

Shadows in the Mist

The Darkest Gateway

MOONRISER WEREWOLF MYSTERIES

Moonrisers

Baying for Blood

THE ENCHANTER CHRONICLES

The Daemon Device

Clockwork Gypsy

Library of the Damned

Medieval Mysteries

THE CRISPIN GUEST MEDIEVAL NOIR MYSTERIES

Veil of Lies / Serpent in the Thorns / The Demon's Parchment

Troubled Bones / Blood Lance / Shadow of the Alchemist

Cup of Blood (a prequel) / The Silence of Stones / A Maiden Weeping

Season of Blood / The Deepest Grave / Traitor's Codex

Sword of Shadows / Spiteful Bones / The Deadliest Sin

Historical Fiction

Though Heaven Fall

Roses in the Tempest

Native Spirit, writing as Anne Castell

LGBTQ Mysteries

THE SKYLER FOXE MYSTERIES writing as Haley Walsh

Foxe Tail / Foxe Hunt / Out-Foxed

Foxe Den: A Holiday Collection / Foxefire / Desert Foxe

Foxe Den 2: Summer Vacation

Crazy Like A Foxe / Stone Cold Foxe/ A Very Merry Foxemas

LIBRARY OF THE DAMNED

JERI WESTERSON

BOOK THREE IN THE ENCHANTER CHRONICLES

ILLUSTRATED BY ROBERT CARRASCO

Dragua Press

This book is a work of fiction. Names, characters, places, and incidents are the products of the author's ridiculously amazing imagination or are used fictitiously. Any resemblance to actual persons, living or dead, is entirely coincidental. Unless those dead had *asked* to be part of this. You never know with dead people, do you?

Cover design by Mayhem Cover Creations

Book design by Jeri Westerson

Illustrations by Robert Carrasco

ISBN: 978-1-7356160-1-8

Sign up for my newsletters at JeriWesterson.com

Dragua Press
PO Box 799
Menifee, CA 92586

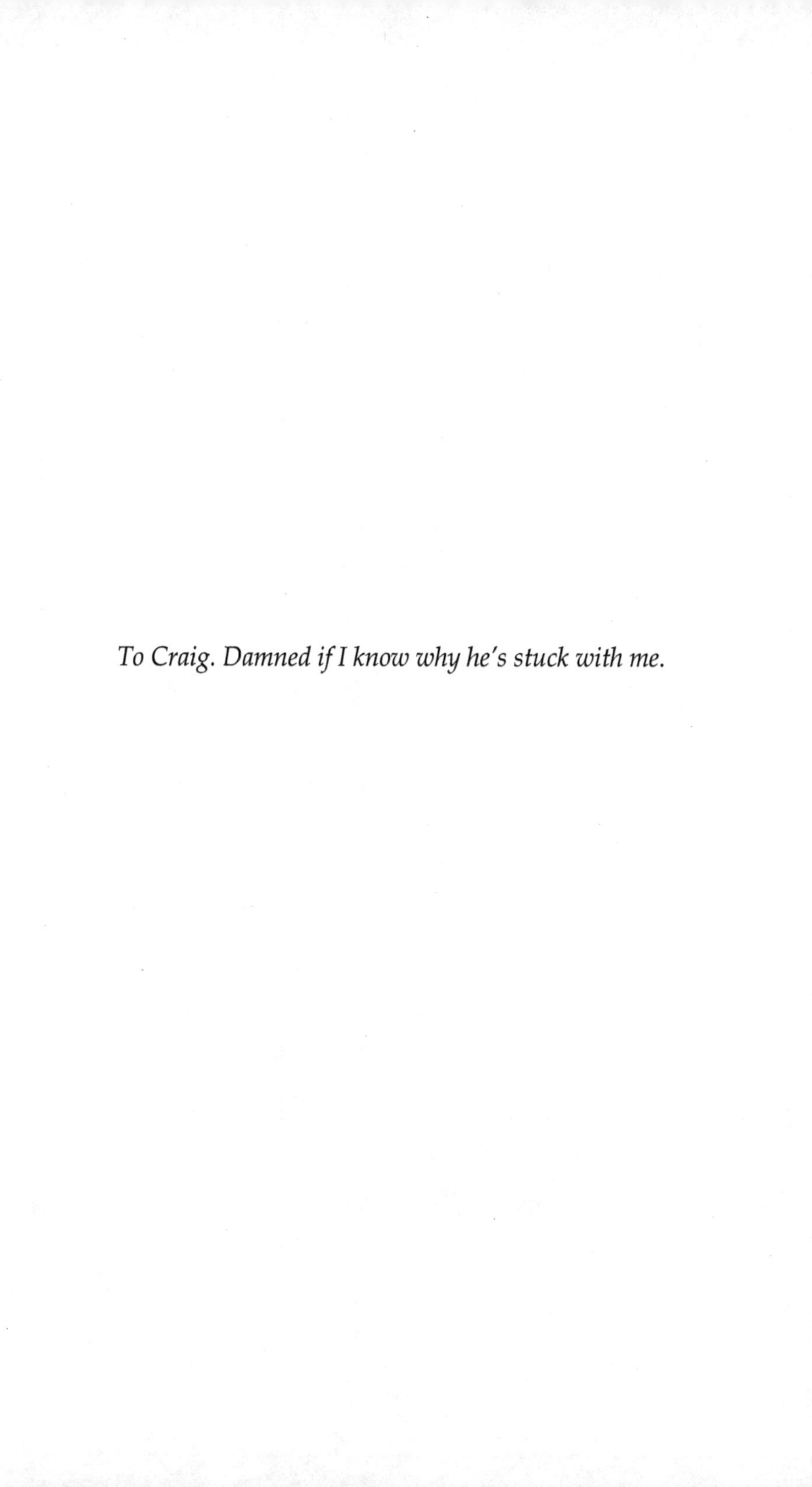

To Craig. Damned if I know why he's stuck with me.

Acknowledgements

Much thanks to Robert Carrasco for the amazing illustrations. I only wish I could have had you do more.

I also wish to extend my thanks to James La Salandra for his careful editing. It's my fault now if I change something. And thanks to my very creative cover designer Mayhem Cover Creations, because she really rocks. And much thanks to my audiobook narrator, Noah James Butler, because he is the true magician to put *his* voice in my head when I write these characters.

And finally, to my beloved husband who graces me with his support and encouragement and who reads it all first before it ever gets to you.

Thanks to you all!

Author's Note

This is the third and last book in the Enchanter Chronicles series, a gaslamp fantasy about the Great Enchanter Leopold Kazsmer and his intriguing collection of friends. It is advised to read the books in order to understand what the Gehenna is going on. If you come to *this* book first, you might be lost until you have read all that has come before. Well, there you are. Fair warning.

Also, as a reminder, a *daemon* is a good guy and a *demon* is a bad guy, though they are pronounced the same. Also, "Alignment Lines" or "Lines of Power" are what they called Ley Lines in this time period.

Glossary

Chuppah - Canopy used in Jewish Weddings, usually to be held outside under the sky.

Crawler - Beggars, usually women, too sick or weary to go begging, but who instead hang about in doorways or on steps in the area of St. Giles, London.

Finger-smith - A pickpocket.

Grenadiers - A specialist soldier first established in the seventeenth century for throwing grenades, and now traditionally a guard at Buckingham Palace.

Major-Domo - The chief steward of a large household or manor.

Tael - Chinese money/weight measurement exchange. Not exactly a coin, but its weight is the value. In 1840, the silver tael weighed about 40 grams.

Ulster Coat - Long overcoat with a short cape at the shoulders over the sleeves.

Wagtail - A prostitute.

Western China, 1884

"MINGLI!"

She heard the madam scream her name—as she always seemed to do. She was probably angry at her for biting off the earlobe of that awful client. He was greasy, his hands calloused, and his face scratchy with stubble. Mingli hadn't liked the way he'd pawed at her, even though she was supposed to accept it in the Lotus House.

She came to her uncle's brothel when she was ten, perhaps eleven. She didn't quite remember and, truly, it didn't matter. She worked in the kitchens and thought that was her lot…until she blossomed at fourteen, and that awakening was the cruelest of all. More cruel than knowing your father had sold you. More cruel than the way your uncle had leered at you when you were only a child and she was forced to strip before him to see if she had any deformities. She recalled every hurt and tallied them like a banker tallied coins.

Grunting farmers, sweating fishermen, rough soldiers. She tallied. She never forgot.

When she was a child, she had known so little of men. Now that she was sixteen, she knew far too much.

"Mingli!" the madam screamed again.

Mingli hid in the pantry cupboard that smelled of spilled vinegar, mold, and the rough sacks of rice, millet, and buckwheat. The beating would come soon enough. She would put it off for as long as she could.

She watched the day turn to night through the missing tile on the roof. The brothel would be busier now, and she could sneak out of her hiding place, just another body among so many…but she decided not to.

The Lotus House catered to farmers, merchants, and soldiers from their little village. It was the better brothels of high rank where the women seldom serviced their clients. Instead, they served them tea with coy looks, played musical instruments, and wrote love poetry. At least, that's what she'd heard from the other girls.

The women who populated the Lotus House were farmgirls, sold off as she was because of too many girl children in one household. Her father was a scientist for the university, but he lived far away in the city and had agreed to her sale to pay debts to her uncle. Such was what her mother had told her.

Somehow, she fell asleep, and by the time she had awakened the whole house was silent. She decided it must be very late for all to have gone to sleep.

Mingli!

The voice again. She had heard it since she came to the brothel, particularly when all was quiet, or she was by herself in the vegetable garden. Sometimes she could almost hear more words. She thought she was going mad, and if she never answered them, then she could salvage a sliver of sanity.

Mingli!

But this time, she couldn't seem to avoid the voice. "Who are you?" she whispered at last.

Ah. Finally, you answer.

"I'm tired and want to sleep."

Do you know who we are?

"The noisy ones," she muttered, trying to get comfortable again on the rice sack.

We are the guardians of the souls of those killed unjustly. We are the yuan gui, spirits with a grievance.

She stiffened, unmoving, too frightened now even to breathe. The *yuan gui.* One was never to talk to them let alone *hear* from them. It was said they were dangerous, deadly. Their very presence was a curse.

We are the lost ones, the unlucky ones. But you will avenge us and in so doing, you will be redeemed.

Without moving she quietly asked, "How?"

You must do as we say. And we must mark you.

She tried to hold back her whimper. "Why? Will it hurt?"

We must. And yes, it will hurt, but for only a moment. And we will help you to leave this place.

"I will leave?"

Yes. All the souls here must be sacrificed to bond you to us.

She thought briefly of the kitchen girls who had befriended her in their way. No one wanted to form permanent friendships in case one of them was punished. It wouldn't do to be friends with someone who was always punished…as Mingli had become.

"All the souls? My…my uncle included?"

Yes. Every one.

"Then yes," she said in a heated rush. "I will do it."

Then we will mark you. You mustn't make a sound.

She didn't have a chance to respond. Instantly, her right shoulder was on fire. She stuffed her sleeve into her mouth and cried into it. The fire continued to burn and she was certain she would die. It burned across her back and down to her left hip. But finally, it was done, leaving the distinct smell of burnt flesh in her nostrils.

She slumped in relief.

It is a beautiful mark. It is in our likeness, a female spirit of exceptional beauty. This is our covenant with you. This makes you mightier than you have ever been, will ever be. You will redeem the lost souls and, in so doing, free yourself. And now…there will be a fire…

She smelled the scent of smoke and sat up. "Fire," she breathed.

You must get up, Mingli. You must make haste to your uncle's room. You must take into your possession a sacred object.

"Why? What is it?"

Get yourself to his room. He lies sleeping.

She stood in the dim light from the hole in the roof, touched the wooden latch and carefully opened the pantry door. She peered through the crack and found the kitchen dark and empty. Only the banked coals in the ovens gave a little glow as she crept through. But before she left, she stared back at the pans on the work table. Quickly, she grabbed a heavy long-handled iron skillet, and crept out of the kitchens and down a corridor. She well knew where her uncle's room was. She had not forgotten her humiliation.

She clutched the handle of the skillet, frowning as she thought of that moment of long ago, of how he had made her feel, that he had done it on purpose to cow her.

Smoke was now moving along the ceiling. It looked like a miniature storm, rippling and roiling along the beams. She thought she'd be coughing by now, but the spirits must have been protecting her, for she didn't feel the choking smoke in her throat or her nose.

She trod quietly, so quietly along the corridor until she came to his door. She opened it easily and stood in the doorway.

Make haste, the spirits urged.

She closed the door behind her and looked about the sitting room. Her uncle had money. The sitting room was adorned in the more fashionable and expensive pieces; chairs and settees, vases, and sculptures, none of which the rest of the house had. The girls who worked the brothel shared a single bed of brick, under which a warm fire could be lit, but the servicing beds were mere cots or pillows.

She crossed over a Persian rug and stopped before his bedroom door. Carefully, she grasped the edge of the door and slid it aside with no sound at all.

The mound under the blankets in the darkened room must have been him. The bed was a huge *kang* monstrosity of spiraling carved bedposts with banked coals below. His snoring continued despite the smoke slowly seeping into the room.

All was dark…until something in a far corner began to glow. Something in a bell jar. She approached it and leaned over to look inside. She thought it was merely a piece of jade, about the size of a *tael*. But on closer examination, it was a carved piece resembling a dragon. It was on a chain.

Take it, Mingli. This is the sacred object we wish for you to take for us.

She adjusted her grip on the frying pan handle and with her other hand, lifted the heavy bell jar lid, setting it aside. She closed her fingers on the cold jade and looked at it.

Make haste, the daemons said again.

She set down the frying pan and put the chain around her neck.

"What are you doing there!"

She snapped her head toward the bed. Her uncle was sitting up and glaring at her.

"Thief!" he cried. "You little whore!" He threw his blankets aside, leapt from the bed, and stomped toward her.

Stop him, said the spirits.

She saw the frying pan where she'd left it, and, in a flash, took it up. She cocked her arm back and swung it toward his head. It made contact with a loud clang.

He fell backward onto the floor, blinking furiously and whimpering. She stood over him, looking at his pathetic expression, and didn't hesitate to rain down blows to his head until he moved no more. Looking at the frying pan in her hand, she tossed it aside.

Run, Mingli. You must escape.

She turned and ran through the bedroom doorway out into the corridor. Flames were consuming the walls and she could hear the screams from the house's inhabitants. She thought only briefly of helping the others when she remembered they must all be sacrificed.

"So be it," she whispered.

That way was barred by fire, but the other way was only filled with smoke. She ran through it, feeling the heat behind her like a pursuing hunter.

There was a window ahead, flanked by flames. She held her arm over her face, charged, and crashed through the shutters, landing on the grass outside and rolling over the bumpy ground until she collided with a boulder at the edge of a pond.

She rubbed her head and stood, looking back at the Lotus House. The inferno lit up the sky, and the roar of the flames almost drowned out the helpless cries and wails within. She watched it dispassionately. Or *was* it so dispassionate, when she discovered tears running down her face? But those must be happy tears, she decided much later.

She felt around for the jade dragon on the end of its chain around her neck, clasped it, and ran for the hills.

Now you are ours, she thought she heard on the wind. It was only much later that she realized she was never to hear those voices again.

PART ONE

THE MAGICIAN

"The very best method for a trick is the easiest method, and it is the method that should be used." —Jean Hugarde (aka Oscar Kellmann, Chin Sun Loo, and Ching Ling Foo), c. 1896

CHAPTER ONE

London, 1891

"MINGLI," WHISPERED LEOPOLD. He reached out for her and found her hand. How he needed her touch just then. She turned and grabbed him into a trembling embrace.

All night long, they had enjoyed such a sweet and affectionate consummation of their love. It had been amazing! Spectacular! Incredible! He had not known such sensations could be had. He had not known such touches could be felt. They had explored one another in the most intimate of ways and it was freeing in a sense he had not thought possible.

For all his posturing on the stage as a man of the world, performing stage magic as well as the real thing, he had been woefully inexperienced with women in general. And with Mingli Zhao—the Special Inspector for Scotland Yard, with her experience and education and galivanting all over the world—that inexperience had made him ashamed...until it hadn't. Until she took him in hand and, well...

Love will out, and they were to be married. Such a strange match and such a uniquely mated one, at that. He, a magician of Jewish-Gypsy heritage; she, a Chinese woman of exceptional talents and verve—but also half-daemon. Both of them walking on the edge of dangerous magics. One night of bliss...before the tattoo on his left wrist abruptly and without warning burned with fire, and the voices of the Unholy Hosts had told him that they wished him to fulfill their agreement.

"Leo," she said, mastering the quiver in her voice. "Leo, we must dress and then you must call upon Eurynomos."

His Mingli. So precise, so calm.

"Yes, yes." How he had wanted to continue on as they had done all night. But he could not...not now. The Unholy Hosts wanted their slave to do their bidding, and he didn't yet know what that was. The price he paid for learning to summon daemons. And now his father was truly lost.

He pulled himself from the bed, standing helpless, naked, defeated. Mingli, efficient yet tender, dressed him in his dressing gown, and somehow found another to clothe herself.

"Call him now, Leo," she said, lifting his arm with the tattoo.

But he had no strength, nothing to focus on.

"Call him," she urged, her voice growing sterner.

Dutifully, he pressed his finger to the double tattoo, and whispered, "Eurynomos."

Instantly, a bright, piercing light rose up from the floor like a doorway, and the daemon stepped through.

He was taller than any man alive, yet he always made certain he was no taller than the room height, for he sported two black, twisting horns like that of an Ibex that reached to the ceiling. His skin was red and scaly, and his bare feet with their sharp, black talons dug into the Persian rug. He was bald and naked except for a black breechclout that nearly reached to the floor. His sharp teeth smiled at first at their appearance—both in dressing gowns and obviously nothing else, standing in Leopold's bedchamber, the bed itself ruffled as much as their hair—until he noticed Leopold's expression.

"Leo, old chap," he exclaimed in his West End baritone. "What's wrong?"

"They want me," he said wearily. He lifted his tattooed wrist to show the beast. The tattoo glowed.

"Oh, gods!" the daemon gasped. "Leo..."

"What am I to do, Eurynomos? What am I to do?"

The beast took him suddenly in his arms. He was warm and strong and encompassing. Leopold almost felt safe there. Almost.

Eurynomos pushed him back to look him in the eye. "What did they say, Leo? What are the exact words?"

Leopold swallowed past a hot lump in his throat. "All they said, Eurynomos, was this; 'The time has come for you to serve us.' And then they went away. The tattoo has not stopped glowing and buzzing beneath my skin from that moment on."

He carefully picked up Leopold's arm and stared at the tattoo, turning the arm slightly this way and that. "And when was this?"

"Mere moments ago."

Eurynomos let Leopold's arm go, put a hand to his own squared chin, and paced.

"Is there any escaping this, Eurynomos?" said Mingli with a strangely tightened voice. "Is there anything Leo can do?"

"I am afraid, Miss Zhao, that Leo is in very great peril."

"Well. He most assuredly will not face it alone."

Leopold jerked toward her. "No. You will not be a part of this. You can't be. I won't let you be."

She adjusted the extra-long cuffs of her dressing gown. "This is not up for debate, Mr. Kazsmer. I have no intention of leaving you to an uncertain fate. Somehow, we will discover how to save you. I am not called a 'Special Inspector' for nothing."

He took her hands and gazed into her eyes. Well, *eye*. The right eye was what he called her "galaxy" eye, changed by an encounter with a magical sword, making it entirely black with the images of galaxies and stars within. She usually wore a special eye patch with a telescoping lens over it during the day. But it was her other eye, her fully human eye, with all the sweetness and bravery within it, that grounded him. "I couldn't go to my fate knowing I had allowed you to step into danger. Mingli, I love you too much for that. Please. Let me go. Please."

She took a deep breath. "Mr. Kazsmer, I have never run from danger. And I certainly don't intend to do so now, what with my own beloved in peril. We *can* find an answer." Though when she looked toward Eurynomos for encouragement there was very little there. After all, Leopold had been in Gehenna when he and Leopold's father had been dragged into the Otherworld and they had first encountered the deadly Unholy Hosts. He knew what it was like. She didn't.

"Mingli..."

"Leo. You know me. You know I am relentless."

His heart was torn. He didn't want her in danger, yet he was encouraged by her certainty. Maybe…just maybe…if anyone could, *she* could find a way…

"We must alert your friends, Leopold," she said. "We must call on Inspector Thacker, Raj, and Suchah. They will come to your aid."

Perhaps. But first things first. He must wash and dress. And suddenly, he was starkly aware of Mingli's presence…and *her* state of undress.

"I say, Eurynomos, perhaps you can entertain Miss Zhao in the next room…"

The daemon blinked at him uncomprehendingly…until understanding bloomed in his eyes. He smiled fondly at his human friend. "Perhaps Miss Zhao can call upon your landlady to bring us coffee. I do like her coffee."

Mingli, not the least fooled, sighed. "I think, rather, that you might leave *us* for a moment, Eurynomos."

"Oh." He looked to Leopold, whose face was stark, but succumbed instead to the piercing glare of Mingli's one eye. "I shall conjure my own coffee, shall I?" He vanished from the room and Mingli gazed at Leopold tenderly.

"You mustn't be embarrassed, Leo. We have no secrets from one another now." She untied the belt and dropped her dressing gown.

He gasped and turned away. "Miss Zhao!"

"By the gods, Leo! We entertained one another in this state of dress all night."

"I know, but…"

He felt her approach, felt her hands on his shoulders, and then her breath at his ear. "Leo," she said softly, seductively. "Part of our being human is the appreciation of one another's…person." She kissed his ear.

Despite his earlier terror, the touch of her lips softened his fear. He turned toward her. She was so luscious, so enchanting. He couldn't stop himself from pressing his lips to hers.

She pulled back with a blush of pink to her cheeks. "Let us both wash and dress. We can do so at the same time."

He could not believe that at this dread time he was aroused by her. "Erm…I…don't like to point this out, but…"

"Oh, Leo," she smirked. "It's very flattering, but we simply don't have time for that."

EMBARRASSED, DESPITE HOW familiar they had gotten last night—it was in the dark, after all, not the light of day!—Leopold nevertheless soldiered through their mutual washing and dressing, though he always had half an eye on his delectable companion, marveling at all the petticoats, laces, ruffles, ribbons—and *corset*—of a woman's clothing ensemble.

She was dressed in no time, faster than he was, with his simple underthings, braces, trousers, tie, and spats.

They both adjusted side by side in the full-length mirror, until their eyes met in the glass. "Is this what it's like," he said quietly, "when one is married? Shared toilet, wardrobe, and…dressing?"

"Well, since I have never been married, I can only speculate. Although many couples of a certain level of society have their own dressing rooms. Own bedrooms, I daresay."

"Oh. Is…is that something you would favor? I suppose, if I ever get out of this, that I should look for a new flat…for the two of us. Or a town house. What would you prefer?"

"I have no preference," she said, buttoning her jacket that fitted snugly over her curves. "And I don't need a separate dressing room and definitely…" She smiled as she strapped on her eye patch. "No separate bedroom. And Leo, we *will* get you out of this."

He loved her for oh-so-many reasons, but perhaps the most for her confidence.

But for all that, he wasn't certain she was capable of keeping that promise.

OUTSIDE HIS BEDCHAMBER, an abashed Thacker, Suchah, and Raj were politely waiting, with just Eurynomos and Suchah partaking of coffee…though the latter didn't look as if he much enjoyed it.

They raised their faces with stark expressions. By this point, even Leopold was feeling somewhat ashamed of his earlier reaction. He pulled his waistcoat taut and stepped forward to pour Mingli a coffee, and then one for himself. He handed her a cup on a saucer.

"Gentlemen, I appreciate your gathering here. I'm sure Eurynomos has acquainted you with the situation. Though my summons from the Unholy Hosts was abrupt, it wasn't entirely unexpected. I don't know what we can do to solve this problem, but I implore you, if you cannot find a way to help *me*, please find a way to help my father. He is still trapped in Gehenna in the lowest depth of it. And I dread to leave him there any longer than necessary."

Raj rose off his chair on his recently discovered brass legs. His pistons whooshed and the governors within his brass ribcage whirred. His face, as always—a painted visage of an Oriental man on porcelain—didn't change expression, but he somehow conveyed his concern with his glass eyes. He wore a turban and a boiled shirt, tie, and tailcoat, but since he used to be ensconced behind a wheeled table laying out tarot cards, he didn't have trousers. "Leo, any of us would be extremely happy to accommodate you," said the automaton in a thick accent of India. "But perhaps it is for us to point out that both perils are not mutually exclusive."

Leopold stilled. *Of course!* If he was to battle the Unholy Hosts he would have to take that fight to Gehenna, and while he was there, he could free his father. "Oh, Raj, my dear, dear friend. You've only pointed out how stupid I am."

"Not a bit of it, Leo. Your mind has been otherwise…occupied." He slid a glance toward Mingli.

"Leo, old son," said Inspector Despenser Thacker in his brash Cockney, pushing back the transparent bowler up his ghostly forehead. As always was the case, he hovered slightly above the floor, not actually standing on it. "You must know we're ready for action any time you say."

Suchah, a little red imp with short horns, small bat-like wings, and webbed feet below a melon-shaped body, looked perplexed. "Leopold Master has our help anytime he needs it. Suchah can help get into Gehenna. It is only beyond the veil."

Leopold's heart swelled. "My friends, you don't know how grateful I am. How ashamed I feel for thinking I would have to go it alone."

Eurynomos, standing nearly to ceiling height now, laid a giant hand on Leopold's shoulder. "I told you that you were not alone, dear friend."

He patted the beast's hand, warm and textured like lizard's skin. "A momentary lapse." He took Mingli's hand and beamed at her. "I won't forget again."

Mingli gave his hand a squeeze before she abruptly released him and began to pace his drawing room, all business again. "The question is not how to get to Gehenna, but how to get someone who is captured there *out* of Gehenna."

Everyone turned toward Eurynomos. The beast sighed. "I know what you're all thinking. Since I am known as the 'Prince of Death' and commander of Gehenna, why don't I simply release Àkos? The simple truth of it, my dear friends, is this: I do not have the power ascribed to me. Yes, I have some, especially over the daemons like myself. But you must understand. Angels—all fallen—are in command of each of the seven levels, and I have no sway there. Nor do I have sway over any of the inhabitants of *Sitra Achra*, where Àkos is being held."

"Where are the Unholy Hosts in this hierarchy?" asked Mingli, unperturbed as usual.

"They are fallen angels. Fallen *arch*angels, to be precise. They have much greater power than the others, and seem to have their own agenda. Over the centuries, they have gotten used to the punishing ways of Gehenna. It changed them. Their power was so concentrated, infused with evil, that they became a power unto themselves. Leo, you've experienced it. Merely looking at them can make mortals ill. Or go mad. No one can interfere with them. Least of all, me."

Mingli folded her arms over her bosom. "It seems very complicated."

"It is, I assure you."

Raj stalked toward him. Leopold was still getting used to the automaton with legs, and since they were very long and slender, longer than proportionally necessary, he appeared more insect than man. "Can you tell us the nature of Gehenna, Eurynomos?" he asked, "I suppose that most of us on the outside harbor many assumptions."

"No doubt. I daresay, even Leopold, who has been there himself, cannot elucidate you, for it is ever-changing. You see, you must imagine it as an ancient nomadic tent, and the levels of Gehenna as the fabric. The tent pole is *Sitra Achra,* holding up the whole but not interfering with the many sections. Yet, even as the dreaded place where all evil comes from and goes to stands as its support, one cannot merely traverse *to Sitra Achra.* One must *fight* one's way to it."

"I remember Gehenna as a completely confusing and nightmarish place," said Leopold quietly. "Gravity had no meaning. Colors made no sense. The very nature of it could drive you mad."

"That is because," said Eurynomos, "it is not designed for living mortals to enter. It is for souls, spirits. Only the dead can make sense of it. But I have been thinking on this problem for over a decade, since last you were there, Leo. I think I can use my powers to smooth it out in your mind. I can't have you going mad, after all. Nor would our Miss Zhao appreciate that."

"Quite," said Mingli.

"But the biggest problem is, getting you back inside. It simply can't be done."

Leopold stared in disbelief at his friend. "What do you mean? I am infused with Earth magic now. I can burst my way through—"

"No, you can't, Leo. I was there to help you through before. But it can't be done now. The Unholy Hosts have closed that loophole. Even if I wanted to let you through, I cannot."

"Not even Suchah?" asked the imp.

Eurynomos shook his enormous head. "Not even you, my impish friend. Only the Unholy Hosts."

"Interesting," said Mingli, still slowly pacing. "Their magic is overpowering."

"Indeed," said the daemon. "The Great Creator made it so. Everything about Gehenna changes constantly. It isn't as if I can draw you a map, for the moment I have done so, you would be lost again."

"That is going to make our job difficult," she said, glancing at Leopold. "But not impossible."

"We should go to Madam Hui Ling," said Leopold abruptly.

Mingli stopped her pacing and turned to him, surprised. "Why...Leo..."

"She is a sorceress. A very powerful one. I recognize that at last. We can't ignore the possibility that she could help us. She has a sense of these things, after all. I wouldn't be surprised if she was already expecting us."

Mingli cocked her head in a most fetching manner. "She may not be able to help."

"We'll have to try. Gentlemen, Miss Zhao and I will see to it immediately. You must, of course, stay here."

"What about me, Leo?" asked Thacker.

"Spense, it might be wise for you to come with Miss Zhao and me. After all, once we've seen Madam Hui Ling, I must go to a graveyard. I will need to obtain…something from it."

CHAPTER TWO

STEPPING INTO THE driving rain, Leopold hailed the cab. He told the cabby the way to the wharves and, even after offering Leopold a skeptical eye, the driver nevertheless urged the horse with a click of his tongue.

Thacker, as usual, appeared halfway in and halfway out of the Hansom cab through the back wall between them. All sat in silence as the cab threaded its way through the soggy traffic of Regent Street toward Piccadilly, passed Trafalgar, and nearly to Waterloo Bridge. He wondered if it wouldn't have been faster taking a dirigible…but no. He detested the sooty, chugging things, even as they loomed overhead, blocking out what little sun there was to be had.

Once they arrived at the dismal streets near the wharves, they disembarked and hurried down the dim avenue, Mingli holding her own umbrella over her head, and Leopold transfiguring his cane into one. Thacker floated along beside them. No one was able to see the spirit except for their immediate friends, and so Leopold never feared taking him along on their many sojourns throughout the city and into Scotland Yard. Or at least as far as he *could* go, for Thacker was restricted by his spirit nature from venturing more than a three-mile radius from the Yard where he had been summoned from death.

They reached the sooty brick building with the steps that went lower than the pavement to a dim door. This time, Leopold pushed through first ahead of Mingli. He quickly glanced at the opium den around them, its red Chinese lanterns hanging here and there that could not pierce the dim gloom, clouded by a layer of smoke drifting waist high. He held a kerchief to his face so as not to inhale the sickly-sweet smoke, and didn't bother searching the faces of the many men and few women spending their drowsy days in the twilight of that most despicable of drugs. He simply trod straight through to the back, stopping for no one, not even the Chinaman who stepped forward to prevent their entering to the back rooms, though the man seemed to recognize Leopold and let him pass.

Leopold plunged through the backmost door, whipping the kerchief away from his face to find Madam Hui Ling already waiting for him. She was much shorter than he, and looked to be at least a hundred years old, perhaps more. Her face was wrinkled and folded in such a way that it didn't seem possible she was anything but a strange waxwork of Madam Tussaud's, but she faced him, arms folded, sucking on a brass waterpipe between her wrinkled lips. She wore a simple red silk tunic, buttoned with ivory disks, with black silk trousers, and embroidered slippers on her tiny feet.

"Mr. Kazsmer," she said in her soft voice. "Miss Zhao. Ah, and your ghostly friend, I see." She bowed her head slightly at a discomfited Thacker. "Come into my parlor. We have much to discuss."

Leopold followed her as she pushed a curtain aside and opened another door. Once again, she took up her place on her chaise lounge with a sigh. She puffed on her pipe, fragrant smoke wreathing her head.

"I have been expecting you for some time. I didn't know it would be so soon."

"Neither did I. I suppose it was foolish of me to think I had time. I came to you since you seem to know everything..."

Madam Hui Ling cocked her head and chuckled. "Not everything, Mr. Kazsmer. But certainly... *some* things." She leaned forward and took his left hand, yanking him forward till he was stumbling toward her. She pushed back his sleeve and cuff, revealing the glowing double Celtic knot of his wretched tattoo. The Eye of Providence sketched on the inside of his wrist looked at the sorceress warily. It had been subtle before, but was fully animated now. Always, Leopold questioned whether the eye had moved. Now there was no doubt at all. "The Unholy Hosts of Gehenna. They have called to you."

He allowed her to hold his arm for a moment more before he gently extricated himself from her claw-like grasp. He sat back in his chair. "Yes. So you realize I must go to Gehenna…but not for the reason you think."

"Your father," she said, puffing more smoke. "I have read the cards, Mr. Kazsmer. I know." She turned her gaze to Mingli. "Come here, my daughter."

Mingli rose from her chair and crouched by the chaise. The old woman reached out and closed her fingers around her wrist. "You wish to go with him?"

"I *will* go with him."

Leopold's heart warmed again at her forceful words.

Madam Hui Ling nodded. "Of course, you shall. For there is much you can do. You know now your true nature, do you not?"

Mingli tensed until she slowly relaxed her shoulders. "Yes."

"But much is still a mystery. You are a half-daemon. It does not happen often. This journey can help you understand it as well." She took a puff of her pipe. "And even you, Inspector Thacker, may benefit."

"Erm…I'm just here to help me friend Kazsmer."

"And very noble it is. You are very fortunate among men, Mr. Kazsmer, to have inspired such loyalty. Including your daemon and impish friend."

Was there nothing she didn't know? Leopold girded himself. "You seem to know much, Madam. Can you not tell me…if I will be successful?"

"Ah, Mr. Kazsmer. The cards tell me a great deal, but the future is not yet written. Paths are chosen that ultimately change the outcome. One has only to choose the *right* path for the *best* outcome. Surely your mechanical friend has told you that."

Yes, she knew *all* of his doings. "Forgive me, Madam, but…I will need all the help I can get to choose that right path. For I must not only save myself, but my father. He has suffered a great deal."

"You will know what to do when the time comes, Mr. Kazsmer. I have faith in you. But faith is a delicate thing. It needs bolstering with solid information. To that end, I will make a recommendation." She sucked on the pipe for a moment and blew out a ring of smoke, before leaning toward him. "You must go to the Library."

"The…library? Which one? And what must I find there?"

She gestured with the pipe. "The Library. Eh, Miss Zhao?"

"Oh!" Mingli seemed to pale. "I take it that we may find a map there."

"And more. If you are to reach Gehenna, you must start there." She reached into a fold of her tunic and pulled out what looked to be a beetle. Leopold wasn't certain whether it was dead or alive, but she nevertheless offered it to Mingli. "Take it. It is the only way forward."

Mingli studied it curiously. Leopold canted toward her. "Miss Zhao…"

The beetle lay in her opened gloved palm, nearly covering her entire hand. It looked plain and brown at first, but as he studied it, he saw, etched on each wing, a drawing of a dragon.

"The *Lóng*," Mingli breathed.

It shuddered and began to make whirring and clicking noises. The etched shells covering the wings snapped opened, revealing a rainbow of jeweled surfaces. Leopold could see gears and brass legs now. The wings deployed, and it rose off her palm, readying to dart away…when she clapped her other palm over it.

"Yes," said Madam Hui Ling. "The dragon beetle. Like the jade object you wear around your neck."

Mingli put one hand instantly to her bodice. The necklace's long chain hid the object deep within her clothing. Leopold knew that she had been told by her household spirits to steal the jade dragon pendant when she was freed from the servitude of her uncle's brothel. He longed to know what it all meant, longed to comfort her and keep her from the pain it seemed to be causing her.

"My dear," he said softly.

She suddenly closed her hand, hiding the beetle. "I'm fine," she assured, unconvincingly.

The old sorceress puffed on her pipe once more. "The beetle will tell you the way to the gate. Once the gate is open…but I see you already know what to do, Mr. Kazsmer."

He didn't know why it surprised him, the things she said. She seemed to be able to read his mind. "Yes. We will be going to a graveyard next."

"Excellent. I wish you well on your journey. Your friends are your strength, Mr. Kazsmer. But I need not tell you that."

"No. It is something I have already learned."

"Good. Make haste. You have no more time to waste. *Zhù nǐ hǎo yùn.*"

Though she said the last out loud in Chinese, he heard it in Hungarian in his mind. "Good luck," she had wished him. He was going to need it.

IT WAS STILL raining when they hailed another cab. "St Dunstan-in-the-East Church," he told the cabby.

They settled in and Mingli as well as Thacker were staring at him. After a long pause, Thacker finally asked, "Why are we going to a graveyard, Leo?"

Mingli straightened her skirts. He was certain she had wanted to ask it first.

He didn't look at either of them. Instead, he stared out the window. "I need to make an Incantation Bowl."

Mingli made a sound of recognition and sat back, nodding. Thacker stared at each in turn. "And what the bloody hell is that? Pardon," he said to Mingli, raising his bowler.

Leopold sighed. "It is a clay bowl covered in magical incantations. It is made from graveyard clay and, usually, it serves to trap demons so they may not enter a certain place, like a home. But in this situation, not only will it trap demons, it will serve to keep open the gate to another realm."

"Oh. Is that all." Thacker pushed back his bowler to scratch his head as he used to do when he was alive. "You just…put it on the ground…"

"No. You bury it with the open side facing downward. It's like cupping your hand to catch a fly." He glanced at Mingli. "What was it you called that beetle? Long?"

"The *Lóng*. It is a Chinese dragon. A potent symbol of power. It is good luck for those who are worthy. Chinese dragons are water spirits, controlling the weather."

"Is that…like the pendant you wear?"

She reached into her *décolletage* and pulled out the lengthy chain and held up the jade dragon. Delicately carved from the stone, it was so finely done it could have been alive. At least, Leopold thought so. She never took it off, even when they had made love last night. *Gods, was that only last night?* It seemed ages ago now. Too long. He had rather spent the time today exploring her body all over again…and letting her do the things she had done to him. It brought heat to cheeks…and then shame. He shouldn't be thinking of that. He should be calculating how to rescue his father while trying to avoid the call of the Unholy Hosts.

"What had Madam Hui Ling meant about some library?" he said hastily. "Is it in London?"

The carriage rattled over the road, tossing Mingli against Leopold for a moment…and through the specter of Thacker. "Do forgive me, Inspector," she said, settling back at her seat.

"Think nothing of it, Miss Zhao. It's this bloody road—begging your pardon." He touched the rim of his bowler again.

She took a deep breath. "She meant…the Library of the Damned."

"The *what?*" cried Leopold and Thacker at the same time.

The carriage abruptly came to a halt, and the cabby looked down through the trap door. "Saint Dunstan's, guv."

Leopold paid the man and he stepped out, offering Mingli his hand to help her. The rain had changed to a light sprinkling. Mingli put up her umbrella, but Leopold decided his topper would do.

When the cab drove away, Leopold glanced up to the eighteenth-century church, its gothic steeple rising into the mist. It was a small church, and one of the few in London that still had its graveyard attached. Too many churches in the city had their burial grounds moved from them, or dug up for new construction of gardens and parks, the stones relocated and the dead beneath quite forgotten.

He walked south of the church and found it: a short wall topped with an iron fence curved along the pavement, capturing within the few headstones and vaults nestled under the protection of the church walls, with a few spindly trees.

He passed through the gate followed by Mingli, but Thacker paused.

Leopold looked back at him. "What is it, Spense?"

Thacker stared at the gate. "I don't know, Leo. I just feel…I can't pass through."

"Stand guard, then," said Mingli, giving him a kind smile.

"I don't understand," said Leopold quietly when they'd gotten several paces away from the pensive spirit. "Why can't he cross? I had hoped for his, er, expertise."

"This is holy ground. There are numerous prayers and magics associated with a graveyard. He's wise to stay where he is."

"Then what of Gehenna?"

"It isn't the same, Leo. It is very much…not the same."

Leopold continued his searching along the ground for the best spot to find clay and spoke over his shoulder to her. "I say, what was this business about a 'Library of the Damned'? What in blazes is that?"

"I wasn't quite certain it truly existed, but if Madam Hui Ling suggested it…well. It must be so." She straightened her hat with its feathers and netting, and planted the tip of her umbrella into the mud.

Thacker drifted by behind the curved wall and iron fence. "Oi, Leo!"

"What is it, Spense?"

"I may not be able to get into the graveyard—and a dread place it is." He gave a shiver. "But I can tell you where the clay is. I can do that much."

"Excellent. Where, then?"

"Right where Miss Zhao is standing."

She looked down and pulled the tip of the umbrella out of the mud. She turned the umbrella to look at the tip. "Jolly good," she said. "Clay."

CHAPTER THREE

LEOPOLD TRANSFIGURED HIS cane into a spade and began to dig, collecting the clay onto a muslin sheet he had laid out on the damp grass.

"You asked about the Library of the Damned," she began. "It is a library situated between the worlds in its own portion of space."

He stopped digging and looked up. "I don't understand."

"Then be quiet and allow me to fully explain."

He shrugged and put his back into it, digging out the sticky clay.

She glanced once at Thacker who seemed to be pressing his face to the bars of the fence in wonder.

"It is said to be a structure fluctuating between the worlds and filled with the archives of the centuries."

Leopold grunted as he dug into the hard clay. "A sort of Library of Alexandria?"

"Not quite. It isn't merely books or scrolls on shelves, or boxes filled with old parchments. It is a strange and dangerous place where answers can be found—but not easily. The answers must be interpreted from the objects provided. The Library is considered an entity. It is alive, and hinders those who seek its secrets."

"That doesn't sound very pleasant."

"I can't imagine that it is. But it's the only way that mortals can find a way into Gehenna."

"How did you ever discover about such a place?"

"I do mounds of research."

He wiped his arm across his brow, leaving a messy swath of clay behind. "That's enough, I think." He donned his frock coat that had been draped over a tombstone, and left more clay on that.

"Leo, come here."

He was unable to ignore such a summons, remembering well what it led to last night, and stood before her. "Yes, my dear?"

She clasped her hands to both his cheeks and leaned in to kiss him. He felt the tingle of magic and gazed at her curiously.

"Now you're presentable again."

He looked down at his coat and noticed that it was clean. "Oh. Thank you. And here I thought you merely wanted to kiss me."

"I did. But there was no need to waste an opportunity."

"If you two are done playing kissy-face..." said Thacker impatiently through the fence.

"Of course," said Leopold. He gathered his clay in the muslin like a Christmas pudding and led the way out of the churchyard.

"Spense, why don't you alert the others to meet us at the Whitechapel lockup. I'll be creating the bowl there, and I can certainly use the help of Eurynomos and Suchah for the Hebrew."

"Right-O. We'll be there before you." He vanished without a sound.

He turned to Mingli. For the first time since morning, they were alone again. "Answer me honestly. Do you think this journey to the Library will work?"

She sighed and turned her head to watch the traffic along the street: carriages; a few riders on horseback; the rattling of the elevated tram as it chugged along its uneven tracks on iron structures that wended around buildings throughout London; the smoke from dirigibles overhead cloaking the avenue in a perpetual haze.

It could have been any street in London. The noise, the smoke, the hurrying people...along with the invisibles: the beggars, the fingersmiths, the crawlers...the latter, gray women perched in doorways and on steps, too weary to even beg.

"Leo, you must understand. What I have read of the Library is that it will fight us every step of the way. The odds of our surviving that to even enter into Gehenna..."

"Oh, I'd rather not hear the odds, if it's all the same to you." He gazed at her profile, the ghastly eye patch with its constantly whirring lens that drew in and out, focusing on God-knew-what; the curve of her creamy cheek with its merest of blush to it; the sheen of her hair forced into mounds of curls at the back of her head. His Mingli. His fiancée. The woman he loved.

"You know," he said dreamily, "you truly are very beautiful."

She turned back to him in surprise and only then offered a small smile. How his heart warmed at such a sight! He couldn't help himself and drew closer, wrapping his free arm around her small waist and pulling her against him. He closed his eyes and inhaled the scent of lilac. His nose caressed that cheek, until he found her lips and kissed her properly.

He felt her gloved hand grasp the back of his neck to keep him there. They indulged in their embrace for far too long. Someone was shouting at them, and he broke from her to look.

A white-haired man in a white collar—the vicar of the parish, no doubt—stood at the gate, raising his fist to them. "What mischief-making is this? This is not a brothel. It is consecrated ground. Away with you!"

Leopold doffed his hat. "I beg your pardon, vicar. We apologize. We were just…"

"Visiting an old relative," said Mingli, turning, her telescoping eye patch still for once.

"Devil woman," he sneered, and gestured toward her eye patch. "With devil devices! Leave this place and take your curses with you."

Leopold felt her tension under the hand he kept at her waist. "Surely a vicar of Christ should be more charitable," spat Leopold stiffly. "We're going."

He nudged her along, still with his hand to the small of her back, but the man would not cease his tirade.

"The likes of her kind—this foreigner—on hallowed ground. Whore of Babylon! I should call the law on you. I should strike you down myself."

Mingli stopped abruptly and pivoted on her heel. She doubled slightly and put a hand to her stomach as if in pain, but seemed to quickly recover. But he could hear something of a growl creep up her throat. She sneered and raised her hand to the vicar. He hadn't noticed before that her nails were particularly long, but they seemed to be testing the seams of her gloves, poking through. She said nothing, but the man suddenly seemed struck dumb and stumbled back. He clawed at his throat, gasping to breathe, when Leopold—checking that *he* had not enchanted the vicious man accidentally—faced Mingli. "You must stop."

Her hand, which was still raised, closed to a fist and fell to her side. The vicar crumpled against the wall of his church, and breathed again.

Mingli didn't wait. She spun and marched through the gate to the kerb where she waved her hand viciously for a cab.

"If demon he thinks me to be, then demon I *shall* be," she rasped.

"But my dear, you aren't…"

She whipped her head toward him. "But I *am*!" Her one true eye glittered with venom…and…had it changed color? "Aren't I, Leo? Half a daemon. No wonder that the *yuan gui* made their bargain with me. They knew, as a daemon, I could accomplish what they wanted. And I have, Leo. I have, all my life now."

"My love…" People along the streets were starting to stare. He gently pulled her away from the kerb and settled them both on a bench outside the graveyard under a tree still dripping from the recent rain. "Mingli, I haven't forgotten your…circumstances. And we will strive to discover why and…well. *How* this happened."

"I don't want to know who my daemon father was, Leo. That certainly isn't necessary. In the end, well…I fear to discover exactly who. It's best left a mystery, if you don't mind." She looked down at her hands and took a shallow breath. "I believe I am succumbing to what the physicians call 'female hysterics." She raised her chin. "It's most unpleasant."

He smiled good-naturedly. "Here now. We all need a good rant every now and then."

"*I* do not rant."

"May I point out that you did a damn good job of it when you thought I'd stood you up." He'd only done it because…well, he had forgotten. After all, at the time, he had only just been attacked by goblins and a clockwork man, not to mention the distress over his father's captivity.

She studied him from under the rim of her hat. "That was entirely justified on my part. One doesn't accept an invitation to my flat and then fail to arrive."

Oh, he had *wanted* to go. "I had a good reason." He offered her a faint smile.

It appeared that she couldn't resist it and smiled back as she rose. "It seems falling in love with you has completely rattled my usual calm demeanor. You're entirely to blame."

"Yes, Miss Zhao," he said, rising to stand beside her.

She adjusted her cape and hat. "We'll be terribly late to meet your friends at the lockup."

Leopold let out a heavy breath. He felt a cad that they hadn't yet addressed her circumstances. Finding out one was half-daemon could fluster the best of them. And his Mingli was always so proper and unfazed. It broke his heart to see it, but it only made him more determined to help.

"I feel foolish indulging in a fit of emotions," she said. "I'm *half*-daemon. Surely I can call upon my human side to keep my emotions in check." She put a finger to her cheek, and her nails seemed to be back to normal. Or perhaps Leopold had only imagined their length before. "On the other hand, it might be advantageous to exploit this knowledge, this... *heritage* of mine. I suppose my daemon side accounts for my small abilities to perform magic."

"It certainly would," he agreed.

"But it's nothing compared to your woes. Oh Leo, I apologize. This is just the sort of thing that convinces me that an overindulgence of emotions only gets in the way of logical and scientific thinking."

"Well, I..." He stopped and sniffed the air. "What is that *smell*?" He turned to look back at the graveyard. It was as if a hole had opened up in a grave or vault. Or perhaps a sewer line had chosen that spot to break open, leaking raw sewage. Yet all appeared to be untouched, and even the ranting vicar had departed.

Mingli covered her nose with a gloved hand. "That is most unpleasant."

But as soon as they turned to face one another, it seemed to dawn on both of them at the same time.

Leopold's tattoo blazed with pain just as the enormous demon, Ogiel, appeared before them with a loud boom.

CHAPTER FOUR

OGIEL, A CLOVEN-HOOFED beast standing nearly as tall as the church roof, with black, reptilian skin that seemed so dark it absorbed all light, glared down on them. A pair of ram's horns spiraled up from his skull and twisted down around his foxlike ears, whilst a pair of clawed bat-wings arched up over his back, flapping slowly. Tusks extended from the edges of his mouth, dripping with drool. He wore the typical ragged breechclout that seemed to be the uniform of all his fellow denizens of Gehenna.

Leopold desperately searched the street, but, thankfully, bystanders couldn't seem to see the beast. He was quite invisible to the uninitiated...except for the smell. An invisible Ogiel had killed Inspector Thacker, after all. Leopold's heart seethed with anger.

"What do you want, Ogiel?"

The demon's voice was gravelly and sour. "The Unholy Hosts have tasked me with telling you their will."

Fear replaced the anger, but Mingli was at his side, her warmth sustaining him. "Well?" he managed to croak.

Ogiel did his version of a smile, with thin lips pulling back over sharpened teeth. His tusks seemed to glisten. "They want you to destroy the world."

"What? What sort of asinine... Wait a moment—why would they send you?"

"I am Ogiel, the Polluted. They thought it fitting to send me as the harbinger of the world's destruction."

"And just how is it I'm to destroy the world? Don't the Unholy Hosts know that there will be no more souls to torment if the world is gone?"

The demon laughed. It was a sound like choking, like a cat expelling a hairball. "They're satisfied with the souls they have. And, of course, there is...*you*. You will last as long as they want you to, an eternal life of torment just for you, Kazsmer."

A chill rattled down his spine. All the speeches, all the words of support would, in the end, mean nothing if Leopold could not free himself from his bargain. The idea of eternal torment...well. It would only make up briefly for putting his father in jeopardy in the first place, but after Àkos was freed it would continue on...and on. He didn't relish the idea of it.

And destroy the world? Mingli was part of this world, along with all of his friends. He'd never do it. But he had to make Ogiel believe he would, or the demon would snatch him now and drag him into Gehenna. The Unholy Hosts could make it happen, even as Eurynomos confessed *he* could not.

"Very well. You've delivered your message," he said in an unsteady voice. "You can return to the pit where you belong."

"I shall dog your steps, Kazsmer. I shall watch you to see you do the bidding of the Unholy Hosts."

"Got a ring in your nose, then?"

He laughed again. "As do you, Mortal." His laughter clanged into the air. "But first, a taste of the doom you are to inflict." The beast turned toward the street and glanced at the oncoming elevated tram. It chugged slowly along its tracks. The poor passengers within were covered with a sprinkling of soot from the steam engine's boiler, and rattled by the uneven railway built with so much haste and so little oversight.

Ogiel stomped toward it, clasped his enormous hand around the tram, and lifted it from the tracks. Screams and panic ensued. The engineer looked desperately at the rails, the engine, but could not understand the cause of the unexpected careering of the tram. A man tried to leap from it and crashed against the ironwork supports, clinging to an upright. Women fainted! Children wailed!

Leopold dropped the clay bundle and rushed into the street, sketching sigils into the air with both his hands, creating a magical trail of gold and sparkles.

Ogiel smiled at Leopold as he raised the tram to hurl it to the ground. But his smile faded as he realized he couldn't let go or move his arms.

"Set it back on the track, Ogiel!" cried Leopold.

"New tricks, Kazsmer?" He fought, swinging his body—or trying to—to free himself.

"Put it back on the tracks…or I shall turn *you* into a tram."

The beast laughed…until he didn't, considering it. "Release me."

"Do it with care or you shall suffer for it."

The demon found he could move his arms again and slowly returned the tram—albeit facing the wrong way—back on the tracks.

"I'll be close, Kazsmer," he sneered before he faded steadily away.

Leopold quickly turned his attention to the man clinging to the elevated ironwork, and with the slashing of more sigils in the air, slowly lowered him to the ground onto his feet.

The man looked all around at his sudden good fortune and hightailed it away.

Making certain no one else was in danger, Leopold rushed away from the street and faded back into the shadows of the tree where Mingli awaited him.

"Well now," she said. "That was useful."

Now that his hot blood had had a chance to cool, he was shaken all over again by the beast's sudden appearance, as well as his deadly message. His hand—so sure and accomplished when put to the test—trembled. He stuffed it into his frock coat pocket. "Use-useful?" he asked, wondering what she could possibly mean.

She slipped her arm in his. Surely she could feel his trembling, but she never mentioned it. "Of course. Now we know what the Unholy Hosts wish of you. Destruction of the world. Simple, eh? I suppose they think you can snap your fingers. Although…I almost think you could," she said under her breath. "Nevertheless," she continued. "It gives us time. And an excuse if they discover that we are going to the Library."

"One can find a way to destroy the world…from the Library?"

"Certainly. Even as antagonistic as the Library is, it is still most useful."

Now he was glad that this Library of the Damned was difficult to get to.

He heard a bell strike from the church behind them and scrambled for his watch in his waistcoat pocket. "Good Lord! Look at the time." He searched the street, which seemed to be empty now that the drama was over, and grabbed up the linen with the clay.

Reaching deep inside his core for the tendrils of magic, he concentrated on it, balled it up, kept it taught and ready to spring. "Perhaps, Miss Zhao, if you will allow me…" He took her gloved hand in his and grasped it tightly. "Now…this might be slightly disorientating. I recommend you close your eyes. Er…eye."

She didn't ask. She didn't protest. She simply gazed at him with the utmost confidence and trust, closed her eye, and raised her face slightly. He resisted the urge to kiss her.

Instead, he closed his own eyes, concentrated on gathering the magic until it was a hot mass pulsating in his chest, thought of the lockup he owned in Whitechapel and, with a deep breath, they both melded into the mist...

…and appeared directly before the lockup's door.

She opened her eye and blinked, her eye patch's lens twirling and adjusting. "Leo! You are becoming quite accomplished."

He was rather surprised himself that it worked. "Thank you. Shall we?"

Flushed with the last bits of magic pulsing in his chest, he walked up to the door first and unlocked it with a wave of his hand.

The daemon, the automaton, the ghost, and the imp, turned.

"Leo, old man," said Eurynomos. "We almost gave you up."

"We were on our way when we encountered Ogiel."

Suchah startled back with a gasp. "Ogiel?"

"Yes. Oh…that's right…You were partners with him."

The imp wrung his hands. "But that was before Leopold Master and Suchah became friends."

"I know," he said kindly. "I'm not accusing you. But perhaps a bit of a warning. He said he would be spying on me. Will that put you in danger?"

Suchah seemed to gird himself and stood straighter. "Ogiel can try. But Suchah is faster. And smarter."

"That's the blighter that…that put me lights out," said Thacker.

"Yes. And he had a message for me from the Unholy Hosts. My task…is to destroy the world."

Raj laughed. Perhaps he had merely been trying to diffuse the situation. Especially with the stunned expression Eurynomos wore. "You could no more destroy the world," said the automaton, "than *I* could."

"I certainly wouldn't know how...and I have no intention of carrying it out. But…I must make it appear as if I am."

"Leo," said Eurynomos in a quiet tone, "this is no laughing matter. As you say, the Unholy Hosts will expect you to try. And I suspect—with your new-found expertise with Earth magic—that it just might be possible."

"Don't be absurd. Of course it isn't possible…"

"Leo. Trust me. It is."

Leopold's breath caught. If he trusted anyone with the truth, it was Eurynomos. And then he remembered their last adventure. Alignment lines. Lines of power. Mingli had warned him that to destroy one would be to create a cascading effect and would most certainly destroy the world. Not that he intended to do so. As long as the Unholy Hosts didn't know, then all was well.

"And I pointed out," Mingli cut in, "that our journey to the Library of the Damned is the perfect cover for our Mr. Kazsmer. Not only can they not follow us there, but they well know it is a place where we can find the means of the world's destruction."

Eurynomos slowly nodded, pointing a clawed finger at her. "Miss Zhao, you might just be right about that."

"I know I am," she said, lifting her nose into the air.

Eurynomos smiled, revealing his sharpened teeth. "I shall never underestimate you again, my dear."

She huffed. "It never ceases to amaze me how *anyone* can underestimate me once they have met me."

Raj laughed again, which fell to mere chuckles once Mingli turned her eye on him.

"Well, the rest of you can talk it out." Leopold doffed his hat, stripped off his coat, and began rolling up his sleeves. "I must make the Incantation Bowl, and I'd appreciate the help of you, Eurynomos and you, too, Suchah."

"Suchah knows nothing of these bowls. But Suchah would be best patrolling, sniffing for Ogiel."

Leopold cast a glance toward Eurynomos, who nodded. "You know best, Suchah. Oh. I was wondering. Would you like me to remove the glyphs I etched into your skin? I mean, since you choose to serve me with your own free will. To tell you the truth, I regret now having done it."

Suchah looked down at the Hebrew glyphs Leopold had cut into his red, scaly belly. It had made Suchah Leopold's slave at his beck and call. But since saving Suchah's life, the little imp had changed allegiance. Leopold hated the idea that the creature might still be in some way compelled to help him.

Suchah rubbed his round stomach, no doubt feeling the incised shapes of the glyphs under his webbed fingers. "Another time, Leopold Master. Now, Suchah is protected. If Suchah encounters Ogiel, he will be able to see that Suchah is at Leopold Master's mercy."

"Ah. That is wise, my little friend."

Suchah smiled. "You see? Suchah *is* smart." He disappeared with a pop. No doubt, he was now secretly patrolling around the perimeter of the lockup.

Leopold set to work, depositing the "pudding" of clay on his work table. He rubbed his hands, bringing the magic from his core and up into his fingertips. When he felt the pleasant and familiar tingle in his fingers, he began drawing sigils in the air. They showered the clay with a sparkling rainfall of magic, whipping up the clay, tumbling it, and forming it carefully with swirls and dips into a bowl form.

Positioning his hands above the bowl he instantly fired it to glowing hot, the smell of warm clay filling the air before it quickly cooled. He used his finger just above the surface to paint Hebrew words deftly and magically in an ever-spiraling pattern from the bottom of the bowl and up its curved sides. Eurynomos stood beside him, touching shoulder to shoulder—and Leopold felt the great warmth of him, like standing too close to a hearth-fire. The daemon murmured softly, encouraging, correcting some of the words so Leopold could flick his fingers and change them as he moved along inside the bowl.

Finally, once the pattern of words came to the very rim, the thing was finished and he lowered his hands. He carefully picked up the still warm ceramic and turned it to examine his handiwork.

"Excellently done, my friend," said Eurynomos.

Raj walked toward it with a whirr of governors and clicks, and the soft release and clamp of his leg joints. "Very fine work, indeed, Leo. What must be done now?"

Mingli took the beetle from the pocket in her jacket and held it forth between her fingers. "We must find the portal to the Library with this."

"But the question is," said Leopold, "who will come with me? Certainly Eurynomos must go."

"And I," said Mingli.

"And I," said Raj.

"Me, too," said Thacker, standing inside the table, though he hadn't noticed.

"And Suchah!" said the imp, appearing before them with a pop of air.

Leopold smiled and his heart beat strong and fast from their encouraging faces. "What a proud company we are. Well, I suppose now is better than later. Miss Zhao, we have but to employ the beetle…"

She held it out with her fingers, arm straight.

They all leaned in, peering at the clockwork insect in her hand, breathless with anticipation.

Nothing happened.

"Suchah sees nothing," said the imp, unnecessarily.

Raj poked at the beetle with his child-like porcelain hand. "Perhaps there is a required incantation."

Mingli narrowed her eye at it. "Madam Hui Ling didn't mention an incantation."

"She didn't say much of anything," Leopold murmured.

Mingli tossed her head and straightened her arm again. "Perhaps concentration on our purpose." She cleared her throat. "*We wish to find the gateway to the Library*!" she declared in a clear, loud voice.

Still nothing.

"Mortal toy is useless," said Suchah with a scowl.

But Leopold blinked, screwed his knuckles into his eyes, and blinked again. "Miss Zhao…you appear to be…transparent."

She turned her head. "So are you, Leo."

Raj looked down at his boiled shirt and tailcoat. "So am I!" he said delightedly.

Thacker huffed. "I can't tell about me."

Before anyone else could speak, Leopold felt a chill rumble down his body. An abrupt tug grasped his core. He tightened his hold on the bowl, when suddenly, all of them were vanishing and tumbling away…

CHAPTER FIVE

THEY ROLLED ALONG wet grass in the woods. *What now?* he wondered, raising his eyes to the trees and retrieving his hat.

He rushed to Mingli to help her up. She brushed off her skirts, straightened her hat, and retrieved her umbrella. "Is the bowl all right?"

It was safely tucked into the crook of Leopold's arm. "It seems to be intact."

Mingli glanced up to the woods surrounding them. "Where do you suppose we are? Are we still in England?"

Eurynomos brushed leaves from his broad chest and black breechclout.

Suchah sat on the ground, webbed feet apart. His tiny wings flapped on his back as he rubbed his head.

Raj seemed to be checking that all his limbs were functioning, and there were extra clicks of gears, escapements, and pistons whooshing.

"Is everyone all right?" asked Leopold.

"Suchah no like this."

"I'm sorry, Suchah. I never expected it."

Mingli looked at the beetle that was still, remarkably, in her hand. "It's glowing. Do you suppose that means we're close?"

"I swear," said Leopold, mostly to himself, "that if I live to become a wise old Mage, I won't give cryptic messages to those who come to me for help."

"I suppose sorceresses and wizards do so in order to test the traveler," said Raj, sagely. "Just in case they are up to no good. It assesses their mettle. If you were not sincere, you wouldn't have tried so hard."

"I believe Raj is perfectly correct," said Mingli.

"I don't give a dash. If I survive this to a ripe old age with whiskers down to my belt, I will be as clear as sunshine to the poor blighters who seek me out."

"Right you are, Leo," said Thacker. "There's too much mumbo-jumbo as there is in this magic business."

"Oh, but Inspector," said Eurynomos, a rakish lilt to his brows, "where's the fun in that?"

Leopold frowned. "Spense, how is it *you're* here…wherever here is? I mean, don't you have a limit to your, er, ghost traveling?"

Thacker held the open edges of his Ulster with both hands and seemed to preen. "I solved that. Every day, I practiced going farther and farther. I thought it a bloody silly rule to begin with. Oh. Begging your pardon, Miss Zhao," he said, touching the brim of his hat.

"Do you mean to say, Inspector," said Raj, looking him up and down, "that you have overruled the limitations of your spiritual form? That is quite extraordinary." He gave a little salute. "My hat is off to you, sir!"

"Leo!" cried Mingli as she was tugged to the right, her arm outstretched with the glowing beetle shuddering and trying to open its wings. "I'm being directed somewhere."

"Let it go. See where it flies." She paused before releasing her fingers on the clockwork beastie and it rose into the air under its own power. Suddenly, it darted away.

They all dashed after it across the grass. The meadow and nearby forest somehow looked familiar to Leopold, and when he heard the toot of the distant train on its trestle, he recognized it at last. "We're near the Romani camp!"

"I do believe you're right," she huffed as she tugged up her skirts to chase after the beetle. The rest of their company hurried to keep up.

Finally, the beetle began to slow. It flew upward, then in a circle, hovering over a particular thicket at the outer edges of the meadow. Then it stopped completely, closing its wing covers. Still glowing, it dropped. Mingli stretched out her arm and caught it before it fell, staring down at it as if it were a compass, because its glow changed as she backed up, took a step ahead…until the beetle glowed brightest.

"I believe this must be it," she said.

Leopold came up beside her and stared at the clockwork insect. "Now what?"

She glanced at him, then at the thicket, and reached her hand with the beetle towards it…

Her hand seemed to grow transparent the farther she thrust it through. "Cold," she breathed. "Yes. This is it."

He knelt with his clay bowl through the thicket—feeling the coldness on his skin—and waved his hand, allowing the magic to dig through the tangle of grass and roots. He turned the bowl upside down, nestled it inside the hole, and waved his hand again to cover it up. The roots, like worms, squiggled and entangled again, and the grass reached for its brethren, clasping, and hiding the hole completely.

"There. That should enable us to pass through the gateway."

"Hold, Leo," said Eurynomos. He moved his hand through the barrier of the thicket and closed his eyes. "This won't hold it open for long. And we must pass *back* through *this* gateway. Since we don't know how long we shall be there, we are taking a chance by relying on the bowl to keep it open."

"What do you suggest we do?"

"We need a soul to keep the barrier from closing."

Leopold scanned the faces of his little troupe. The only two he was certain had souls were Mingli and himself. Perhaps Raj had one, but it wasn't known for certain. And Thacker…a ghost once had a soul, but was it elsewhere? He wasn't certain of that either.

"There's no one here that we can leave behind."

"I will stay," said Mingli.

Leopold felt the fool. "After all my protestations to keep you safe from this journey, I…I am loath to leave you behind. I don't know what dangers await at the threshold."

"And, I hate to point this out," said Eurynomos apologetically, "but she's the only one who can find the Library."

"Oh blast," he muttered.

As they all lowered their heads to think, the distant sound of music reached their meadow. The Romani were singing their songs, playing their instruments. The mournful tune sung in Hungarian was one familiar to

Leopold. It told of lost friends and long distances between family, roaming the world as they did.

But then Leopold got a thought.

He turned to his friends. "Wait here. I'll be back in a moment."

HE FOLLOWED THE old track of trodden grass and mud where many a member of the caravan had come through the brake to cut wood, and finally emerged into the Gypsy camp. The familiar scent of the fires and the cooking pot struck him first, and then the look of the wagons with their peeling paint, the snuffling of the horses and goats, the dogs, the smoke lingering as it always did like a ring around the beaten caravans.

They were also busily hitching the horses to those very wagons, dousing the perpetual fire in the center of the ring. They were preparing to leave.

One of the men noticed him and raised his arm in greeting. Then other men, playing their gambling games, also turned to greet him. As if he had never been away. As if he'd never left at all. He knew that if he desired it, he could easily join them again, be a part of them, travel as they did to all the corners of England, Wales, and Scotland…

Could he run from the Unholy Hosts there? Was it possible? But no. They were everywhere, and they had sent their messenger Ogiel, who was following Leopold to make certain they knew where he was.

He headed directly to the mostly green wagon that belonged to his uncle. The man himself was not sitting on his steps, smoking his terrible tobacco as he was wont to do. It was a little too cold for that. So Leopold stood on the bottom step and knocked on the Dutch doors.

The top door creaked open, and Yanko himself stood there in his shirt sleeves and threadbare braces. The pipe hung from his lips and wispy white smoke lingered around his beard-stubbled chin, large nose, and bleary gray eyes. He actually looked happy to see Leopold.

"Leopold! Nephew! It is good to see you," he said in heavily accented English. "Come in, come in. I get you tea."

He accepted the invitation and stepped through into the warm interior, closing the door behind him. He warmed his hands at the wood stove as he had been accustomed to doing for all the years he'd lived there.

"Where is your charming fiancée? She's grown on me, Leopold. And she's very pretty…and smells nice."

"I'm glad, Uncle Yanko. Oh, thank you." He took the chipped cup and saucer and sat in the chair he used to use. The tea was hot and sweetened and it warmed him very well indeed. "I have a lot to tell you in very little time."

"Always you are rushing here and there. I thought this fiancée of yours would slow you down."

He glanced around the familiar room, with its shabby eloquence. He had been ashamed of it once, ashamed of living in the dirt and poverty of the camp, but now it was glazed with the glow of nostalgia, even when his years at the Gypsy camp hadn't been all that endearing. All at once, he realized that he might never see this wagon again.

He took another scalding sip before setting the cup back in the saucer. "Uncle Yanko, I have some very serious business to discuss with you."

"Always serious with you, Nephew."

"I'm afraid I was always a very serious fellow." He tried a smile. He didn't know if it worked.

Yanko eyed him carefully under his bushy brows. "It looks serious. Well then. Tell me."

"Part of it is about…my father." He waited for the inevitable scoffing about his *Jewish* father…but it never came. Yanko merely watched him. "You see, Uncle, we all thought he was dead. And…I never really explained to you the circumstances…"

"I can imagine the circumstances."

Leopold shook his head. "But it's important now that you *know* them. Fully."

Yanko sighed, took a bottle from inside his patched waistcoat, and poured some of the contents into his tea. Gin. Leopold might have objected once to this practice, but not now.

He sat back in his chair and sighed. "My father and I…we learned the practice of summoning daemons."

Yanko snorted. "This I know. I tried to discourage this when you came to the camp."

"And perhaps you were wise to do so. It's what trapped him there. I thought he was killed, beset upon by the demon hordes. I saw it myself."

He raised his left hand, letting the cuff and sleeve slide away to reveal the tattoo.

Yanko's eyes widened. "The tattoo! It glows."

"Yes. The first bargain I made protected me from the denizens of Gehenna. It was because my father made a bargain to stay in order to free *me*. I made a second bargain more recently to save my friend. And now…" He looked at it, turned his arm to look at the All-Seeing Eye…that looked back at him.

Yanko startled from his chair and pointed at it.

"It's all right, Uncle. It can't hurt *you*."

"What have you done, Leopold?"

"My bargain…was badly made. To save my friend, I had to become…" He swallowed. "Become a slave to the Unholy Hosts of Gehenna."

"Leopold, Leopold…" He crossed himself twice. "Was that the red demon who came to you here in the camp?"

"Oh no. That was my friend, Eurynomos. He taught me how to be a gentleman. He's helped me with my magic act. He made me a success."

"And all for naught."

He lowered his face. "So it would seem. These Unholy Hosts have called in their marker. I must now submit to them. And it's most inconvenient, because I have only just learned that my father isn't dead, but instead trapped in Gehenna."

"What is this Gehenna you kept talking of? Is it Hell?"

"Not quite. In Jewish mysticism, it is a place of punishment, but for only briefly. He…he shouldn't be there. It's a horrible place. I fear he will have been driven mad."

Yanko looked aghast. "Are you telling me he has been there nearly twenty years?"

"Yes. And I must free him. And now I can. But I am also running one step ahead of these Unholy Hosts who want me, not just for the task they set, but to torment me for all eternity."

"We must go at once to a priest!"

"No, Uncle, not a priest. And not a rabbi. It is far too late for that. And in any case, they can't help me. My friends have agreed to go with me to Gehenna. And now…I need *your* help."

His bushy white brows rose. "You want *me* to go to this place with you?"

"Oh no. I wouldn't ask that of you. But we have found a portal that will take us there. I have put spells around it to keep it open, but only a soul can keep it open for as long as we need."

The brows lowered but still danced a bit. "How long do you need?"

"That's just it. I don't know."

"But the caravan, Leopold. We are leaving."

"I don't know who else to turn to, Uncle Yanko."

He rubbed his chin and paced. "What must I do?"

"Well, you would have to…stand, or, I suppose, sit in a chair *on* the threshold."

"There is a door?"

"Of sorts. It's invisible. But we have little time to spare. I'll be running from the demons after me, and trying to get to my father at the same time. It will be difficult. I…I might not ever return."

"What have you done, Leopold?"

Leopold ran his hand over the back of his neck. His hairs seemed to stand up all the time now. He realized it might be the presence of Ogiel, watching him. "I know it was foolish, Uncle. I was too young to know any better the first time, and did the best I could…when I began to summon daemons. But these were the good kind—" Yanko scoffed and shook his head. "I know you don't believe me but there are *good* daemons. But…I made errors and…and accidentally summoned bad ones. But later, six months ago, to save my friend—the good daemon Eurynomos—I had to sacrifice myself. He didn't want me to do it, but I had no other choice. They like their sacrifices in Gehenna."

"What if the caravan leaves without me?"

It sounded so plaintive, and when he looked up at his uncle, he realized what a tired old man he was. His beard stubble was white, the bags under his eyes drooped. "Oh. I'm sorry, Uncle. It's…it's selfish of me to ask this of you. I'm sorry. Forgive me. Don't think anything more about it." He rose, put his hat back on his head, and turned toward the door.

"Leopold. I am an old man. I have no family left…but you. Why…why was *I* never enough?"

Leopold blinked. He could *hear* the sudden sadness in his uncle's voice but it did not seem to harmonize with his experience of him. Leopold leaned against the door, sagging. His gaze couldn't rise to the old man's eyes. "You…you hated me. I was a burden to you."

Yanko frowned and shook his head. "This is not true, Leopold. When…when my sister married your father, she took everything from me. I had no wife, no children. She even took *you* away. She would not have you visit the camp. At first, I blamed your J— Hmm. Your father for this. But later, I discovered it was her. *She* did not want you at the camp, learning our ways. I never see you. So…when I had to take you in at last, I try to be a father to you, but I don't know how. I did my best. I…I failed, I see. But…I always love you, Nephew, because my sister is part of you. I see her when I look into your eyes. Especially when you are angry with me." He chuckled sadly. "Those are her eyes, right enough. Older brother, very protective. *Too* protective." He nodded, seeming to remember. "Ah." He raised and lowered his arms. "That time is gone. I wanted to be father to you, Leopold. But you summoned your demon, you left us. Why was *I* not enough?"

Leopold never realized there might be another side to it, that Yanko was not just a cruel uncle, but a man. Only a man, who suffered from the loss as much as Leopold had. He stared at Yanko, eyes raking over his shabby clothes—the patches at his knees, the braces, the familiar waistcoat that was too short for him, revealing his stained shirt below it—and saw him anew.

Leopold took his time, swallowing past a warm lump in his throat, before he answered. "I…I never knew how you felt, Uncle Yanko. I could have used some expression of that love and understanding when I was growing to an adult. But I did…I *do* love my parents. Couldn't you understand that?"

"Yes. Of course, yes." He ran his large, calloused hand over his mouth and day-old beard stubble. "I only wonder…if it's too late?"

"Oh, Uncle. It's never too late." Leopold reached out and pulled the man into an embrace. Yanko smelled strongly of that acrid pipe tobacco he liked so well…and gin. Those large hands that had most often been used to box his ears or grab his arm in a bruising grip, patted Leopold ever-so-gently on his back.

After a long moment, when Leopold felt forgiveness flow through him, he stepped back from the bewildered old man. "But...I must go. His suffering... I die a little every day thinking of it. I must find someone who can guard the gate." He moved again toward the door, but that strong hand clasped his shoulder and turned him back.

"I can do this."

"But...the caravan?"

"Bah!" He waved his hand. "Someday, they be back. I wait for them too."

"Uncle, it might be weeks. You can't sit there all alone."

He raised a finger and nodded. "Come. I have idea." He grabbed his coat hanging by the door, and his dented hat with the scarf beside it, and donned them all before he led the way.

They trod across the camp to what Leopold remembered was Mrs. Antalek's caravan and knocked smartly on the door.

Miklos Antalek answered it. He was no longer full of clockwork and metal plates. The curse that Leopold had unknowingly cast upon him thirteen years ago when Leopold was still a young boy, had been reversed. He was a man again, and he looked at Yanko and then at Leopold with some alarm.

"What do you want, Kazsmer?"

Yanko pushed Leopold aside. "Leopold needs your help. He has demon problems and I must sit in a magic portal to keep it open. But the caravan is leaving."

"What is this you say?" Zsófia Antalek pushed her much larger son out of the doorway. "Leopold needs our help?"

"Mother, I can take care of this."

"But the caravan is leaving," she said.

"I will stay with Yanko and keep this demon gate open."

"You will not!"

"Mother..."

"You will not stay alone. *I* will stay too!"

Miklos raised his brows. "But...the caravan..."

"The caravan, the caravan. What do we care of that? I lived at the edge of the caravan, not a part of them anyway, these last thirteen years. What do I care?"

"Mrs. Antalek," said Leopold. "That is very generous of you."

"Is your pretty Mingli going with you? Oh, I knew she would. She is a woman to keep hold of, Mr. Kazsmer. Maybe she has a sister for Miklos."

"Mother!"

She pushed Miklos nearly off the steps. "You go with Mr. Kazsmer and Mr. Péntek. They tell you what to do. I will unhitch the horses."

Faced with her stubbornness, Miklos had no choice but to grab his coat, pull it on, and follow.

Leopold led them back to the meadow, and realized only when they'd turned the corner at some trees that he should have warned them both what to expect.

Yanko stopped dead. "Two demons! And…what in hell is that brass thing with legs?"

CHAPTER SIX

"UNCLE YANKO, YOU remember my Miss Zhao."

Distractedly, staring at Eurynomos and Suchah, he embraced Mingli. "Of course. One cannot forget the Scotland Yard rozzer."

"And…er…this is my very dear friend that I told you about…Eurynomos."

The daemon had shrunk down to man-size. Even his tall horns seemed shorter. Instead of extending his hand to shake, the daemon simply bowed with great dignity. "Mister Péntek. How pleased I am to finally meet you face to face. I must thank you for your care of Leopold when he was a child."

Yanko narrowed his eyes. "I know you. I see you before, when Leopold conjure you."

"As a small matter of correction, he did not 'conjure' me, but 'summoned' me. To some it is a subtle distinction, but I assure you, there is a great deal of difference."

"As you say. Leopold calls you his friend, credits you with making him a successful man. I find this hard to believe."

"Oh, my friend, it is true. Though I learned more about him than I ever taught. I was gratified to have the opportunity, which I much enjoyed. I will never have children, of course. Teaching Leopold, I felt as if I had."

Yanko flinched at that. Leopold was sorry that Yanko had been so unable to show his affection, if what he had said was true. And here was Eurynomos, seeming to cast the remark off as if it had been a simple task.

He thought it best to move Yanko along. "And this, Uncle, is another good friend of mine, Raj. He is an automated man who is quite alive."

Raj bowed and extended his small porcelain hand to shake. Yanko merely stared at it. "I, too, am pleased to meet you…Mister Péntek, is it?"

"What is an 'automated man'? You look like a toy."

"I am very much more than that, I assure you. I work with the use of gears, pistons, and pulleys. But the heart of me is magic. It is not known when or who created me. I find the mystery…fascinating."

"And you call yourself Leopold's friend?"

"Indeed. We have been together for some years." He extended one of his shiny, brass legs. "My legs are new!" he said proudly.

"And here we have Suchah," said Leopold, shaking his head at Raj, "He's an imp. A sort of…demon chappy."

Suchah postured, nearly mirroring Yanko's own gesture of hands-on-hips, with a skeptical expression. He looked the Romani man up and down with a sneer. "Suchah no like this man. You were cruel to Leopold Master."

"Er…Suchah…"

"Is that what he tell you?" said Yanko, bending over to stare the imp in the face. "That I was cruel to him? Do you know how sullen and angry a young man can be? A boy must be ruled with hard discipline!"

Suchah folded his arms over his chest. "Suchah. No. Like. *You*."

Yanko straightened and chuckled. "This one is the only one telling the truth. I might like him. If he wasn't a demon from Hell."

Leopold was about to defend the impertinent imp when Miklos stepped forward. "He's all right, Yanko," he said in his strong Hungarian accent. It was strange to hear his voice without the filter of his formerly mechanical self, when he was the clockwork man. "We fought a war together. He helped us all."

"A war? What war?"

"Between the faeries and the goblins," offered Raj…*un*helpfully.

"Faeries and…" Yanko shook his head. As he opened his mouth to argue the point, he squinted in Thacker's direction. Lifting an arm, he pointed. "What is that?"

"You can see him?"

"A foggy figure…coming into more detail. A…a rozzer?"

Surprised to be seen, Thacker tipped his bowler. "Detective Inspector Despenser Thacker of Scotland Yard, sir. Well…*formerly* of Scotland Yard."

"You're a ghost…" Yanko paled.

Mingli trotted forward to grab his arm to steady him. "Never mind that for now, Mr. Péntek. Just know that your nephew is a very important man, who has saved the world twice. And now he's called upon to save it a third time."

"*You* saved the world?" he said sarcastically. But then Yanko paused, roving his eyes over Leopold's unusual company. "You…you saved the world?"

"I've always had the good help of my friends. And now…we must do it again."

"And all I need do is sit in your threshold?" He looked around. "I don't see a door."

"It's there," said Miklos, pointing.

Surprised, Leopold turned to him. "Miklos…how can you see it? *I* can't even really see it."

The man's eyes seemed to look far away. "I can still…*feel*…the magic sometimes. I know when *you* are doing it. Even when you are in London."

Raj stalked up with a whirr of gears that made Miklos flinch, probably remembering his own former mechanical existence. "You can feel Leopold perform magic even that distantly?"

"I don't know. I think I do. Is that…is that…strange?"

"Mr. Antalek," said Mingli brusquely, "I shouldn't be surprised. Or distressed. You lived with his magic within you for over a decade. Some of it was bound to rub off. And now, Mr. Péntek…"

"Call me Uncle Yanko. You are soon to be my niece."

"Thank you very much," she said, tilting her head in a bow. "Uncle Yanko, let us show you where you are to stand. Or sit. We shall have to arrange for you to have a comfortable chair. I'm afraid you won't be allowed to leave it for long periods of time."

"I will take turns with him," said Miklos.

They stared at Miklos for long moments before Mingli, still keeping hold of Yanko's arm, walked with him to the edge of the meadow where the trees began. She pointed. "Here."

"I will bring him a chair from his wagon," said Miklos. "And I shall bring him food and drink and sit with him. You play cards, Yanko?"

"I beat you at cards," the old man muttered.

THE SUN WAS setting in streaks of orange across the sky, as the crescent moon—climbing all day behind the clouds—suddenly emerged. Zsófia had already built a cooking fire in the meadow, and looked up at the silver disk. "A full moon is better for such a journey, but a waxing moon has good fortune attached to it as well," she said, stirring her pot.

"There will be no moon where we are going," said Mingli, sipping her tea.

Leopold glanced at her and at his friends, politely sipping their tea or miming the experience, as Raj did out of politeness, for he could not drink. Neither could the ghost of Inspector Thacker, nor could he even grasp and pick up saucer and cup. Eurynomos held his teacup like a vicar, with pinky finger—and its talon—extended.

But they all seemed to be looking at Leopold expectantly. What was he waiting for? They had found the portal, his Incantation Bowl was in place, and a soul was guarding the opening. He supposed he couldn't put it off any longer.

He rose and meticulously straightened his waistcoat, adjusted his frock coat, and secured his cravat. He strode to where Yanko sat in the chair from his caravan, a pipe hanging from his lips, a week-old *London Times* in his hands. Leopold stood over him, watching him slowly read and mouth the words before him, waiting for him to look up. When he did, narrowing his eyes at his nephew, Leopold withdrew a magician's wand from an inside pocket of his coat. It was made of wood, polished and stained to a shiny black. "Uncle," he said solemnly, and proffering the wand to him, "this is the first wand I ever made myself. I created it from the Talmudic four species—the date palm, the myrtle, the willow, and polished with the oil of the citron. This will provide you with some protection."

Yanko did not yet take it and looked upon it with suspicion. "What protection do I need?"

"Well…I might have failed to mention that there is a particularly nasty demon after me. His name is Ogiel and he is very dangerous."

"He's the one what killed me," said Thacker.

Yanko frowned at the ghost. "He kill you? Did you have this wand?"

"No, mate. Never knew that demons or wands existed, or that Leo here was involved in such."

"I don't like your unholy magic things, Leopold."

"I'd take it, if I were you," said Thacker. "Just as an aside, I found that listening to Kazsmer is the best course of action."

"This is blasphemy."

"No, Uncle. It's protection. And these are *Jewish* talismans. Like it or not, it is part of the Old Testament. That's the Bible you claim to read."

"I *do* read it, Nephew. You see me, night after night, read the Bible."

"I recall you misquoting it."

"No one can read all those words. Too many words in one place." He scowled before he snatched the wand from Leopold's hand. He turned the wand over and over. "How do you work this thing?"

"You don't 'work' it, Uncle. If Ogiel or any other demon shows up demanding to know where I am, you simply present it, thus." He took it back from Yanko and aimed it toward the invisible threat, like a swordsman in an *en garde* position. "That's all." He gave it back.

Yanko cocked his head from side to side. "You make this magic you do sound hard, when it is easy."

"That's right, Uncle. It is all very easy." But even as he turned toward his friends, the uneasiness that had been with him all day suddenly magnified. His neck hairs stood up, and he spun.

The twilight air shimmered, an unholy smell filled the meadow, and a large figure abruptly materialized. He didn't have to fully form for Leopold to realize it was Ogiel.

Eurynomos rushed forward to stand in front of him, rising in height. "Polluted One," cried Eurynomos, "why are you here and not in your realm of *Sitra Achra*?"

"I come…because I was called. By the Unholy Ones."

"Begone!" He waved his hands as smoke drifted off of his shoulders. "Go back to Gehenna where you belong!"

"I don't do your bidding, Prince of Death. I do the bidding of the Unholy Ones."

"Like Hell, you don't!" Eurynomos grew, bigger than Leopold had ever seen him grow. He was now taller than the trees, and terrifying in his aspect, with pointed teeth bared, and eyes glossing over to a solid black. His shoulders grew wider and smoked outrageously now. "I COMMAND YOU!" he bellowed, voice echoing over the countryside.

But Ogiel was not impressed. He folded his arms across his broad, naked chest and narrowed his eyes. "Why do you defend this…this…*Mortal*? He is not worth your time or your concern." His eyes flicked over Suchah and he frowned. "Oh! Are you captive to this flesh creature, little friend?"

Suchah wrung his webbed hands and minced forward. "Oh, it is most terrible, Ogiel."

"Then come with me. Do not fear this weak Mortal. He will be the slave of the Unholy Hosts soon enough."

Suchah looked back warily to Leopold and bit his lip with sharp teeth. "Alas, Suchah is now *his* slave. You see these glyphs." He gestured to his belly. "Suchah may not leave this flesh creature's side."

"Cruel and evil Mortal!" cried Ogiel. He snarled at Leopold.

Leopold thought it was rather terrifying and even though he tried to put on a brave face, he found himself stepping back.

Suchah shrugged, giving his actor's performance. "Suchah suffers, it is true."

"Then I am glad of this Mortal's fate. For here is the Prince of Death, who is also slave to this flesh creature."

"I do what I like, Foul One," said Eurynomos. "And I choose to defend this mortal for my own reasons."

Ogiel chuckled. "He is your pet. Or…are you his?"

Eurynomos did not take the bait, but he loomed over the beast, gnashing his teeth. "There are consequences to every action, Ogiel. Yours will be dire. I will see to that."

"You can do nothing. I have the protection of the Unholy Ones."

"Are you certain? Are you *very* certain?" Eurynomos took a step back, wound his whole body, and whipped back, sending a pulse of magic crashing and crackling all over the demon with tendrils of blue lightning.

For a moment, nothing happened, and Ogiel's smile grew wide, tusks glistening. "You see…" he said, until he realized that something was indeed wrong and he frowned, slapping at the little shards of lightning crackling anew.

"What is this?" he yelled, slapping more furiously at the sparks and pops erupting all over his black, scaly skin. "What have you done?"

"I warned you, Ogiel," said Eurynomos. He walked forward, blocking his friends from view. Behind him, he waved at them to go to the portal.

I suppose it's now or never, thought Leopold. He grabbed Mingli's hand and ran with her. Raj and Thacker followed, and then Suchah snuck away.

Ogiel jumped and yipped at the painful magic roiling over him. Eurynomos laughed as he shrank, and soon enough he left the demon to his fate and followed Leopold.

Leopold clasped tight to Mingli's hand, rushed past his uncle sitting on his chair in the portal's threshold with mouth agape—offered him a silent apology—and leapt into the unknown.

PART TWO

THE LIBRARY

"Libraries are not made; they grow." –Augustine Birrell (1850-1933)

CHAPTER SEVEN

LEOPOLD HESITATED. MAYBE he should go back to help Yanko...but even as he contemplated it, he was pulled inexorably forward. He tried to spin around but found it impossible to do anything but move forward. Miklos remained behind. *He* could help, this he knew. That would have to be enough. Still, he sent up a prayer for Yanko *and* Miklos.

And then his mind caught up to what he was seeing, and he didn't think anymore.

It wasn't what he imagined. He didn't even know what he *could* have imagined. Stars and galaxies twinkled all around them in a black sky... No, not "sky" precisely. They seemed to be floating in the celestial sphere as one would see through a telescope into a night sky. It was above them, below them, all around them. It was like Mingli's injured eye, beautiful and terrible in its aspect. They hung suspended in a shower of gases like a rainbow cloud. Before them lay a core of light, and instinctively, he felt they should aim for that.

"Mingli," he said, and yet his voice sounded very far away, even to him. "Do we go forward, to that bright core?"

"Yes," she said, "swimming" forward, for he suddenly realized he wasn't standing upon anything at all, and was free to move about in this way as if underwater. It made him giddy, and he, too, moved his arms and legs, propelling himself forward. He tumbled, twisting into rolls, head over heels, and laughing all the while.

"This is very interesting," said Raj. He splayed his arms and legs and slowly rotated, looking all around him at the stars above and below.

"There's nothing to it," said Thacker, whose regular mode of progress must be compared to this, Leopold speculated.

It was the daemon and imp who found it unpleasant.

"Let us hurry, Leopold," said Eurynomos, struggling to move his bulky body forward.

Suchah found that his wings did little good, and he was forced to try to swim, all ungainly arms, legs, and tail, furiously flailing in the ether.

Leopold smiled and held tight to Mingli's hand. She, too, looked amazed at her surroundings. "Did you expect this?" he asked.

She shook her head. There was a bit of a glow, an aura around her – around all of his friends, even Thacker. "I didn't know what to expect," she said. "I've only read about it. The details were sketchy at best."

"But it's wonderous!" he said, glancing all around him. He felt part of the universe, and he supposed that the Library would be something fantastical as this, even with all the dangers Mingli warned him of.

Thacker suddenly came up alongside him. "Now you know what it is to be a ghost."

"Is this how it feels?"

"Well, to move, at any rate. You can't feel anything." He poked Leopold to prove it, and pulled back his hand in surprise.

"What's wrong, Spense?"

"I…I *did* feel that."

"Come to think of it…so did I. Do it again."

Cautiously, he brought his hand up and poked Leopold in the shoulder with an index finger. "Gor-blimey!"

Eurynomos flowed up to them, seeming to take control of his locomotion at last. "We have entered the place between the worlds, Leo. The rules do not apply. Your Inspector Thacker can move as a mortal again. I daresay, you can probably *walk* once we reach the Library, Inspector."

"I'll be buggered. Oh! Begging your pardon, Miss Zhao." He raised his bowler.

Mingli merely smirked at him.

"How much longer, Leopold Master?" Suchah rolled up beside him, tumbling a bit.

Leopold glanced at the bright core. He thought he could see…a building through it? "Mingli, my dear. Am I seeing rightly?"

"Yes. The building should be visible. Ah yes. I see it too."

"It looks something like St Paul's crossed with the Old Royal Naval College in Greenwich."

"It will look like whatever the observer expects. Now we shall all see it in something of Christopher Wren's style. If I had come upon it first, it might look something like the Imperial Palace in the Forbidden City, for I should be expecting that."

"This is fascinating," breathed Leopold. All his fears fell away, at least for the moment. His natural curiosity took over and he scoured the building growing larger before them.

A dome stood on pillars atop the roof, and immediately below the dome was a large clock face…with multiple hands all spinning in different directions. The structure was surrounded by wide lengths of steps reaching the front doors visible under a pediment on the front of the building.

"There is no way to know who made it and why it is here," said Mingli. "Even trying to find out in the Library itself—so I've read—is impossible. As I told you before, the Library is alive. For all we know, it invented itself."

"How can that be?" ask Raj, now swimming on his back and using his legs to push himself along. He looked to Leopold like some enormous water bug.

"How can any of it be?" she asked. "How can Gehenna and our world be?"

Raj put a hand to his cheek. "I wonder if I could find out about myself?"

"I wish we had the time, old man," said Leopold. "But we have one job to do and must do it quickly. I can't have the Unholy Hosts knowing what I'm at."

"Of course, Leopold. I forget myself. The idea of seeking knowledge, or my being able to do so myself without the fear of being captured or destroyed, had me thinking heady thoughts."

"I know. I wish we could."

"Don't worry, Leo. I am here to help you and your father. Not to indulge in my own whims."

Now he felt guilty. Perhaps Raj could wander off on his own...but no. It wasn't any kind of normal library, even if it might look like one. They had to stay together, for safety's sake.

Despite Mingli's assurances she looked tense, strained. He could see it on her face. He grasped her hand again as they flew closer. The bright light was fading, and they found themselves suddenly standing on solid ground, looking up at the vast width of steps leading up to the front entry. The library floated alone, not on any sort of plain or street, but as if it were floating on an immense sea under an overcast sky.

Leopold stepped forward onto the first marble riser when Eurynomos' hand grabbed his arm. "Leo, you must be careful. Not even the simplest thing can be trusted..."

But even as the daemon said so, Leopold felt himself sinking, and when he looked down, his feet were entirely encased in the now solid marble step. "*A francba az összes*!" he swore, twisting and yanking to try to pull himself free.

"One moment, Leo," said the daemon. He seemed to silently consult with Mingli. "Leo," said Eurynomos. "I want you to close your eyes and imagine yourself free."

"Do what? Why, that's absurd."

"We've come to the very heart of absurd. Indulge me, old friend. And don't struggle."

"Very well." He closed his eyes and tried to stand perfectly straight, resisting the urge to pull at his feet. He did as his friend said, and imagined himself free of the marble, walking up the steps normally, reaching the entrance, and opening the door.

"You have great powers of concentration," cooed the beast. "You may open your eyes."

When he did, he was no longer entrapped on the first step, but was standing—with all of his friends—at the entrance.

"What the devil was that?"

Mingli bent to examine his feet, eye patch telescope whirring, lenses and filters clicking madly. "I fear some traps will be mere illusions. But I also fear, we will not be able to tell one from the other."

"That's…that's…damnable."

"Indeed," said Eurynomos. "Hence the name, Library…of the Damned."

Leopold cast a glance to all his companions. "We could all easily be trapped here for all eternity. There is no wandering off. We must all stay together. It's imperative."

"So I see," said Raj. He sounded shaken.

But Thacker was looking down at his own feet. Feet he once again possessed instead of a vague tail of ectoplasm. "Look, Leo. It looks like me again."

"Oh Spense." As Leopold examined his friend, Thacker didn't seem so transparent. He truly did look like his old self.

"I can feel the floor, too." He stamped his foot a few times. "I can feel the bloody floor. Begging your pardon, Miss."

"I'm glad you can feel the bloody floor," said Mingli, offering him a smile.

Thacker glanced at her with an equally wide smile. "Well all right, then."

Leopold reached for the door, when Eurynomos stepped forward. "Allow me." He placed his large hand on the latch and pushed it open. It made no sound but the soft whoosh of the giant door moving through air. Inside there was an expanse of marble floor under a dome where light filtered in. And all around the rotunda, were bookshelves radiating from the center like the spokes of a wheel. This was repeated over and over in several levels climbing into the dome, with spiral staircases set about every ten feet.

"Is any of this real?" asked Leopold.

Mingli was suddenly beside him. Her eye patch with its telescoping lens, whirring and clicking as it moved in and out, searched the room. It reminded him of his own multi-dimensional spectacles, and he drew them from the pocket in his waistcoat. Placing them over his eyes, he moved the different lenses on stalks mounted to the frame one at a time over each eye. Suddenly, the space before him took on an entirely different appearance. There was no rotunda, there were no spoking book shelves, and no marble floor. What lay before him was far more interesting.

"Are you seeing this too, Mingli?"

"Yes, I think I am. What of you, Eurynomos?"

"I can see between the veils of deception, Miss Zhao. And it serves to remind us how very clever this Library is."

Before him, Leopold observed that, instead of the magnificent marble floors and florid columns, everything was made of old, dark, and desiccated wood in several levels. And the staircases that had at first gone from bottom floor to upper floor—which some still did—many more seemed to go sideways into impossible spaces...sideways onto sideways corridors. Still other levels lay perpendicular to the one they were standing on, but had doors on what should have been the floor. An arch, opened to the outside, lay on its side, and a tree growing outside that window also lay on its side, as if each level, each *face* of each *level*, had its own geometry, its own physical domain.

Staircases crisscrossed over their heads, and one could not be fathomed from the other, for some seemed perfectly normal while others were sideways or upside down.

"It's completely insane," Leopold whispered.

Plain, rounded columns of wood soared into the varying heights, but didn't seem to make sense once they got there, as if they had moved between the other columns in mismatched perspective.

He realized that this must be the *real* Library.

"Nothing is as it seems," Mingli breathed.

"Not at all," he replied. "Suchah, Raj, Thacker...can you see only a bright marble rotunda, or this other mish-mash of floors and staircases, cutting into the gloom?"

"Suchah sees. It is not the brightly lit rotunda, as Leopold Master says."

"No indeed," said Raj. "But I was obliged to take a second look. Nothing *is* as it first appears."

"I don't know about no rotunda," said Thacker. "But I've only ever seen this puzzle of stairs and floors before us. And it ain't bright in here neither. And it's all made of wood."

"Interesting," said Raj. "Then it is only the mortals who see it as it is not."

"I shouldn't rely on that," said Eurynomos. "I have known several fallen angels who love to play these tricks, and it works on daemons as well."

"So even though you can see through this deception now," said Leopold, "you're saying that as we move through this space..."

"Raj and I and Suchah and perhaps even Inspector Thacker, *will* be deceived. The Library will learn, you see."

It was fascinating and terrifying at the same time. Every one of them *could* spend an eternity here if they took the wrong turn or were separately deceived. "This is a most forbidding place."

Out of curiosity, he removed the spectacles to look around...and the marble rotunda had vanished. In its place was the dark wood and impossible staircases.

"Well...where do we look first?"

CHAPTER EIGHT

"THAT, MY DEAR boy," said Eurynomos, scratching his square chin, "is the crux of it."

Leopold found himself turning in circles, glancing up to the many visible galleries and suspecting there were many more he couldn't see. "Maybe there's someone here, like a librarian."

Raj imitated his posture, turning to look above. "And how should we find *them*?"

"It's been my experience in libraries and archives that when you least expect it, a librarian will turn up out of thin air to shush you should you make a noise." Leopold cast a glance around once more before he put his hand to the side of his face, took a deep breath, and loudly called out, "Hello!"

Instantly a black figure swooped down from the gallery above, startling Leopold so badly that he fell against Eurynomos, who had grown in size to his usual ten feet. A squawk rang out from the interloper, and the entire company seemed surprised to be accosted by a raven.

The raven circled them again before alighting on the stained tile floor. It walked imperiously across the tiles before them, extending its neck and cawing,

"Is that your librarian, Leo?" asked Raj, walking forward, curious. Mingli caught his arm and pulled him back.

"I've no idea," he said out of the side of his mouth. He straightened his coat, stepped forward, and doffed his hat. "I say, greetings. I am

Leopold Kazsmer, and these," he said sweeping his arm toward them, "are my friends. I wish to ask a question, if I may?"

The raven fixed its dark bead of an eye on Leopold and croaked a sound.

"Er…well then. We are looking for the means to get into Gehenna. Can you direct us to the proper—"

The bird spread its wings and suddenly took flight, leaving a black feather behind. The bird circled above them and landed on the rickety railing of a sideways gallery. It cawed several more times before it flew into the depths of the shadows on that floor.

Suchah ambled forward and grasped the feather. He opened his mouth with the intention of eating it, when Eurynomos snatched it from his hand. "Stay your hunger, my little friend. This could prove useful." He tucked it into the top of his breechclout.

Leopold looked up into the galleries and sighed. "It's looks like we'll have to start up there. Will we…will we fall if we try to stand in the different gravities?" He glanced at Eurynomos, but the beast only shrugged.

"Very well. Then let's find the nearest staircase."

He led the way to the bank of stairs dimly lit by a flickering candle on a sconce beneath a low ceiling. He followed the stairs with his eyes first, calculating which one among the many followed its winding way to the floor they wanted, even as it dipped and rose above each stair, like an intricate plait. "This one, I think."

They all followed, Thacker expressing particular delight that he could feel each step as he ascended. Leopold found that the steps themselves were rickety. It could be an illusion, he reasoned, but it certainly felt real, and just as he thought it—

"Damn!" cried Mingli, stepping through it. Leopold caught her as she teetered. "Thank you, Leo." She adjusted her hat that had gone askew and, using her umbrella to steady herself, leapt lightly up to the next step, looking back to the broken one. "If this is, indeed, real, the fragile nature of these stairways must be observed."

"We'll be careful," he said. Leopold was certain which floor the raven had flown to and he kept his eye on it as they climbed. The staircase did, indeed, seem to tilt into the next area as it changed its allegiance to the gravity of the sideways gallery, but just as the stairs rounded a corner, it was plain that it would not reach the destination they sought.

"Wait, everyone. This is the wrong stair."

"Can't be," said Thacker.

"It is. It's now that one down there."

Mingli leaned over the rail, glancing at the now sideways stair that seemed to twist into an upside-down stairway. "I was certain it was the one we're on."

"So was I. But we'll have to go back."

Thacker leaned over as well, smoothing his hands over the rail and smiling at the novelty. "What if we just jump down to that one?"

Eurynomos joined them, and leaned over the trio as they looked over the side. "We might end up falling right through."

"Suchah will look." The imp's fluttering wings took him into the air and clumsily lowered him to the stair. He stomped around on the steps up and down. "They are solid," he yelled.

Leopold looked at Mingli. "It isn't far. Do you want to take the chance?"

"Every step we take in the Library is a chance. I say we do it."

"Right, then. I'll go first…"

But Eurynomos had already leapt over them and landed with a heavy thud, standing sideways. He looked at his footing. "Seems to be solid enough. Come on."

Leopold clutched the rail and swung over, landing feet first, but being steadied by Eurynomos. "Miss Zhao," said Leopold, "it's quite all right."

"I'm coming then." Over the rail she went, her skirts filling with air and seeming to help her land more delicately, but he suspected, rather, that it was her natural grace.

Thacker remained above. "Come along now, Spense."

But Thacker seemed to hesitate.

"What's wrong? There's plenty of room."

"Well now," he said. "I…I could do it as a ghost, Bob's-your-uncle. But I don't seem to float no more."

"Spense…are you afraid of heights?"

"Now I like that! I've gotten you out of more scrapes and nonsense..."

"It's all right, Spense. You can do it."

"Come along, ghost man," said Suchah. "You can cheat this like you cheat at cards."

"I don't cheat at cards, you little whelp. I'll show you."

"Show Suchah, then." The little imp rested his hands on his hips.

"Yes, Inspector," said Raj behind him. "Let's show him." He grabbed Thacker by his upper arms at a run.

"Wait! Wait!" he cried.

But Raj shoved the both of them over the side and, still clamped tightly to Thacker, they landed none-too-gently on the stairway, sideways, and rolled into a lump. Thacker untangled from Raj and scrambled to his feet. "Why, you mechanical menace! Don't you ever do that to me again!"

Raj popped up to his feet. "That was thrilling! I'd *love* to do it again." But he must have noticed how distressed Thacker was and attempted to brush off his coat.

"Get your little boy's hands off me." He pushed Raj's hands aside and pointed a finger into his porcelain face. "You could have broken yourself. Cracked your little head in two. This is no place for fun and games, my lad."

"You are absolutely right, Inspector. My apologies."

Thacker straightened his Ulster and then his bowler. "That's right. And don't forget it."

"Spoken like a rozzer," muttered Leopold.

Mingli elbowed him.

They started up the staircase—which was now to the side where they had been before, and Leopold marveled that the gravity seemed perfectly normal—but with Eurynomos in the front, he started to slow down and blocked the others.

"Oi, Eurynomos," ventured Leopold.

"I don't mean to alarm you, Leo, but this staircase isn't the right one either. Unless we defy the law of physics...again."

"What?" He shouldered the daemon aside and looked up. But he was right. This staircase didn't go to that floor either. And he was certain it had. "We are being toyed with, for I was certain this was the right stair."

"But it's that one over there," said Thacker, pointing to another farther staircase that clearly went to that second floor.

"We'll be at this all day," Leopold muttered.

"Or an eternity," said Eurynomos. "Look, old man, why don't I go to that floor and look about for information?"

Leopold shook his head. "We shouldn't separate."

"We shouldn't," the daemon agreed, "but I think it inevitable that we do. Otherwise, we will be entrapped by these diabolical devices the whole of our time here. And who knows how much time has already passed?"

"He's right," said Mingli. "It just may be that we must split up."

"But you said—"

"I know. But we might have to take that chance."

"Very well. Then Spense should go with Eurynomos, Raj go with Suchah, and I shall go with Miss Zhao."

"That's all very well," said Thacker, "but what exactly are we looking for?"

"A map of Gehenna."

"And weapons," said the daemon. "One can't be too careful in Gehenna."

"Weapons," muttered Raj. "I don't like weapons."

Mingli raised her chin. "Bear in mind that they may not at first appear to *be* weapons."

"Ah!" he said. "I see your point, Miss Zhao. Not your ordinary weapon, surely. That will be far more interesting."

"Right," said Leopold. "Eurynomos, you take the Inspector up to that floor. Miss Zhao and I will continue on this staircase, and Raj and Suchah, find a different staircase. And we'll meet back in the rotunda in an hour's time."

Leopold looked down over the staircase, but the tiled floor had changed again. It was now a wooden floor and looked entirely different from when they left it. "Dash it all!"

"That is a problem," said Eurynomos, peering over the side. "Perhaps we should meet outside the Library on the steps."

"What if those have changed?" asked Raj.

Leopold raised his arm, and a ball of light erupted from his hand, rose to the ceiling, and exploded into sparks. "My magic still works. Follow that."

"Right," said Thacker. He patted the daemon's muscled arm. "Let's go, then." He held tight to that arm and closed his eyes as Eurynomos made the leap to the other stair. They landed none too steadily but the daemon signaled that they were all right.

Suchah took Raj's arm and fluttered off their staircase in search of another, while Leopold faced Mingli. "Up we go. Or…to the side, I suppose."

"Lead the way, Leo."

Leopold kept half an eye on the steps before him and the other half on his friends disappearing into the gloom of the other confusing staircases.

"Leo, this might be an instance where our eyes deceive us so much that we cannot go on. Best to close our eyes as we proceed."

"We've walked right into Lewis Carroll's world."

"It's all absurd. We have no choice."

"Perhaps we'll find a mad tea party," he mumbled. There wasn't any way to reach the end of the staircase that seemed to be going down and up at the same time. He let go of the rails, grabbed her hand, and closed his eyes. "I certainly hope this works."

He moved his foot carefully up the next riser…and the next…slowly feeling his way forward, visualizing in his mind stepping off onto the gallery. When he slid his foot forward and encountered no more risers, he opened his eyes and startled back. A raven, sitting on a bust of Athena, cawed at him.

Mingli joined him. "This bird is certainly insistent."

Leopold thought it the better part of valor to doff his hat once more. "Greetings again. Or…are you a different bird? Forgive me for not being able to tell. But we are strangers here, in urgent need of a map of Gehenna. I'm hoping the Library is in possession of such a thing; a changeable map to help us find our way. It is a humanitarian effort to save someone who isn't dead and doesn't belong there."

The raven gave its raucous call again, spread its wings, and took to the air. It dropped a feather, and he barely noticed when Mingli swooped down to snatch it up, as he hurried to follow the bird.

It flapped at a seemingly leisurely pace as Leopold trotted after it. Was it foolish to think the bird understood him? Not any more foolish than a deceptive staircase, he supposed.

The bird banked and veered in a circle above him and finally alighted on a rickety display case, with a crack in its glass door. The only item within the many shelves was a small, round porcelain portrait of some unidentifiable woman of means from the last century wearing a benevolent smile. The empty shelves were covered in a layer of dust and the cabinet itself could have been from the eighteenth century, with Queen Anne-style legs.

"Do we need to find this woman?" muttered Leopold.

"I shouldn't think so," said Mingli. "Look at the style of her hair and dress. She'd be long dead by now, at any rate."

"But we *are* to go to the place of dead souls."

"Hmm." She reached forth to grasp the door's knob and Leopold made a sound of disapproval. "Really, Leo. We can't be afraid of everything or we'll accomplish nothing."

"I truly don't want my fiancée to be hurt by any trickery here."

"The raven led us to this spot. Somehow, I feel a benign sense from it." Yet, she was cautious when her gloved fingers closed over the knob. When nothing happened, she carefully pulled the door opened. Leopold was almost certain some evil spirits would emerge, but still nothing happened.

She reached in and snatched the portrait. They both crowded together over it. The frame was gilt and fashioned into a tiny rope pattern in a perfect circle, no bigger than the palm of Mingli's hand.

She flipped it over but there was no clue as to whom the woman was or the artist. "Should I open the back?" she asked.

"Here, let's take it to that table. I shouldn't like to drop it and break it. God knows what curse may fly out of it."

She agreed and they moved toward the table. There, Mingli carefully set the portrait down on its face. Leopold bent down to look at it. "There doesn't seem to be any way to open it..."

Mingli reached under her skirts and withdrew a small leather case strapped to the inside of her thigh.

"Miss Zhao, you seem to have an abundance of hiding places…under your skirts."

She smiled. "That's how I keep the mystery about me."

"You do indeed," he muttered.

"Now, Leo, observe." From the case, she withdrew a small turnscrew and an awl. She worked at the back with the flat edge of the turnscrew, but could not appear to gain purchase. She then picked up the awl and traced the edge with the point. At last, the tool was able to get underneath part of the seam and she gently forced the tip in, levering the seam open.

Abruptly, the cover flipped off and landed on the table on its edge, spinning like a top, until it finally fell over with a clang.

Mingli bent over it and made a small sound. "Oh. That's unusual."

"What?" said Leopold. But he saw it too.

What seemed like a simple portrait was instead a strange device with clockwork inside. Tiny, thin gears turned a tooth at a time, but instead of an escapement that ticked the hands one step further each minute in a watch, it had a miniature gyroscope.

"Now *that's* intriguing," said Leopold, poking a finger near it. "Why should it need a gyroscope? It isn't a compass. It's not a watch, that I can see. And it's got more than one winding spring. And what in blazes is *that*?"

Suddenly, it seemed to come to life, vibrating on the table. They both drew back as it danced and twitched. And then, without warning, it shot forward with a whirring sound and imbedded itself in the wall.

They both trotted forward to inspect it.

"It's in the wall a good four inches." He grasped it by its edges and jerked his hand back. Beads of blood rose up from the skin of his fingers. "The edge is like a razor."

Mingli retreated to the table and brought back a pair of tweezers. She grasped the thing with them and pulled it from the wall. It was still vibrating as she laid it on the table and snapped the back on it. She was able to pick it up from the table by grasping the face and back with two fingers. "It's not the map we were hoping for. But it is a weapon."

"Strange." He painted a sigil in the air with his good hand over the injured one and healed it instantly. "Would you like me to carry it?"

But she had already dropped it into a pocket in her close-fitting jacket. "No need. I'll see to it."

Leopold glanced all around into the shadowy and dusty recesses. "Look here. There's a door."

Mingli approached. "Is it unlocked?"

"We'll soon find out." He reached for the dull brass knob and tried to turn it. "Might be…no, wait. It's just rusty." He put his back into it and finally loosened it. It crackled and crunched and finally clicked and opened when he pushed.

The interior was dark and he could not fathom the size of the room let alone what might be inside it. Except…a movement caught his attention, and he spied something in the distance in a sliver of light. It was…another person.

CHAPTER NINE

"HELLO?" SAID LEOPOLD.

But the silhouetted figure didn't answer. It simply stood there, looking at him.

"I say…hello?" He raised his hand.

The figure raised his hand, too.

"Leo!" Mingli poked him in the back. "What are you doing? You don't know whether they are friend or foe."

"I've got to give them the benefit of the doubt. After all, they're here in the Library with us."

He pulled Mingli in and motioned for her to close the door behind her.

Suddenly, the figure in the distance fell to darkness.

"Hello? Are you still here?"

Still no answer.

They moved forward. "Make a light, Leo."

He snapped his fingers and a ball of light appeared before them, bobbing in the air.

The figure in the distance came into view again…and there was another.

"They still haven't responded," said Mingli. Slowly, she drew the sword from her umbrella.

To his left, another two figures appeared in the gloom.

"Leo…"

"I see them." He cleared his throat and spoke in his loud stage voice. "We mean you no harm, and we expect the same courtesy. We are only looking for…a particular object. We won't bother you in your own search.

The shadowy figures only stood quietly immobile.

Another set of figures appeared to their right, like shadows.

They only seemed to move when Leopold or Mingli moved into the room.

"Leo..."

"Yes, my dear?"

Mingli sheathed her rapier into the umbrella again, watching carefully what the figures on three sides of them did. She raised her arm and the shorter of the figures on the three sides raised *their* arms. She lowered hers and raised the other arm...and the others did so in turn. "Leo, raise your light high into the ceiling."

He flipped his hand and the light lifted, radiating light across the space.

Immediately, three sets of Leopolds and Minglis were illuminated, mirroring everything the originals did.

"What the..." Leopold strode forward. Another three sets of Minglis and Leopolds appeared, mirroring their movements. The more he moved, the more sets of their mirrored selves appeared. Soon, a battalion of Leopolds and Minglis crowded the space. He rushed forward, and thinking they were mere illusions, he expected to plough through them. Except that they *weren't* illusions, and he slammed into one Leopold and staggered back. All the others in the room staggered back, hitting other Leopolds like carroms.

"Mingli," he cried, looking back over his shoulder. "For God's sake don't move!"

He looked all around. He was surrounded by false Leopolds—who were also looking around as he was doing—with Minglis at their sides.

"I'm coming back toward you."

"Be careful, Leo."

Even as he made his way toward Mingli, the other Leopolds moved in tandem. Soon they had surrounded him in a crush. "Open the door, Miss Zhao!" he cried, shoving Leopolds out of the way, but the more he pushed, the more *they* pushed at him, and he found himself stumbling forward with more Leopolds stumbling into him. "Stop it, you monsters. Good God, is that how my mustache truly looks?"

"Keep talking, Mr. Kazsmer!" Mingli had her gun in hand.

"Don't shoot! You might hit me!"

"Thank you for speaking up." She aimed and shot three Leopolds in succession between the original and her. They dropped and Leopold stumbled over their lifeless bodies. He looked back as he finally rejoined her. "I say, that's very unpleasant, looking at one's own corpse."

"I never miss."

"Open the door."

She didn't turn to look, but opened it behind her, keeping the pistol aimed at the Leopolds approaching and Minglis raising pistols in their hands.

"Not that door!"

It was too late. There had been another door beside the one they had entered, and he followed her, seeing no other alternative.

Instantly he was thrown into confusion. The gravity had changed and they fell to their sides as the floor at their feet changed to a wall…or what *was* a wall.

"A little disorienting," he gasped.

"All a trap to confound. Had we gone too far into the other room we wouldn't have been able to distinguish the original from the copy."

"I fear you are right. I would say that caution is utmost, but… I hate to point out that we've already lost our way again by going through the wrong door."

She scanned the darkness. "I'm afraid I didn't notice there was another door."

"Well, we're here now. Might as well explore it to see if that ruddy map is here." He threw a ball of light up to the ceiling and the two of them stilled.

All around them, on every wall and hanging above, were clocks of every variety, though their hands were all running at different speeds and in different directions.

"I dread to think what this means," said Leopold, trying not to touch the various clocks. The ticking sound was suddenly loud and disorienting.

"I hear something," said Mingli.

"Yes, that blasted ticking."

"No. It's something else."

"Look! There's a door."

They started for it, avoiding touching any of the clocks. But then Leopold heard it too. A strange whooshing sort of noise.

"What do you suppose *that* is?"

"Duck, Leo!"

He didn't question. He bent double.

A huge pendulum swept by him. He felt the air from it move over his face. "Good God!"

"Caution, Leo. There may be more."

Even as he looked up he could not see where the pendulum came from, but he heard the whirr of something that sounded like a governor, and saw the flash of enormous gears ahead.

"They're blocking the door."

"Only sometimes. They move away from it, see?"

The gears moved, rolling along a set of still more gears just peeking out of the floor, back and forth in a ticking rhythm.

Leopold sighed. "Of course, we don't know where that door leads."

"I suppose we could go back to the other room and take our chances."

He didn't take but a second to decide. "Let's go forward."

They both stood before the door, waiting for the gears to move aside again.

"This is a very dangerous place, Leo. I certainly didn't want to lose you. Though the prospect of *several* of you…"

He couldn't believe what he was hearing. "Miss Zhao!" he admonished, even as he reddened.

She shrugged. "I was only letting my imagination get the better of me. It helps to cut the fear."

"I see." And then he allowed himself to imagine several Minglis… "I…I get your point." He pulled his collar away from his suddenly hot neck.

The gears began to move. "Are you ready?" she asked.

"Yes."

He hadn't heard it. Neither had she, because when a second pendulum brushed inches from them, it swept up Mingli with it.

"Mingli!"

But she had disappeared into the gloom. "Mingli!" If something happened to her, he'd never forgive himself.

The door opened and she stood in the archway.

"Hurry through, Leo."

"Wait a moment. How do I know it's the real you?"

She leaned in, grabbed his hand, and tugged. He fell through the archway at yet another gravity angle, tumbling to the floor. When he looked up, he realized it was in the original corridor. She tried to let go of his hand but he held it tight. "How do I know you are my Mingli."

She pulled hard on his hand until he fell forward and his mouth fell against hers. She kissed him hard and thoroughly. He sat back with a gasp. "Well…" he said, thoughtfully, "if not the original, you'll do."

"Oh, I see. Thank you very much."

He helped her to her feet and she brushed off her skirts. "When the pendulum took me, I saw a window through to this corridor. I let go of the pendulum and barely caught the sill. It was a ways down, but I managed to jump without injury. Are we ready to proceed?"

He dusted off his own trousers. "I suppose so."

They moved down the decidedly shadowed corridor when Leopold's neck hairs rose. He slowed and covertly glancing over his shoulder. In a particularly darkened corner, he thought he detected movement.

"Wait just a moment," he whispered. Mingli turned without speaking, watching Leopold carefully. He looked back into that darkened corner, and the longer he looked, the more his eyes adjusted. And he thought he saw…eyes. Yes, they reflected what little light there was to be had.

And then they blinked.

"Who *are* you?" he demanded sternly. "Show yourself." Yet, as soon as he said it, he didn't want them to do as commanded. The feeling he had creeping over his skin seemed to be telling him that he very much didn't want them to be showing themselves.

He girded his courage and flexed his fingers, ready to sketch an incantation into the air.

The eyes blinked at him for another few, tense moments…before they faded into the utter blackness and didn't appear again.

"Does it suffice to say," offered Mingli, "that this place gives me the shivers?"

"That very much sums it up." He stared into that corner a heartbeat longer before he swallowed nervously and backed away.

The rest of the corridor seemed to be lightening again. That was because a dusty window came into view behind some pillars and he was pleasantly surprised to spy some books at last. It was a window alcove with a lower ceiling where a regiment of bookcases nestled. He and Mingli started toward them. "Perhaps we can find some answers over there."

He looked closely in the gloom, but none of the shelves were marked. The bookcases themselves seemed old. They were double bookcases—bookshelves placed on opposite sides—with desks attached and pew-like seating, resembling reading carrels in a library or monastery, especially with the lower ceiling in the alcove. The books, too, seemed quite old, as he expected, and were chained to the shelves along bars at each shelf level.

"I remember similar bookcases from Oxford," she said, taking down a hefty volume and resting it on the desk. "The books there are medieval—most of them—and the chains were to prevent poor students from stealing and selling them. They were quite valuable, as one could imagine for books that had to be copied out by hand. I suppose the same problem persists even in a Library of the Damned."

"I should think so," said Leopold.

She ran her finger along the spine, examining the Latin scrawled along it, and put that same finger to her lips thoughtfully. "Leo, I think you should stand back."

"Why?"

She glanced at him before she moved to the side away from the front of the book, and opened it.

A dart shot up from the book and embedded itself above them on one of the low wooden ceiling vaults. Had she or Leopold been sitting directly before the book, they would have been darted.

Leopold stared at it open-mouthed, reached up, and pulled the still quivering dart from the ceiling. He turned it this way and that. "How did you know?"

She turned the spine toward him so he could read it. "Morpheus" it said.

"And from that you surmised…"

"I have encountered the like before." She closed the cover. "The books themselves are traps for the unwary."

He shook his head, aghast. "Why should such a thing be? Can't they just keep miscreants from getting into the Library in the first place with guards or something?"

"Perhaps the heart of the individual cannot be determined from the outset. Only those wary and clever enough may use the Library. Or perhaps…*we* are perceived as miscreants, daring to cross the threshold at all."

"Well, that's all dashed inconvenient. And not fair to those who are innocent of such things."

"That's why I'm here. To keep you safe."

He tugged at his lapels. "I'm not that innocent," he grumbled.

Her hand was suddenly on his cheek. "My dear, sweet Leopold. Of course you are."

He readied a rejoinder on his lips, but melted instead under her loving gaze. "Well…" he huffed instead.

As usual, she abruptly turned away from him, just as he was thinking of stealing a kiss. "Perhaps the bookcases have large volumes of maps." She strolled to the other side of the first bookcase and perused the spines. When that didn't satisfy, she moved on to the next.

Leopold went to the bookcase at the other end and scanned the shelves. "I see ancient books of magic here."

She leaned out, only her head appearing from the side of the bookcase. "Surely you don't need those."

"I don't, actually."

"Leo, I've wondered. Just how is it you perform magic? I see you gesture. It looks as if you are painting runes or something similar in the air."

"Well…yes. Sigils of ancient origin. Sometimes Hebrew glyphs. Before I discovered Earth magic, I had to recite Hebrew or Latin incantations. But now I can form in my mind what I wish to do and the sigils suggest themselves to me, almost bypassing my brain and going directly to my hands."

"Interesting. And is this what Eurynomos taught you?"

"Not so much taught me, but made me aware of, opened my mind to it. He said I was a natural Adept."

"A Mage?"

"I suppose. I really haven't thought too much about the mechanics of it. It simply…came to me."

He ducked his head back before he thought more and stuck it out again. "I say, Mingli…"

"Yes?" She thrust her head out as well.

"How…how do you do yours?"

She nodded. "Much the same way," she said, thinking. "But I have no need to sketch sigils. When I think it, it simply happens. Only my magic is not quite as elaborate or refined as yours. Nor as strictly controllable."

"Due to your…your…" He gestured vaguely.

A frown line appeared between her brows. "My daemon side."

"Er…yes."

"I suppose I should be grateful for it." She ducked back behind the bookcase.

But she didn't sound grateful. He supposed he couldn't blame her. First these ghosts with a grievance vexed her with their mission…and that tattoo that wended its way sensually down her back and hip. And then to discover she was part daemon…well! Anyone would have been vexed. He longed to comfort her, but he reasoned that an embrace and a kiss wouldn't relieve the questions and fears she might be harboring.

He thrust his neck out again and inquired softly, "Mingli?"

Slowly her head appeared again, and by the expression on her face, he knew she had closed the veil on her emotions.

"Mingli…my dear, you know you can talk to me about all of it. Every bit of it. I love you. And I will do anything I can to relieve your suffering. Even if it's just to listen to you speak of it. You know that, don't you?"

Her flat expression softened, and she lowered her eye under a fan of lashes. "I do know it, Leo. Forgive me for being terse with you."

"Oh, but you weren't! I just thought…"

She raised that eye again and refrained from spinning the telescope on the eye patch. "I know. And I love you, too." She smiled and slowly pulled back behind the bookcase once again.

He grinned. "She loves me," he whispered dreamily. Even after last night, he could scarcely believe it.

Raucous cawing. He startled back and looked up at the top of the bookcase. The raven was looking down at him and snapping its beak.

"What is it?" he asked.

It flapped, rising inches off the topmost moulding and landing again.

And then, with a loud crack and the sliding of wood on wood, the bookcase began to move.

ROBERT CARRASCO 2021

CHAPTER TEN

IT SLID AWAY from Leopold and toward…

"Mingli!"

"Leo, the bookcase is moving toward me."

"Get out of there!"

"It appears that my arm has become entangled in a book's chain and I can't seem to move."

Just as he made to leave the carrel, a piece of the moulding slid in front of him, entrapping his ankle.

"I appear to be trapped as well." He looked behind him and *that* bookcase began to move toward *him*. "I seem to be in rather the same predicament."

"Can you use your magic?"

He wrote a sigil in the air over his entrapped ankle, but nothing happened. "Didn't do a bloody thing, I'm afraid."

"Well…that's unfortunate."

He pushed at the bookcase, knowing full well that it would do nothing. Glancing up, the raven was still there, watching him with a gleaming bead of an eye. "Can't *you* do something?"

"I'm trying," said Mingli.

"No, my dear. Not you. The bird."

"Oh? Is the raven there?"

"Yes. It either tried to warn me…or is laughing at our predicament."

"I don't believe it's the latter."

"Then it bally well can *do* something."

"It may not...be allowed to...inside the laws...of this place." She seemed to be struggling, trying to loosen herself from the chains.

"I'm going to try something, Mingli." He closed his eyes, drew the proper sigils, and then tossed the magic over the top of the bookcases toward her. "Did your chains loosen?"

"No, but thank you for trying."

The carrel touched the back of his legs as it moved ever closer. He flattened his back against the seat that had trapped his ankle. "This seems a rather unpleasant way to go," he muttered.

He looked down at his glowing tattoo and inspiration hit. He pushed up the sleeve, touched the Eye of Providence, and yelled, "Eurynomos! Suchah!"

Instantly the daemon and the imp appeared. "What does Leopold Master...shit!"

"Good Lord!" cried Eurynomos.

"Yes. Can you both manage to disable these bookcases? I fear Miss Zhao is in grave distress."

Eurynomos whirled around the corner. Leopold could only see the daemon's talons curl over the edge as he worked hard to push them back. Suchah worked to free Leopold's ankle, but after much grunting and straining by both daemon and imp, neither were successful.

"Concentrate on freeing Miss Zhao, Eurynomos."

He could hear the daemon grabbing the chain. "Miss Zhao, you appear to be well-tangled," said Eurynomos in his usual polite tones.

"I assure you, it wasn't my doing."

"Of that, I have no doubt. It saddens me to say, that I fear I shall have to destroy this book that binds you so."

"I'd rather anything but that."

"I'm very much afraid it must be done."

Leopold cringed at the sound of tearing parchment and leather. Suddenly, Eurynomos grew taller than the shelves. He grasped Mingli by her waist with his larger hands and set her down atop the bookcase and burst his way free of them, just as they closed upon the space she had occupied with a crack of splintering wood.

As soon as the bookcases met and crashed, Leopold's ankle was released. He sprang upward upon the seat and caught Mingli just as she tumbled from the top.

"I've got you," he said with a grunt, holding her like some damsel in distress—he chuckled at the very thought—then leapt away as the other bookcase continued forward to crush the seat he had stood upon.

When he landed on his feet upon the floor, Mingli took advantage of the situation and hung her arms around his neck to deliver a noisy kiss.

"Ack!" snarled Suchah, turning his head away. "Must you?"

Leopold wore a dreamy expression. "Yes, she must."

He reluctantly set her down—she didn't seem to weigh anything at all—and they both looked back at the compacting bookcases that hadn't seemed to stop, as books and shelves, seat and desk, kept on cracking and fracturing into a decided mess.

"What was the point of that?" cried Leopold, saddened at the destruction of the books.

"The point, my dear man, is to lay an example forth of what can happen when the proprieties are not observed," said a small, hollow voice.

Everyone turned to the raven, its black feathers seeming to swallow up the candlelight. Its hackles ruffled and its slightly curved beak opened. "I trust you understand me," it said.

Leopold slowly doffed his hat and leaned over. "By Jove, you *can* talk."

"Mortals. They always state the obvious."

"But…forgive me, if you could talk, why didn't you speak before?"

"Had to test your mettle. See what you were about. It's not just anyone who can reach the Library. Some are good…while some are evil."

Leopold opened his mouth to speak when movement caught the corner of his eye, and he looked upward.

All along the railings of every level, corvids began to appear. An army of ravens looked down upon them, some cawing, some chortling.

"We are the librarians," said the raven.

"Well," said Leopold, returning his hat to his head. "I am pleased to formerly meet you."

"We see that your search is sincere and that you have a love of books and mean them no harm."

"But you just crushed these old books on a whim!"

"Crushed which old books?" the raven enquired, cocking its head.

"Why, those..." He gestured toward the ruined bookcases...and found them entirely intact and back in their original positions, the desks and seats also quite unharmed.

"Leopold!" Suchah was busy retrieving Raj and set him down upon the tiled floor. "Leo, are you all right?"

"We're quite all right now. And...we've met the librarians."

"The corvids. Yes, I see them."

"What of Spense?"

"I was with Suchah," said the automaton.

"Oi, Leo!"

Leopold raised his head, and saw Thacker standing at a railing over the rotunda, broadly waving his bowler. The ghost cast suspicious glances at the birds on either side of him.

"Come down, Spense. We need to talk."

It wasn't long—now that the tricks and traps were stalled—that Thacker was able to descend a staircase (that clearly would not have descended directly to them before) and joined the others. They stopped beside their companions to examine the raven standing on the floor at their feet.

The galleries above no longer appeared topsy-turvy, no longer leading up the wall and ceilings, with upside down passages and sideways arches to angled corridors. It looked now to be any normal library, with gravity firmly on one dimension.

"You seek a map," said the bird. It glanced at Eurynomos. "But we know you, Prince of Death. How is it that *you* need a map?"

"Gehenna, my dear corvid, is ever-changing, much as does the Library. But the Unholy Hosts seemed to have seized power and have made it more difficult."

Leopold whipped his head around to stare at Eurynomos. "You didn't tell me that."

The daemon shrugged. "There didn't seem to be much point. You were going to go regardless."

"You're telling me that the Unholy Hosts are now in *charge* of Gehenna? You're telling me this *now*?"

Mingli's lilac-infused presence came up beside him. "Leo, he's right. You had no choice but to come. I suppose it complicates things when we get there."

"They'll never release my father," he muttered.

"As corvids, we have no reason to venture to Gehenna," said the bird. The other corvids above on the railings chucked and rumbled their acknowledgement of this truth. "But we are aware there is a certain logic—or laws, if you will—to every place in the universe. Yes, even the Library of the Damned has its logic and rules. Perhaps you will find this useful as you venture on, Mr. Kazsmer."

The talking raven seemed to ease his fears somewhat. It wasn't that it was amusing to see an animal perform such a "trick", but that it was so reasonable about it.

"You are most gracious," he said to the bird with a slight bow. "But a map is foremost on all our minds. Is there such a thing? And may we have the use of it?"

The bird raised its head to its fellows, and the many corvids above flapped and chuckled, hackles puffing.

After some discussion and cawing, the bird faced them once more. "It has been decided. You are deemed worthy to continue. Perhaps you should try the mews below."

The corvid hopped aside, revealing a trap door.

Leopold swallowed. "You mean for us to…to go in there?"

"The way forward sometimes means…down."

"Very well. I thank you…I thank you all…" he said, raising his hat to the birds above.

"Once you find what you need, Mr. Kazsmer, you must remember…You are safe within the Library. Once you leave it, the denizens of Gehenna can find you again."

"Is there nothing here that can stall them?"

"That is for you to find. The objects in the Library speak only to the finder."

Leopold mulled that, and glanced toward Mingli. It cheered him considerably to find that she was smirking.

"And Prince of Death," said the raven.

Eurynomos shrank to Leopold's size and took a knee as he leaned in toward the bird. "Yes, Wise One?"

"Refer to the Talmud. Much wisdom can be found there." It spread its wings, and flapped, rising from the floor and swooping in a circle to meet the others on the first floor above.

One by one, the ravens flew off and disappeared into the natural gloom of the place. Shafts of light harboring motes of dust—and the occasional drifting feather—were all that remained of them.

They all stared at the trap door and Leopold leaned down to pull it open by its iron ring. He laid the door back and peered into the darkness. He created a ball of light, revealing a ladder.

He glanced toward his companions. "My friends, we have no choice but to go."

"You first, Leo," said Eurynomos. "I'll take the rearguard."

Leopold lowered himself down the ladder. Once the ball of light breached the portal, it shone out to the vast undercroft. Bookshelves, tables, display cases, locked cabinets…as far as the eye could see, much like the secret archives in the bowels of Scotland Yard.

Raj came next, his brass legs shining from the ball of light. Suchah, then Mingli, Thacker—who *did* have to climb in the mysterious architecture of the Library that made even spirits as weak as mortals—and lastly Eurynomos.

When Leopold reached the bottom, he had believed the raven would appear before them again to lead the way. Or he had hoped it would be there. But it wasn't. He walked around in a circle, directing the ball of light. The glow only revealed a nimbus of illumination for about fifteen feet and died off into a gloom so deep no eye could penetrate it. He tried his spectacles, but they could only do so much, giving him another ten feet before it became a haze of tangled shadows. He took them off and stuffed them away again.

Once everyone had descended the stairs Leopold faced them. "We're on our own again. I suppose it wouldn't hurt to spread out and look. Now mind you, it's not likely to be out in the open and obvious."

"I suggest we still move in pairs," said Raj. "It seems more prudent that way."

"If everyone agrees?" They all nodded. "Very well. I'll be with Miss Zhao."

"Suchah will stay with *that*." He pointed to Raj, who sighed.

"Must I remind you, my impish friend, that I am not a 'that'? I am Raj."

"Must go," he said, tugging on Raj's arm. The automaton's pistons and spinning governors whooshed into the distance.

"Then it's you and me again, Inspector," said Eurynomos.

They each took different directions, Eurynomos creating his own ball of light to bob ahead of him. Raj and Suchah didn't seem to need light.

"Here *we* are again, Miss Zhao," said Leopold to his companion.

"I'm glad you chose me. That way I can keep an eye on you."

He paused. "Is that a…joke?"

With a smirk, she blinked said solitary eye. "Possibly."

He slid an arm around her waist and dragged her in against him. Ordinarily, he would never dream of doing such a thing, but these times were different. He knew he might be dead…or enslaved…tomorrow. *Take it while you can, Leopold.* "Do keep your eye on me, my love, and watch me carefully as I take advantage of our being alone." He leaned in slowly, watching her one eye watching him with its thick fan of lashes, watched it slowly close as she lifted her face to receive his kiss.

It wasn't quick, this intended kiss…but a lingering one, the way she herself had taught him, with an opened mouth and insistent caresses. As their kissing became more intensified and with mutual heat growing between them, he gradually drew back with a deep sigh. "You do have an effect on me, Miss Zhao."

"Would you be surprised to know," she said breathlessly, "you have the same effect on me?"

He smiled gently. "Not surprised at this point. Pleased, rather. I do love you, after all."

She put a hand to his cheek. "And I love you. Never forget that, Leo."

She said it simply, but he couldn't help but hear the underlying warning that came with it: that it might be the last time she *could* say it. Instead of showing his fear, he kept his smile in place and smoothed his mustache. "I won't." He gave her a short kiss to seal their love and then released her.

She straightened her hat, took a deep breath, and looked around the undercroft. "Where do you suppose we would find such a map?"

"Would it be in a place of honor?"

"It may be no more special than any other item in the Library."

"I suppose that's true. But I shall go under the assumption that it *is* a grand find. Therefore, I think we should check all the displays and cabinets."

She shrugged. "Why not? There's one there."

They ventured forth toward a large cabinet with glass doors and peered inside. The only object within was some sort of skull, from an animal or…extinct creature. The head was large with horns and bulbous features. It could even be that of a demon, Leopold decided. There was a card displayed with it explaining what it was, he presumed, but it was written in a language and alphabet he had never seen before.

He glanced at Mingli to confirm it, and she seemed to agree with a raise of her slender eyebrow.

They moved on, walking carefully in the dark. Occasionally, he spotted the others with their bobbing lights, but they soon disappeared behind book stacks and display cases.

He wondered, whether in this vast archive, they would be able to find what they sought at all.

"I know what you're thinking," said Mingli so suddenly he startled.

"Confound it, woman. Can you really read my mind?"

She chuckled. "Not in the strictest sense. But I seem to know you in particular. And you're wondering if this exercise is all for naught. It isn't. For one, it got you away from the prying eyes of the Unholy Hosts. Which gave *me* the chance to pause and consider other alternatives for you."

He stopped. "What do you mean?"

"I mean, I considered whether it was the wisest thing to have you go into the lion's den. Into Gehenna at all."

"But I must go. I must save my father."

"But you have us now to do that task. I began to consider if finding another place to live—in this realm or another—would be the best alternative to save your soul."

He blinked. He could do little else as his mind tried to dig into her bizarre proposal. "Live…in another…realm…"

"Leo." She squared with him, her telescoping eyepatch whirring and refocusing elsewhere. "After having found you, my…my soul mate… after so many years of a solitary life, years of assuming I would…*could*…never have this…I wasn't about to give you up so easily. The Unholy Hosts are *angels. Fallen* angels, so your daemon friend says."

"They never seemed like angels. They seemed like horrific creatures, with…with tentacles and horrid faces, though I tried desperately never to look at them directly."

"Their choice has made them as ugly outside as they are within. But they are still angels. Do you realize what that means? They have incredible power. And a very overwrought chip on their shoulders. They have no morality. They are pure narcissism. What pleases them is the only currency they know or care about."

He swallowed. "I have been studiously trying *not* to think on the details," he said softly.

"Leo, I apologize for speaking so frankly…"

"No, my dear. Never apologize for that. It's one of the many things I love about you."

She nodded, licked her delectable lips, before she began again. "If we could find peace in some other place…some other completely different plane of existence, we might be able to foil the advances of the Unholy Hosts…"

He took her arms, simply holding her, gazing into her face, a face he had come to find such joy in—to wake up to, to enjoy the simple pleasures of tea with. He couldn't imagine a life without that face looking at him with love each day, each hour. "Mingli…I can't express how grateful I am for your considering this option for me. For us.

But…I can't run forever. Nor do I wish to leave England, my home, behind. And so…we must find a way for me to defeat this bargain I made with them." He dropped his gaze down to his shiny shoes and spats with their sparkling black buttons, before he looked up again. "Every place, every being has rules that apply to them. The Unholy Hosts are no different. You say they are pure narcissism. You say that they are fallen angels. And yet, they must abide by their own set of rules, just as the raven said about the Library of the Damned. They have power, but not unlimited power, for there is a power greater than theirs. I ask that you put your magnificent mind into solving that problem. Because I fully intend to live the rest of my days beside you *in London*, going on adventures, growing old with you, and loving you."

Her one eye glossed and her plump lip quivered. She pulled away from him and looked up into the gloom, trying to hide her hand as it swiped at that eye. "Well," she said after a long interval of looking about, her body facing away from him. "If that is what you want, Mr. Kazsmer, I have but to obey. I will put my mind to it, as you say, and come up with a more…earthbound…solution."

They wandered, the bobbing globe of light seeming to illuminate each small portion of a world of stacks and cabinets, before it swept away and opened a view of the next place…and the next. Would they ever find it?

That familiar shiver crept up his neck and Leopold found himself snapping his head behind him and staring once again into a black-shadowed recess and at a pair of eyes glaring back at him.

"This really is unconscionable!" he yelled, proud of himself for keeping his voice from quavering. "Dammit! Show yourself."

The eyes merely blinked at him and slowly backed away until the shadows consumed them.

Leopold expelled a long breath. "I don't like it, Miss Zhao."

"Nor do I."

"I…I suppose we have little choice but to press on." Yet, even as he moved his light to illuminate their path of empty spaces, he was beginning to think that they would simply have to take their chances with Eurynomos as their guide and venture into Gehenna without a map…when the light swept over a jar with a disembodied hand floating inside of it, sitting on a lone cabinet.

He walked forward. Of itself, the hand seemed withered…with a bit of a claw about the nails. It was an ordinary-sized hand, just a little unpleasant to look at. And then he turned his eyes to the cabinet it rested upon.

It wasn't ornate, and was as dusty as all the others. It stood alone, unadorned, not even a wall to rest against. He wouldn't have even bothered except for the hand in the jar…and the strange doors. There were no handles, no locks. Only an unusual carved-out shape—in mirror images—on each door.

"Mingli," he said, drawing her back from the edge of the light. "Look at this."

He ran his fingers over the strange, indented shapes. "What do you suppose it means?"

She wiped the dust from the door's glass. Inside was a single scroll of ancient origin. Not parchment. Perhaps…papyrus?

She crouched by the shapes and ran her gloved fingers over them. "It's strange, isn't it? But…familiar."

"I don't see a way to open the cabinet." He pushed on the indentations but nothing happened. He ran his hands up the side at the door, then below it on its long legs. "I thought there might be a hidden switch."

"I wonder if we could smash this glass," she said.

"That doesn't seem in line with what the ravens would like."

"You're right, of course. Hmm. Ravens." She opened her jacket and plucked out the feather she had saved.

"What are you doing?"

She placed the feather into one of the indentations. It fit perfectly. Yet nothing else happened.

"Call Eurynomos," she said, cocking her head as she studied it.

He touched his finger to the tattoo and said the daemon's name.

Instantly, Eurynomos and Thacker appeared. "Yes, Leopold… Oh! This is interesting."

Mingli glanced over her shoulder at the daemon. "Do you see?"

"I do indeed." He withdrew the feather he had saved from Suchah and leaned down to press it into the other indentation.

A strip of bright light sprang from the seam between the doors and they slowly opened like petals of a flower.

When they'd opened completely, a light emanated from within the cabinet and shone down on the scroll.

"Leopold, I do believe you've found it," breathed Eurynomos.

Leopold reached in and grasped the scroll…that immediately crumbled in his hands.

CHAPTER ELEVEN

HE WATCHED THE pieces flake and flutter to the floor. *No!* he cried in his head, all his hopes crumbling with them.

His heart clenched, seeming to create a knot in his chest, in his core. But the knot was more than simple anxiety. It was, in fact, balled up power that suddenly surged within him, starting as a warm hum in his belly before stretching, growing inside his torso. It suddenly blasted out of his chest and encompassed the litter of papyrus into a ball of churning light. The particles suspended in the air, in the light, and slowly turned. As the cloud of flaked papyrus rotated, they gradually came together. Each seam sizzled and drew tight to another piece. Like a puzzle, the proper pieces found their mates and fizzed and flashed as they adhered. One by one, the pieces gathered until the scroll was whole again. And when it had completed itself, the ball of light dispersed and the scroll gently landed into Leopold's open palm.

Eurynomos' eyes gleamed. "Your power is...*extraordinary,* my friend."

"I didn't even...I mean I had nothing to do with it."

"I think you did. There's more to you than even *you* realize."

Suchah arrived with Raj. "Suchah heard your call, Leopold Master."

"But I didn't call you," he said, still looking at the scroll.

Suchah exchanged a curious glance with Raj.

"What have you found, Leo?" said the automaton. His hands were full of varying books and objects he tried vainly to stuff into his coat.

Leopold absently wrote a golden sigil in the air and a carpet bag dropped into his hand. "If you're going to 'borrow' from the Library, old man, best to have a bag handy." He tossed it to the automaton.

Leopold returned his attention back to the scroll and studied it. There was no trace that the papyrus had ever disintegrated into pieces. "I think this is the way into Gehenna."

Eurynomos moved to look over his shoulder. "By Isaiah and Daniel! That's exactly what it is. The librarians must truly favor you."

"They led us here," he said quietly.

He unrolled the scroll and looked at the faded inked lines and markings. Even as he watched, the lines rearranged themselves, the markings flying to different parts of the page.

"It follows the changes," breathed Eurynomos. "We'll be able to find the gates, the rivers."

Leopold locked eyes with the daemon. "We can do this."

Eurynomos nodded. "Yes."

He rolled up the papyrus and carefully stored it in one of his many inside coat pockets. When he turned to the others, he was surprised Thacker had something in *his* hand.

"Spense! You're…holding something."

Thacker looked down at the object. "Strange, ain't it? I can feel it."

"What is it?"

"It appears to all the world as a stereoscopic card viewer, but when you look inside…Well. You ask it to show you people."

Leopold took it. A wooden instrument with an apparatus that fit over the eyes with dual lenses. That end had a handle below a wooden rail where a platform for a dual optic card could slide up and down it. The card held an image of a galaxy.

Leopold glanced once at his friends before he raised the viewer and pressed the eye piece to his face. The galaxy image—instead of having the effect as if it were in its own space, free of its background—became blurry. "Show me…Queen Victoria!"

As Leopold moved the card along the slide the image changed. It was a moving picture…of the queen! There didn't appear to be any sound, but the aged queen seemed to be enjoying tea with her husband, Prince Albert.

He tore it away from his face. "That's remarkable!"

"Showed you something, didn't it?" said Thacker. "Showed you what you asked to see."

He breathed hard and raised his eyes to Thacker. "Yes. I think that can be very handy. With this," said Leopold distantly, "I can see…my father."

Eurynomos suddenly snatched it from his hand. "All in good time, Leo. For we don't yet know if the ones we view can become aware of us, the viewer. Our rescue of Àkos still needs to be shrouded in secrecy."

Leopold nodded. "You're right, of course. It's just that…I long to see him."

The daemon patted his shoulder. "I know, old chap. Best I carry it, then. I wouldn't want you to be tempted."

They all headed toward the ladder. Leopold touched the old wood and looked up into the shaft.

Each climbed—first Thacker, then Raj, then Mingli, then Leopold. Suchah flew on his own, but kept looking back at Leopold.

They had climbed ten feet up…fifteen feet…when Mingli's foot broke through a rung and she teetered. Leopold grabbed her ankle, Suchah latched onto one arm, and she was able to right herself.

She glanced back over her shoulder. "Crisis averted," she said with a smile.

They reached the Library rotunda again and climbed out. A raven was awaiting them.

"You have what you need?" asked the bird.

Raj clutched the bulging carpet bag to his chest while Leopold patted his coat. "We do. I thank you most heartily for your help."

The raven bowed its head.

"Oh, er, one thing." He crouched down and spoke confidentially. "One or two times I saw…well, it seems silly now, but I felt something like an evil presence, with only eyes staring at me out of a black abyss."

"Ah," said the raven. "It wasn't the *actual* presence of the Unholy Hosts, only the manifestation of what they represent. I'm afraid their evil is so palpable that it reveals itself even here. It is Evil itself stalking you, Mr. Kazsmer. Do not fear it here in the Library. Rather, be cautious of it once you leave our precincts."

Leopold rose and thanked them again.

"Good luck, Mr. Kazsmer. I hope the universe is looking kindly upon you and your companions. The exit you seek, is that way." It raised a wing, and with a little difficulty, pointed to an arched portico with a small light hanging from the inside arch.

Leopold doffed his hat and bowed. The bird flew off, disappearing into the gloom near the vaulted ceiling.

He gathered his friends. "Through that door is our way forward. I suppose it's too late to turn back now."

Thacker straightened his bowler. "Lead on, Leopold. To wherever the hell we're going."

Wherever the Gehenna *we're going,* he thought with little amusement. That was *precisely* where they *were* going.

PART THREE

GEHENNA

"And they have built the high places of Tophet, which is in the Valley of Gehenna, to burn their sons and daughters in the fire…" –Jeremiah 7:31

CHAPTER TWELVE

LEOPOLD DEFERRED TO Eurynomos to choose one of three gates.

"What *are* these gates?" asked Mingli.

"Well, Miss Zhao, one opens to the deserts, one to the sea, and one to the Valley of Ben Hinnom outside the walls of Jerusalem. It is this last one we seek."

"To go to Jerusalem?"

"Well, that isn't precisely where it sets one down. Jerusalem is the proper gate to Gehenna. Gehenna, not unlike the Library of the Damned, is a living entity *between* the worlds not of it, yearning for the souls of the righteous, a craving that cannot *be* sated, for it is the *broken* souls—those that need their scales balanced from what evil they did on earth—that must ultimately go there to be cleansed. You see, it is a terrible cycle, for once those souls are released, Gehenna hungers to keep them. Gehenna *wants* to keep Àkos Kazsmer."

Raj shook his head. "But that's horrible."

"Yes. And so it wanted also to keep Leopold. But we won't let that happen, will we?"

Eurynomos, grown to his ten feet again, ushered the company around him like a mother hen gathers its chicks. "Are we all ready now? Good. Stay close to me. I shall go first, but I want you, Leopold, to be right beside me. When we pass through this gate, do not slow, do not stop...no matter what you see."

Leopold exchanged worried glances with Thacker.

Suddenly, Suchah was between them. "Do not worry, Leopold Master and Cheating Ghost. Suchah is here to help."

"Thanks," said Thacker nervously, "...you...you little blighter."

Suchah smiled with his sharp teeth, but even he didn't look too certain about it.

"The gates are guarded by fallen angels," Eurynomos continued. "The one we will pass through is guarded by Nasagiel. He will make demands. Let *me* speak for us."

As they walked forward, an image of an ancient arch appeared. It was made of the golden stone of the desert, but parts of it were broken, crumbling. The arch barely held on from its tilted keystone.

Leopold longed to hold Mingli's hand, but he thought better of it. If any were made aware that she was important to him, might they do her harm? His mouth was dry and he wished he had a brandy about now, but he felt Eurynomos' presence, the sheer strength and will of him, and it gave him courage.

As they passed under the crumbling structure, the pleasant aspect of the Library fell away, and the heat of a desert blasted them. Leopold felt a wash of perspiration over his torso in its layers of clothing…until the initial unpleasantness drifted to the background.

The world seemed to tilt in a sickening way, and he remembered all over again how outrageous was the landscape of Gehenna—far worse than that of the Library.

The disorienting ground gave way to visions of fire, and beasts opening their jaws and baring fearsome teeth…to the feeling of falling and hundreds of hands grasping him. He remembered this. He feared this. He longed to escape when something blew in his face. When he opened his eyes again, the face of Eurynomos filled his vision. "Steady on, my friend."

It helped. Whatever quality the daemon's breath held it seemed to calm him, ground him. And he didn't see the visions assailing him anymore.

Except when a wide-shouldered beast rose up at the edge of three diverging rivers. No, it wasn't a vision. It was a real creature. He had hair on his shoulders, light-colored, and twisted horns on his head. But as the company neared him—and the beast's eyes were steely and hooded as he watched them with an unwavering glare—Leopold realized with some horror that the horns on his head weren't horns at all, but the twisted remnants of what once had to have been a halo. *This* was the angel Nasagiel.

His face was square and hard, scarred by battles, with a broken nose and heavy brows. His shoulders were unnaturally wide and covered in what Leopold had at first thought was blond hair, but was, in fact, the remnants of wings that had fused into a tangled mass for an eternity upon his shoulders. He was definitely more beast-like than angel. His hardened voice confirmed it. There was no longer compassion there.

"Prince of Death," he said in a low growl, "why do you trespass my gate? And what are these?"

"I pass with the immunity bestowed upon me from on high. And these are mortals that accompany me…because I wish it so."

"They are not allowed," said Nasagiel with some relish. His jaw moved as if already tasting their flesh.

"They *are* allowed…because I wish it."

The hairs on his shoulders that seemed to remember that they were once wings, rustled, stood on end. "You think you may break the rules when it pleases you? I know you, Prince of Death. I am not impressed by you."

"You need neither be impressed nor disappointed by me. I play my part, as *you* must, in guarding this gate. Allow me and my company to pass or suffer the consequences."

Nasagiel frowned. He reached for the coiled whip hanging from a belt that held up his breechclout. For a fearful second, Leopold expected him to draw it. He readied a spell to deflect its menace. Yet instead of pulling it free, he merely rested his gnarled hand there. With a growl from deep in his throat, he stepped aside, and Eurynomos stalked forward. Leopold scrambled to catch up to his long strides, even as he stumbled from the imbalance between what his eyes were seeing and what his feet felt. He kept his eye on the angel and looked back at his companions. Everyone was silent, with eyes averted from the celestial being as they walked in step with one another, loath to be left behind.

Mingli seemed to clutch her belly in pain again, but he dared not succor her, lest she fall under Nasagiel's eye.

Once they had passed him at some distance Leopold turned back to his friends.

"That was terrifying," he muttered.

"There's more to come, old chap, as you know. But stand before me. You, too, Miss Zhao. I must prepare your minds for what is to come."

Mingli moved carefully forward, leaning heavily on her umbrella, to stand beside Leopold. "Are you quite well, my dear?" he asked.

"As right as I can be."

He knew she, too, was struggling to stay upright in the topsy-turvy dimensions. There were distant trees, but they weren't emerging from the ground. Instead, they lay on their sides, floating. And likewise, mountains in the distance didn't look right, as if they were standing on their heads, small points on the ground, enormous foundations in the air. None of it looked right. None of it was the right colors. It could make one quite mad.

Eurynomos raised his hands and put one on the side of Mingli's head and the other on the side of Leopold's. The daemon leaned forward nearly resting his forehead on theirs and murmured a Hebrew incantation. It rumbled not in words in Leopold's head and down to his chest, but in sensations of warmth, like a cloak. He had already breathed on them to help them acclimate to their confused surroundings, but with this spell, Leopold hoped all would make more sense. Leopold recalled well how nauseating his time in Gehenna had been and how devastating it had been to his balance, his decisions, even his language at first. Eurynomos had done this for him before, so he wouldn't go mad. He appreciated it even more now.

Eurynomos released them and stepped back. "That should help the both of you to better cope. Only those who are pure of soul go mad in the confusions they will witness in Gehenna. And Leopold, I did get to your father before he was dragged to the pit of *Sitra Achra*. But I don't know if my spell was able to last this long."

"You did your best, old friend."

"But today, we will do better."

They all approached the shore where the three rivers split apart and an unusual boat awaited.

"Eurynomos," said Leopold. "Is this boat…made of…*stone*?"

"Yes. That is because the rivers are most unusual. They are each of gall, pitch, or poison."

"Which one will we take?"

"We will take the one of poison. It's the tributaries one must look out for. Get in, everyone. I will direct us to the right way. And don't touch the water."

They all climbed in, Leopold and Mingli at the bow and the others cramming in behind them. Eurynomos pushed them off and waded through before he climbed onto the stern, temporarily lowering the back end of the boat, before he was settled.

Leopold leaned over the bow and looked at the side of the boat in the water. "A stone boat," he muttered, marveling that it would float at all. He ran his hand along the top edge of it.

He felt Mingli's hands on his shoulders gently pulling him back. "It wouldn't do at all if you came all this way merely to perish in this river."

He patted her hand. "With you looking after me, I feel perfectly safe."

Eurynomos took up his place in the stern and used a large paddle as both motor and rudder. "The current is taking us there, so not much need to paddle, only steer," he said. "Now that we are here, my friends, I think it best to explain how things work here in Gehenna. Each of the seven levels is guarded by a princely and punishing angel, with each level intended for each kind of sin. The souls here suffer for only twelve months, and are punished for their sins every day but the Sabbath, except those who had desecrated the Sabbath."

Raj stretched out his legs, looking at them admiringly. "So the souls that are here are sinners."

"No, not at all. There are the Righteous, the Wicked, and the *Beinonim*, or those in between. You see, the Righteous must travel to the first level, *Sheol*, the grave, where all souls must begin their journey. But the Righteous dead are only there long enough to plead for the rest of the sinners, to ease their punishment. They move off quickly to their reward of enlightenment with the Creator. You see, all souls are recorded in the Book of Life along their journey as living beings. And depending on one's merits, they either leave Gehenna or must traverse the levels until twelve months have passed."

"And do their prayers work?" asked Mingli. "Those of the Righteous?"

"Why, of *course.*" Eurynomos gave her a humble bow.

"If this '*Sheol*' is the first level," said Thacker, "what's the next, then?"

"*Abaddon,*" said Eurynomos. "Destruction. I do most of my work there."

Leopold shivered at the thought of his benign friend doing harm. But as he explained to Leopold when he was much younger, he looked at it as helping those souls to move on to a better reward.

"Then *Beer Shachat,*" Leopold recited mechanically, "the Well of Destruction, where the ten wicked nations must enter: Seir, Ammon, Moab, Ishmael, Esau… and more who refused to accept the Torah. Then *Bor Sh'on,* the Pit of Turmoil. And then *Tit ha-Yeven,* a slurry of mud in the Abyss of Despair. A place for slanderers, traitors, and bribe-takers. Then *Domah,* the Silence, and finally *Tevel,* the earthly garden and exit. And, of course, *Sitra Achra,* whence all evil comes, and where all evil goes."

They all fell silent…until Thacker piped up. "Sounds like a hell of a place."

There was a pause before a titter of laughter bubbled up in their pensive throats.

"I am curious," said Raj. "I must assume in some respects, that I might have a soul, or a partial soul at least by benefit of being alive and sentient. How is one to know?"

Eurynomos gazed down at the automaton with a tender smile. "I can assure you, my friend, that you do indeed have a soul. I can sense it. But it is a different sort than that of mortals. Gehenna is a place of cleansing. All manner of souls report here."

"May I ask," said Mingli, as tentatively as Leopold had ever heard her, "how is it that you—out of all the souls on our planet—that you attuned yourself to Àkos and Leopold?"

"Ah, that one is easy. When Àkos first began to summon daemons, I sensed something different, dare I say, even *special* about them. It was their sincerity. Their…kindness. For there were no foul intentions with Kazsmer senior, nor his son. And it was their ability with magic. Not many mortals can cross the threshold of true magic to be able to manipulate it. Àkos could have been a fine Mage had he sought out that particular practice. Did you ever notice how you gravitated toward magician out of all the vocations you could have tried for, Leo?"

Leopold stared off into the distance of low plains and long shadows of a desert landscape, with distant mountains hugging the horizon in a perpetual blue haze. All the mountains and the few trees seemed to have righted themselves. "I've never thought about it. I certainly wasn't interested in the Romani's thieving ways, nor even my father's interest in teaching. It was…a natural course, as you say."

"Yes. And I enjoyed teaching you the ways of it. Had I known you could have attuned yourself to Earth magic, I certainly would have extended your tutelage. I suppose it didn't occur to me."

"You did me a favor, Eurynomos. The only thing I minded about Gehenna magic was that it faded. And…the blood sacrifice."

"Now I'm curious," said the daemon. "Can you feel your Earth magic here?"

Leopold closed his eyes and concentrated. "Yes, I can feel it. I wonder if I can—"

A swell suddenly lifted the boat, tilted it one way and then the other.

"What the bloody hell was that?" cried Thacker.

A head of a beast, shaped like an arrowhead, arose from the water, snaking a forked tongue past its jagged teeth. It plunged again under the boat, with sinuous arches of an eel-like body surrounding their craft.

Leopold didn't hesitate to sign sigils in the air, and was pleased and relieved when he saw their golden signature shimmering before him. He supposed that answered that question, for it was Earth magic that came to the fore, not Gehenna magic.

He blinked curiously at the long-staffed trident that crystalized in his hands.

He glanced at Eurynomos. "I hadn't expected that."

"Your magic works here…just not in the way you expect."

"Good to know." He positioned the weapon in his hand and scoured the now empty waves still rocking the boat.

"Best to strike when you see 'em," said Thacker, almost floating over the edge of the bow, and using his fists to box at the air.

"I'm trying," Leopold muttered, eyes sharp for anything that looked even remotely like the creature through the undulating waves.

Mingli reached under her skirts and brought up her pistol. She stood back-to-back with Leopold, aiming into the water.

"Does your right eye tell you anything?" he asked.

He heard the lens spin and adjust. "No. It doesn't seem useful in this environment."

"Well, that's a pity."

Raj suddenly pointed. "There!"

The water seemed to boil ahead of them and out came the head of the beast. Eurynomos steered away from it, but the coils of its body cradled the boat, keeping it from paddling away.

Eurynomos beat the tail with his oar, but Leopold was ready. Cocking back his arm, he hurled the spear forward…but it missed, soaring passed the serpent. The beast opened its jaws and darted toward Leopold. He felt the graze of fangs tear through his trouser leg and jerked back, landing unceremoniously on top of Mingli.

"Oof!"

"Oh, my dear! I'm so sorry."

He helped her up and brushed down her skirts. "Leo, forget about me. Mind the water!"

The creature rose again from the churning waves, hissing and showing its fangs in a most threatening manner. The boat rocked precariously, and Mingli and Raj avoided the poisoned water splashing over the sides.

It snapped again at Leopold, who barely escaped being bitten.

"Those fangs are poisonous, Leo!" cried Eurynomos. "If he merely breaks through the skin…"

"I'm trying to be careful," hissed Leopold, scrambling away from the snapping jaws as it reached into the boat. He tried to paint sigils in the air, but those teeth kept coming closer.

Shots rang out, and a surge of power blasted the serpent's face. It sank below the waves again, but its sinuous body undulated all around the boat.

Mingli held her pistol up by her cheek, a pleased expression on her face.

"Beastie comes again," warned Suchah.

Lying at the bottom of the boat, Leopold hurriedly signed his sigils and another trident formed in his hand.

The beast rose from the water high into the air, before plunging down toward Leopold, jaws snapping.

He had no time to rise to his feet. The mouth full of sharp teeth descended and Leopold fended off those jaws with his feet, making sure they weren't in the way of the fangs. He closed his eyes, yelled, and jabbed the trident forth.

It struck into something solid and he opened his eyes. The spear sank deep into the upper palate of the serpent and it screamed as it whipped its head around, trying to dislodge the trident. Leopold quickly signed again, gripped the newest trident that appeared in his hands, and shoved it into the creature's neck. It cried out again. Black blood flowed from the wound, and the head listed to one side as it slowly sunk below the waves.

Leopold scrambled to his feet and searched over the side of the bow, careful of the water that had splashed all over it. Still, he could not see the head amidst the dark water.

Eurynomos used the end of his oar to push the rest of the coils off of the boat and paddled quickly away.

Leopold rubbed his hands anxiously. "I'd never had to physically confront a beast before," he babbled. "Always, I simply used magic means. I expected to this time. Only…that trident appeared instead."

"I saw you accomplish much with a sword," said Mingli with a bit of pride in her voice. "And a broken one at that. With an evil man, no less."

"Yes. It seemed fairer then. This…" He shook his head and sat again.

"In this life you lead, old man," said Eurynomos, spearing the bulky boat through the water, "you must expect to get your hands dirty."

"I suppose. It just never occurred to me before. And, I suppose, it was a bit cowardly of me, using magic from a distance. One must take responsibility, mustn't one?"

Mingli raised her face into the hot wind. "All my life I've had to fight. With my hands alone, sometimes. It makes the winning of one's life more gratifying."

"That's one way to look at it," said Thacker into his mustache. Raj elbowed him.

Suchah perched with his webbed feet at the bow. "The serpent wanted to kill us all. You did good, Leopold Master."

"Eurynomos, did you and Suchah have to traverse this each time I summoned you?"

"Oh no, dear boy. When summoned, I can simply appear anywhere necessary. Seldom have I ever traversed these waters or through the gates."

"Then…you don't know the way either?"

"Hence the need for the map. Let's take a look at it now."

Leopold turned to the stern and took the scroll from his coat pocket. He unfurled it and gave it to Eurynomos.

Suchah fluttered over to the daemon and looked at it over his shoulder. "We're making good progress," said Eurynomos. "We should reach *Sheol* in a tick."

"The grave," said Thacker with a wince.

"The whole venture is entirely fascinating," said Mingli with a widened eye.

Leopold shook his head at his beautiful fiancée, marveling again how lucky he was to have captured the interest of such an intriguing woman. His glance passed over her and caught a glimpse of Raj reading from a small leatherbound book. "What's that you've got there, Raj?"

The automaton looked up, blinking his glass eyes. "I obtained a book from the Library about fallen angels. It is most absorbing. I thought it best, since we will be encountering them, to do some additional research."

"Have you found anything helpful?"

"Not as yet. But I believe that this will prove useful."

"Very well, then. Carry on." He gripped the edge of the boat and used that vantage to survey the river and both banks ahead. "Where do we disembark, Eurynomos?"

"See to the left, just ahead? Where the dark clouds have gathered?"

"It figures it would be dark clouds."

"Don't be so gloomy, Leo. We are finally reaching Gehenna proper."

"Is that anything to celebrate?" said Thacker. "We're here to do a job. Not take a Sunday picnic."

"Right you are, Inspector! I merely meant that the sooner we get into the heart of Gehenna, the sooner we can make things right for Leo…and Àkos."

"Should Suchah fly ahead and tell Mister Kazsmer about our coming rescue?" asked the imp, a little hesitantly.

Everyone turned to look at him.

"Suchah," said Leopold. "You can *do* that?"

The imp shrugged. "Of course."

Leopold glanced anxiously toward the daemon. "What do you think, Eurynomos? Should he go?"

"Like you, Leo, I hope to comfort Àkos. But…I fear that it would give warning as to our intentions. I can't imagine that word has not already gone out that strangers are here. Nasagiel is no friend to us."

Raj lifted the book he was reading without taking his eyes from it. "It seems the fallen angels have no other purpose here but to punish. Their falling has changed them. They…they seem to like it. If you wish for my advice, I say we do not give them any reason to suspect why we are here. It will be difficult enough passing through each level where we must confront each angel."

Leopold's spirits fell, but he saw the sense in what Raj was saying. "Look, Suchah, thank you for offering, but I think it best we maintain the element of surprise for as long as we can."

Suchah's wings fluttered, and he landed back on his seat with a splat. "Whatever Leopold Master wishes," he said with a scowl.

Eurynomos maneuvered the boat toward the shore and it jolted into the sandy bank. "Remember, don't touch the water. You'll need to walk up to the bow and leap."

Leopold went first and offered a hand to Mingli who surely needed no help, but was graceful in accepting it. She leapt over the bow like a gazelle or prima ballerina. Thacker was next and seemed to do more gliding than he had in the Library, even becoming a little transparent again. Suchah fluttered over the bow and Raj, with his long legs, easily navigated over the edge of the stone boat without touching a drop of water.

Eurynomos was last and waded effortlessly—with no ill effects—through the poisoned water, whereupon he turned around and shoved the boat back into the waves. It skimmed away from the shore and floated free.

Eurynomos looked at Leopold's questioning expression. "So the inhabitants of *Sheol* don't get any ideas."

"*Can* they escape?"

"Not really. But why make them suffer more? There would be additional punishments for those who tried to escape. I would not put temptation in the way of them."

"I am curious, Eurynomos," said Raj, walking along and reading at the same time. His legs creaked and hissed as pistons worked. "There is the idea of 'Hell' and 'Gehenna' as places of punishment. Hell, as I understand the mythology, is supposed to be eternal punishment for great sins, whereas Gehenna only punishes for twelve months. Why is this so?"

"Well, the Talmud states that there can be no *eternal* punishment for a *finite* life. How can man's punishment on earth in the courts of law be fairer than that designated by the Creator? Therefore, only twelve months, though there are allowances for exceptionally bad people."

"That does seem fair."

"But sins would be in the eye of the beholder," said Mingli. "Cloth woven from different threads, for one, seemed to be some remnant of a forgotten law, a heinous act back in the biblical days of the Old Testament, whereas today it doesn't seem so much of a sin, but rather as fashion, taste, and expediency."

"Precisely, Miss Zhao," said Eurynomos, shortening the length of his strides to match that of his companions. "Gehenna does change. As I explained before, it is ever-changing."

"Ah. I thought that merely meant its topography."

"It encompasses all change."

"So I suppose it has its own logic. If you were suffering in Gehenna for something you did in biblical times, it doesn't make sense to continue to be punished for it if times on our plane had changed."

"Exactly."

"Still, any sort of punishment once you are dead and can't change it or plead one's case, seems extreme to me."

Thacker approached to walk/float alongside her. "You would be more generous?"

"Yes, I think I would be. Instead, I should shoot thunderbolts down to punish the sinner while they're alive…when it counted the most and when they could mend their ways."

Leopold chuckled "And what a fiercesome goddess you would be, my dear."

She turned her spinning telescopic eye on him in a most forbidding manner, and he almost laughed outright. Until he cast his eyes upon the landscape before them.

The clouds lowered and the land itself grew black and bleak. Gravestones—many of them tilted and decaying—were sprinkled along the plains as far as the eye could see. And suddenly they were surrounded by them. The shore of the river was lost to sight below a rise, and there was nothing but graves, tombs, and gray bareness.

He suddenly thought of Thacker and turned only to find him floating alone and glassy-eyed behind them. "Spense? How are you bearing up, my friend?"

Thacker was as subdued as Leopold had ever seen him. When he reached the inspector, he was looking down at his feet…feet that were no longer there. He had reverted back to his ghostly aspect. "Spense?"

Slowly, Thacker looked up. "I feel strange, Leo. Like me feet are made of lead."

Leopold looked down at his ectoplasmic tail where Thacker's feet should have been. "Er…"

Mingli was suddenly there beside Thacker, and though she tried, she couldn't put her arm in his as she had done in the Library. "Come along, Inspector. This is just another mystery to solve, and we need your expertise."

He nodded vaguely. "All right, then." He slowly moved along. Leopold consulted with Raj, and while he was quietly explaining to the automaton to keep an eye on Thacker, Suchah had already moved to flutter alongside of the ghost.

"Cheating Ghost is falling behind," said the imp.

Thacker suddenly came back to himself. "If you call me 'cheating-bloody-ghost' one more time, you little blighter, I'll…"

The imp chuckled and Thacker seemed to figure it out.

He patted Suchah on the head—or seemed to try—and floated along with him.

Leopold scanned the landscape and there appeared to be blurry patches. He rubbed his knuckles into his eyes and looked again. No, there *did* appear to be spots here and there in a blur, but as he continued to squint at them, they slowly came into focus…as spirits, much like Thacker. Hundreds of them. Thousands.

"Dear God," he breathed.

Eurynomos was suddenly beside him. "Remember, all souls come here first, Leo," he said softly. "Did you expect anything less?"

"I just…I didn't…it wasn't this way when I was here before."

"That's because your summoning went awry and you and Àkos ended up in a quite different place. But this is the way through. And we must traverse it." He gathered his companions with a sweep of his eyes over them. "You must not talk to the souls here. None of you." He gave a particular stern look at Thacker. "*None* of you. Even if they call out to you…and they will. Do not look at them, do not engage them. Walk on. Do you all understand me?"

It was Mingli who asked, "And what happens if we—"

"Forgive me, Miss Zhao, but we must hurry. Let us go now." He stepped forward in a quickened pace. Leopold grasped her hand and held it close to him. Thacker came after and Raj and Suchah trailed behind.

As they neared the blurry spirits, Leopold saw many drawing nearer. He turned his gaze away and kept it on Eurynomos. It seemed the only safe way was to go forward. But then the spirits began to gather round them. Some reached out with beseeching gestures.

"Pardon, guv, but do you know where I am?"

"You haven't seen my sister, have you?"

"I can't be here. I simply can't!"

"Won't you help me?"

He hadn't expected them to have voices. They were even more transparent than Thacker, and certainly not as well defined, as if their limbs simply wouldn't stay together with their bodies. Their voices were far away and hollow-sounding; their aspects, miserable.

He felt compelled to help them, to say some words of comfort, but he believed Eurynomos when he spoke of them, and kept his mouth tightly shut. He tried not to look at them but some passed directly through him and he shivered at the cold sensation.

Mingli kept her head down. He knew her natural curiosity would compel her to look at everything, analyze what she saw. Heeding Eurynomos' words meant that she had to completely shun the sensations, to avert her gaze lest she look the spirits in the eye.

But, of course, she followed the dictates of the *yuan gui*. Were they truly ghosts—ghosts with a grievance? Or were they more like demons...or gods?

They didn't seem to notice Raj, but many of them took to following Thacker, who was growing irritated at their attention.

"Keep calm, Spense," said Leopold out of the side of his mouth.

"They're all over me."

"Inspector," said Eurynomos, "you must ignore them. It's imperative that you do."

"But it's like...ants buzzing all over me!"

"Spense..."

"Leave me alone, you bloody spirits!"

The company stopped, looked back, and held their collective breaths.

And then Thacker was fallen upon by hundreds of spirits and suddenly dragged away into the heart of *Sheol*.

CHAPTER THIRTEEN

"SPENSE!" CRIED LEOPOLD. He looked desperately at his friends. "We must rescue him."

"Wait, Leopold."

It was Eurynomos who spoke, and he wore a sorrowful expression.

"No," Leopold rasped between gritted teeth. "You can't be telling me he is lost to us. I refuse to accept that."

"I haven't the means to wrest him from the hordes of *Sheol*."

"You're supposed to be this Prince of Death. Well, *act* princely!"

"Leo..."

"Wait," said Raj, keeping his finger in place at his book. "I think I have the means. I have collected many artifacts from the Library of the Damned. Surely this is the perfect opportunity to use some of them. Come with me." He stretched out his legs with the sound of ratcheting, and began to run.

Leopold didn't hesitate. He pursued the automaton. He didn't look back at the rest of his company, but he heard their running steps behind him. Even Eurynomos caught up to him and paced alongside. "I forgot," he said contritely, "that we are not alone, that our friends are with us."

Leopold was ready. No matter what spell it took, he'd be ready. He flexed his fingers as he ran, prepared to fling his magic to stop the dead souls from snatching Thacker away forever. He'd not let it happen. *Not on my watch*, he thought grimly.

The air seemed to grow denser, darker. Spense glowed more than the other spirits but they were moving away at remarkable speed. "I...I don't know if we'll be able to catch up..." panted Leopold.

Raj turned his head 180 degrees to speak to Leopold. "It doesn't matter, Leo. I can run much faster." He spun his head to the front again and all at once, his legs were a blur as he sped ahead.

"What does he have in mind?" Leopold wondered aloud.

All at once, he felt warm, scaly arms around him as he and Mingli were scooped up into the daemon's arms. "It will be much faster if I convey you," Eurynomos rumbled, and soon, he and Mingli were zooming through the enclosing darkness, tombstones whizzing by them. Leopold caught a glimpse of Suchah and his madly flapping wings at Eurynomos' shoulder.

They soon caught up to Raj who had clearly mastered his new-found legs and, with mechanical precision, caught up to Thacker. The inspector was struggling with the spirits. "Get off o' me, you bloody ghosts! Hands off!"

"You are different."

"Tell us who you are."

"How do we leave this place?"

"I'll have you all arrested, is what I'll do. It's the nick for all of you."

"Help us!"

"Free us!"

Raj sprinted ahead of Thacker and the inspector swiveled his head to watch as best he could, confined as he was in the grasp of the new spirits. "Raj? What the bloody hell is going on?"

"Inspector, do not look directly into the light."

"What light?"

Raj removed a small object from his coat. An orb made of brass. He turned his torso back toward the inspector, even as his lower body ran forward. He placed the orb in the palm of one hand and compressed a button on the top of it with the other.

The top slid down into the bottom half and a light so vibrant and bright exploded from the opening. Thacker turned his head away, but the spirits were not so lucky. The light seemed to mesmerize them and, one by one, they loosened their grasp of the inspector to fly into the beams of light. Once Thacker was loose, Raj closed the sphere with a snap and the light was gone. He slowed and Thacker, still moving from momentum, began to slow as well.

"Spense!" Leopold leapt from the arms of the daemon and hit the ground running until he caught up with the ghost at last. He longed to embrace him but knew he no longer could.

"Spense, are you all right?"

"Bloody, *bloody* ghosts!" he sputtered. "Grasping and begging. Ack! Like some streets in London, with their beggars and wagtails. I feel dirty."

Leopold sighed with relief. "But you're all right?"

"'Course I am!" He dusted off his transparent Ulster, revealing the gaping hole in his chest where Ogiel's claws had pierced and killed his living body. Leopold had forgotten that this was visible, for the ghost kept his coat closed for the most part.

"Raj? What is that?" Thacker pointed toward the orb.

"This? I was curious about its properties when I encountered it in the Library, but I rightly presumed that the newly dead would be attracted to bright light. The dead have left the light of the Earth's sun, after all, and would naturally be engrossed by it." Raj threw it up in the air and caught it. "A most interesting and unassuming object, is it not?" He turned it a few times before dropping it again into his carpet bag.

Eurynomos stared down his nose at Thacker. "Did I not implore you all *not* to engage, look at, or speak to the newly dead?"

"I tried, Eurynomos. I really tried. But they were fawning all over me like drooling puppies."

"They are attracted to you because…well. Not to put too fine a point on it…you yourself are a spirit. But you are freer than they are. You can go about where you wish, whilst they cannot."

"It's horrible, is what it is," he said with a shiver.

"I know. But there are some things we cannot change."

He shook out his coat, straightened his bowler, and ran his hand down his brushy mustache. "All right, then. I'll do better. Where to now?"

"Your mad dash helped us more than hurt," said Eurynomos, looking into the distance. "I think we are close to the gate to *Abaddon*."

"I say, Eurynomos," said Leopold, straightening his own topper and frock coat. "If *Sitra Achra* is the tentpole to this place, then why can we not go directly there?"

"The tentpole was merely a metaphor for that which is unexplainable. Consider our path more of a spiral."

"But is that not also a metaphor," said Mingli.

"No. Give me the map, Leopold."

Leopold withdrew the map from the inside pocket of his coat and handed it to the daemon once more.

Eurynomos unrolled it and showed it to him while the others gathered closely around. "You see?"

The map was suddenly three-dimensional. As the daemon turned the map this way and that, the markings floated off the page, showing the way as a spiral. But then they moved again, presumably because Gehenna's topography had moved. And yet, though different, it was still in the manner of a spiral.

Raj was facing all the way forward with all parts of his body again. "But *Abaddon* is where *you* reign, is it not, my daemon friend?"

"I do. But I must not look as if I favor any one of you. You must look for all of Gehenna as my prisoners that I am rushing forward."

"Suchah can help. Suchah has moved prisoners through Gehenna before."

"Right you are. Be a good fellow, and arrange some chains for our friends."

Suchah smiled with what Leopold could only describe as an evil grin, and chains appeared in his open hands. "Come and get your shackles, Leopold Master."

"Er..."

"You do trust Suchah, then?"

Leopold swallowed with just the merest of doubts pricking his senses. "Of course, I do." He thrust out his hands. But he murmured a protection charm…just in case.

The manacles shot out and encircled his wrists. He thought they might be like those in his magical paraphernalia; secretly breakaway. But they were definitely solid and impenetrable. Seeing them on Mingli's wrists made his heart flare with anger. But…he *did* trust Suchah in the end. He reckoned the imp was experiencing true friendship for the first time in a very long life. He hoped he would be loath to give it up.

"And now…you appear to be our prisoners," said Eurynomos with just that little gleam in *his* eyes. He certainly trusted Eurynomos too, but it did make him wonder about the beast. For all his posturing, he wasn't a man at all. And, in the end, his vocation in *Abaddon* was to make life difficult for the sinning souls that came his way.

Leopold glanced toward Mingli, but her eye was shining with curiosity. Yes, she was enjoying the novelty of it all. He supposed he could try to be a little more like her—for indeed, he, too, enjoyed their adventures. It was just that, this time, there was someone else at stake if he failed.

Chains encircled Raj's hands, though he barely seemed to notice with his nose in his book.

"The gate is near," said Eurynomos. "As always, I implore you *not* to speak. Is that clear?"

Everyone glanced at Thacker. "Oi! Whatcha all looking at me for?" He shuffled, a good trick with no feet. "Aww. I won't chatter. You can count on me, Eurynomos."

With their shackles secured and chains dragging, the company followed Eurynomos' sturdy strides, while Suchah held the ends of their chains like a page boy in a king's processional. The gate lay ahead and there was a slightly brighter glow at the horizon through the arch. The tombstones had dwindled to nothing, and no glow of spirits—or souls, Leopold corrected himself—were present. The gate itself must deter the souls from venturing forth. It had an aura about it. Not necessarily malevolent, but certainly not welcoming. He supposed these fallen angels and demons were responsible for ushering souls forward to the many levels.

"And was it like this when you were here last?" asked Mingli, still glancing about curiously.

"No. Or…at least I don't remember it being so. But I was young and frightened and only concerned for my father's welfare. In all truthfulness, I don't recall much of it. Only that it was so muddled I nearly went mad."

"Well…it certainly is fascinating. And quite arcane. It seems a more sensible Creator would change it for the better."

"I beg you, Miss Zhao," he said, speaking quietly, "not to bring the Creator into it. I certainly don't want to catch His…or Her…attention."

"I thought you were an agnostic?"

"Not at all. Though I have not met the Creator, I've certainly met His minions. I am simply of the opinion that religion has nothing to do with me, nor I with it. But I must admit…I might have to work on that opinion."

"Pish tosh. You were correct the first time."

"I can't understand you, Miss Zhao. Here you are faced with the evidence of your eyes."

"I was a little older than you when you were last in Gehenna, when I encountered the *yuan gui*. Gods, spirits, demons, ghosts—whatever it is they are—took me from a dreadful circumstance and guided me to help others. That was real. That was my earthly life, Leo. I've experienced all the punishment that I deserve, and any other deity that says otherwise must prove their point with evidence and logic. Therefore, I do not practice any faith. If anything, they owe *me* a bit of obeisance."

He stared at her and her fiercely proud expression and admitted to himself. with a shake of his head that he couldn't find fault with her argument. What good would it do him now to offer supplication to a Creator that had not released his father from Leopold's long-ago mistake?

Even so, he breathed a whispered prayer without even thinking on it when, as they passed through the gate, a buzz tickled over his skin, and they left the land of the dead behind. The air was a little fresher – not as dense with sorrow and loss as *Sheol* – but no garden either. It was still a barren plain, with beaten soil as if many riders had trampled through when the soil was mud. Perhaps they had. This was the place of destruction, after all.

"The Destruction here is the taking down and building up of the sinner," announced Eurynomos. "In *Sheol*, they were made aware that their earthly body was no more. But in *Abaddon*, they are taught that the sin that they carried within them, must be excised. Their pride is destroyed from them and they are taught humility. Those that learn the lesson are freed from Gehenna at this point. Those more stubborn and full of sin, must move on through the levels."

As we are doing, thought Leopold. He wondered if this would count to his own soul on the final hour when *he* died. Or would he have to travel the journey all over again?

Or…If the Unholy Hosts got their way, he wouldn't be permitted to die, but spend an eternity as the whipping boy of these fallen angels.

"If we make good time here," Eurynomos went on, "we shall arrive at the gate of *Beer Shachat* in no time at all."

All at once, an explosion rocked the plains, and a rain of soil and rocks showered down upon them as they lay on the ground from the blast.

The dust, becoming a veil where landscape features changed to gray shapes, showed yet another form. That of a figure with widened shoulders. It stepped forward through the dust and became clearer, though Leopold dreaded that clarity.

This one was not like the last fallen angel they had encountered. It brought with it an air of anxiety, an aura of dread. Its head was misshapen, and all around it, it seemed to have…something like tentacles testing the air about it, moving, reaching. The air grew darker and denser…

Eurynomos gasped. "Radueriel… Unholy Host."

CHAPTER FOURTEEN

THE FALLEN ARCHANGEL stepped forward, each step another shattering of the ground. He swept his glance over Leopold's company with white glowing eyes. His jaw was wide and misshapen with tentacles, and a long line of drool.

"What have you brought here, Eurynomos?" His voice was like ice and sent a shard of frost through Leopold's gut. He thought it the wisest thing to stay on the ground, and grabbed Mingli's chains in order to keep her there beside him.

Eurynomos rose to his full height and gave a slight nod to the angel. "These are my special prisoners, Radueriel. They have nothing to do with you..."

The angel stepped within a hairsbreadth of Eurynomos, cutting off his explanation, and tilting his ugly head to stare at the daemon.

"Why do you lie to me, Prince of Death? I am an Unholy Host. I know who this is." And he pointed a finger with a claw on it at Leopold. So...it *did* have hands. Yes, on second glance, the things that seemed like tentacles were the remnants of robes. Or wings. He couldn't be certain.

And suddenly, with his heart in his mouth, Leopold was lifted off the ground and into the air. His chains kept him earthbound, but the magic strained at them.

"And so I am taking him to the Council," said Eurynomos.

"The Council? That has nothing to do with me or any of the other Unholy Hosts. Kazsmer was to fulfill his mission and destroy the world. He has not done so." The angel turned its burning eyes on Leopold. "That means more punishment, Mortal. More pain. More horror. You cannot break with our covenant. We will show you what it means to lie to an archangel."

Stark cold speared through Leopold's heart, and all he wanted to do was scurry to some rocky shelter and crawl into their shadows and, in his fear, hide from everything.

"I realize that mortal matters may be difficult for you to understand, Unholy One," said Eurynomos calmly.

"What are you talking about? Release him to me now."

"I'm afraid I can't do that. We are all playing our parts in Gehenna. I must play mine, you must play yours…for however long it lasts."

"What does that mean? I know you, too, Prince of Death. You are the friend of mortals. He saved you with the bargain that will destroy him."

"And so he did. And so my allegiance is to him…not to you. Indeed, you have no jurisdiction over him whilst I have custody. You know the law."

Radueriel took a step toward the floating Leopold, but the angel jerked to a stop and turned his head. "I will keep my eye on you, Eurynomos." To Leopold, he said, "And Ashmedai will keep his eye on *you*. You still have a task to perform, Mortal." Abruptly, he clenched his fist, and the spell was cut. Leopold fell to the ground with a cry of pain.

"You think that is pain, Kazsmer? Try this." With a mere gesture of his hand, Leopold's tattoo burst with fire.

He cried out in agony. The fire was real, singing his cuff, but it also seemed to steal into the rest of his body, traveling along his every vein and nerve endings, and spreading pain throughout his muscles and joints.

Mingli was immediately at his side.

"Until you fulfill your task, Mortal. Remember what awaits you." The Unholy Host dissipated into the dust and disappeared.

The pain assaulting Leopold's body suddenly stopped. He lay back exhausted and felt Mingli's cool hand soothing his brow. No, he couldn't do this for an eternity. He *had* to free himself from their sadistic punishment.

"Damn," growled Eurynomos. "Now Ashmedai will be on our tail. I had hoped to get through more of Gehenna without being detected."

Leopold slowly sat up with help from Mingli. The memory of the wracking pain made his muscles twitch involuntarily. "*That* was an Unholy Host?"

"Yes."

He blinked, hugging himself to stop the trembling. "I…I somehow expected he would be far uglier. Although…he was certainly ugly enough."

"Radueriel is not the oldest. The older ones…well..."

"I saw them before. Not very clearly, but their figures, their outlines…they were far more hideous…"

"That's what comes of being a fallen one. They lose all their angelic sensibilities and come to love their punishing ways. And that destroys them even further."

Leopold got to his feet unsteadily and shook off his manacles. They fell to the ground with a clank.

Suchah swooped in, picked them up, then stared at Leopold.

"If he is an archangel…"

"He is. He can make more angels with a mere utterance."

"But…I thought only…only the Creator could—"

Eurynomos stooped to grasp Leopold's chains. "And *I* thought only a daemon could loosen these bonds."

Leopold scanned his friends, and only Leopold had been freed from his fetters. "Oh. I never even noticed when I'd done that." He waved his hand and both Mingli's and Raj's shackles disappeared.

Suchah looked as if he would say something, but Eurynomos shushed him.

Leopold noticed Mingli holding her stomach again. "My dear, are you quite all right?"

"It's nothing. I'm fine."

"It's not nothing. You keep holding your…your middle."

"It's just a little pain."

"It looks like a lot of pain."

"I fear it is those hysterics again. Every time you are put into danger, my stomach roils."

He slid his arm around her and she uncharacteristically leaned into him. "Everything that can be done is being done. We are fighting our way toward my father. That is of utmost importance to me. Oh, I knew I should never have brought you here."

"I think you will find," she said, sounding like her old self, "that it is impossible to naysay me."

He chuckled. "I suppose you're right. But…I can't help feeling that I've brought you to your doom."

"Well, in the scheme of things, I've been bringing my own doom upon myself for some years now. But Leo." She pushed away to square with him. "I would never have stood by and allowed you to go on your own. I love you too much. And…it's a funny thing, this love." She reached up and smoothed a finger over his mustache. "I thought it wasn't my lot. That it was for other people. Nothing has surprised me more." She smiled suddenly and lowered her hand. Leopold was sad to see it go. "Do you know…I'd seen you perform before we'd ever met."

"No you didn't."

"I did. You looked so smart and so handsome on the stage with your boiled shirt and tailcoat. I liked the addition of the mustache."

Gone were the memories of his recent encounter with the archangel. All he saw was Mingli. He couldn't help but touch said mustache with a smoothing finger. He realized that she must have returned to the theatre to see him for several years. "You really did? You saw me perform?"

"Yes. And I began to suspect that you were utilizing more than tricks. That there was real magic underlying your performances, enhancing them. You certainly intrigued me."

He reached out and pushed wayward strands of her hair out of her face as an excuse to touch her, to get closer. "I'm so glad I did."

"And that's when I began looking into your history. But there was little to find other than your association with Detective Inspector Thacker and your relation to Gypsies."

They gazed at one another intently. "Then you know that you mustn't worry about me."

"But Ashmedai..."

"You mustn't worry." He leaned into her and kissed her petal-soft cheek. Then he moved to take more...until someone cleared their throat.

The cloud of contentment that surrounded him dissipated into the ether, and Gehenna returned to fill his sight. When he looked over his shoulder, everyone was staring at them. Eurynomos, with his red skin, seemed to be blushing.

Then Suchah flew up into his view and stared with bulging eyes. "Why does Leopold Master try to eat this woman?"

Leopold sputtered and Mingli put her hand to her mouth the hide a smile.

"I'm not...er...it's...I'm showing my affection for her. It's called a kiss."

"To Suchah, it looked like you were eating her."

Raj's hand tapped Suchah on the shoulder. "I'll explain it to you later, my friend."

Suchah sighed and rolled his eyes. "What humans get up to is not of interest. Was merely telling Leopold Master that Suchah can keep Ashmedai away."

Leopold shed his embarrassment and straightened. "How's that, Suchah?"

"Suchah can lure him away with a plan. A plan to tell him to ambush Leopold Master where Leopold Master will not be."

"Can you truly do that, Suchah?"

"Suchah is smarter than Ashmedai. *Much* smarter than most demons."

Leopold looked to Eurynomos for reassurance, but the beast looked pensive. "What's wrong, Eurynomos?"

"Radueriel will tell the others. We haven't much time."

"Can't we somehow skip the other levels and go directly to *Sitra Achra* now?"

Before the daemon could answer, Raj—with nose was still in his book—piped up with, "Yes!"

Even Eurynomos was stunned. "Raj, what do you mean? I was leading us on the most straightforward path."

"Let us see the map again," said Raj, lowering his book.

Leopold withdrew it from his coat and unrolled it for the automaton. Again, it showed a three-dimensional view. Raj studied it carefully. "According to this most interesting book I am reading, the map works in two ways. It shows us the path. But…" He reached into the transparent drawing hovering above the papyrus. "But it can also be manipulated *from* the map itself. Observe."

With his small porcelain hand, he carefully nudged the gate to *Sitra Achra* closer to *Abaddon*. He inched it along until it moved where he stopped it. He slid it more, and soon it appeared—at least on the map—very close to their present position.

Everyone peered over Leopold's arms to stare at the map. The gate stayed. And suddenly, the ground shook beneath their feet. They held on to each other to keep their footing, and raised their heads as the sliding of rocks and gravel sounded nearby.

Behind them, a stone arch, much like the others they encountered, appeared out of the rising dust. Yet this one was of black stone, slimy with mold and moss, and crumbling from neglect.

Leopold left Mingli holding the map as he walked slowly toward the gate. Around it was still the view of *Abaddon*, but *through* the gate was a wasteland of red, fiery skies and streaks of black clouds. The flat plains rose up into cinder cones that dripped a steady flow of brightly glowing lava.

His gorge rose. Yes, he'd definitely seen this before. His father was there. Àkos Kazsmer. And as fearful as the prospect was, Leopold was going to save him.

CHAPTER FIFTEEN

LEOPOLD COULDN'T TAKE his eyes off the horrifying landscape when he asked, "Eurynomos, how do we find him?"

"Leo," said Thacker. "Use the stereo-optic thing-um-bobs."

Eurynomos handed it to him and Leopold held it to his face, seeing again the three-dimensional image of a galaxy. "Show me Àkos!"

Slowly, the image blurred and changed. A cavern, and within, a stone bowl with flames licking out of it. A figure sat on a rock, stoop-shouldered, surrounded by gloom. As the image cleared, Leopold could see that the man's hair was completely white…as was the mustache and long beard. Leopold carefully studied the face and…a warm lump caught in his throat. It was his father! But how he had *aged*! Frown lines ran along his forehead, crows' feet at his eyes. He was doing something but Leopold couldn't tell what…until he discerned it. He was miming serving tea to imaginary guests.

"Leo," said the soft voice of Mingli at his ear. "Have you found him?"

He pulled the viewer away from his eyes and handed it wordlessly to Eurynomos. He couldn't speak. He thought he would be overjoyed to see his father…and he was. And yet…he was so different, so changed. And Leopold had been responsible for it.

He wiped harshly at the tears on his cheeks, licked his lips, and straightened his coat. "Do you know where that is, Eurynomos?" he rasped.

"I…yes. I think I recollect that place. But we must hurry. Your magic has certainly brought the attention of demons here. And the Unholy Hosts know you're present."

"Then take us. As swiftly as you can."

Raj closed his book on his finger, marking the place. "Perhaps Leopold can use his magic to create a conveyance. Since they already know you're here."

He stared at Raj for a long moment before his words made sense. Leopold nodded and calmed, closing his eyes. In his mind, he imagined something that could move them all. An image of a carriage pulled by horses rose up in his thoughts. The sigils formed in his head and he signed them, feeling the magic surge within him and release through his fingertips. When he opened his eyes, he startled back.

Before him was a chariot of sorts, but horses did not draw the strange and organically swirled architecture of the chariot, but instead giant lizards, whipping their tails and darting forked tongues.

Thacker drew up and looked it over. "Crickey, Leo. What goes on in that mind of yours?"

"I don't know. I certainly didn't ask for this."

Mingli examined the lizards with their rippling scales and undulating tails…from a decent distance. "Obviously your Earth magic becomes slightly twisted when working in Gehenna."

Slightly? he thought.

"I suggest we cut short our arguments," said Eurynomos, "and instead get in."

The company all fit in the high sides of the chariot, though Suchah and Thacker chose to fly close to it rather than crowd in.

Taking the reins, Leopold rolled them in his fingers. "Are we all ready?" When the answer was affirmative, he swallowed hard, raised the reins, and snapped them down on the reptiles. "Gee-up, there!" he called. Amazingly, the lizards broke into a clumsy pace, bodies undulating back and forth, but gaining speed.

"Lizard conveyance," whispered Mingli, astonishment on her face.

"Better than walking, I suppose," said Leopold, spreading his feet apart for balance and wrapping the reins around his hands. It wasn't the most comfortable of rides, for the reptiles' gait made the chariot buck and rock. But it moved along at a respectable clip and Leopold was satisfied that they would make good time. But…to where?

"Eurynomos?"

"Yes, Leo. We are heading in the right direction. Do you see those hills there in the distance? That is our destination."

A chill rippled down his spine. He remembered hills, and a canyon, and demons falling upon his father. "That…that same canyon then?"

A warm hand with claws that never touched him, rested on his shoulder. "Yes, Leo," he said quietly. "The same."

Mingli reached down and unsheathed her gun, examining the strange bulb with the green liquid that stood where the chamber should have been. "Don't worry, Leo. This is precisely what this gun is for; demons."

The chariot made a startling rise and fall, and he nearly lost his balance. "If we all make it there in one piece."

Raj's nose was in his book again. His brass legs seemed to be able to keep his balance well. "Never fear, Leo. I am forming a plan." He raised his face just enough to catch the attention of Eurynomos, who leaned over him curiously to look over the page Raj was reading.

Leopold moved with the rhythm of the chariot and pondered. He tried to recall everything he could remember about that day seventeen years ago. He well remembered the terror he felt, but he tried to look at it now with the eyes of an adult, not a frightened child.

Yes, he remembered well the canyon's sheer walls and their dark rock, almost black and streaked with purple. He remembered the smell of sulfur and the glow of fire in the sky from countless volcanos erupting in the distance.

And he remembered the dark, indistinct shapes of the Unholy Hosts. And the vague sense of tentacles. The face of Radueriel certainly confirmed that. His stomach roiled at the memory. For the blurry sight of them had sickened him, and sickened him again when he received the second mark on his wrist.

Not a child, he told himself. No, this time he was a man, and he would stand up to anything barring his way. He was no child to be scared off by creatures in the dark. *He* was a creature in the dark now. With his Earth magic, he was a fearsome Mage. And not even an archangel would get in his way.

And dammit, he wasn't even going to *look* as if he was destroying the world. He utterly refused to be cowed by these evil beings.

"Leo." Mingli's voice was quiet beside him. "There's...suddenly something about your bearing. A confidence that seems to be building in you. I can sense it. And I find it...very attractive."

He looked at her, surprised. And a bit pleased with the lascivious look to her eye. He lifted his brows. "Why, Miss Zhao," he said with a smirk. "Do control yourself."

She gave him an answering smirk, but she leaned against him as a reassuring presence.

The shadows lengthened but the sky didn't seem to change. When Leopold looked back, he realized why.

A score of flying creatures seemed to be pursuing them. Their bat-wings spread wide to flap in long strokes, and their eyes and faces were intent. Each one was different in figure and visage. Horns, tusks, long tongues, beaks, scales, and sharp teeth all. Like a murmuration of starlings, they formed the shape of one immense demon.

"Eurynomos..."

The daemon looked over his shoulder. "Damn!"

Suchah screwed up his eyes. "Minions of Ashmedai. Suchah will help delay them."

Before Leopold could ask, the imp zoomed up into the sky to intercept the creatures, flying toward them. He watched as Suchah circled them, slowing their progress. His little wings flapped hard as he maneuvered in and out of the demons, talking the whole time. Leopold could not hear what he said, but he noticed his hands working fast, and when he pointed in the opposite direction, all the beasts turned to look and they suddenly changed direction with focused intention.

Suchah flew with them for a while, until he slowly and carefully dropped farther and farther back, hovered in the air as they out-paced him, and then dropped out of the sky to rejoin their chariot.

"You see?" he said, perching on the front of the chariot. "Suchah is smarter than most demons."

"What did you tell them?" asked Leopold.

"Made an illusion of this chariot and sent it in the other direction. Most demons too stupid to question what they see." He raised his chin, and strutted.

"Suchah, you are amazing. Thank you!" He patted the imp's shoulder and the creature gazed up at Leopold in adoration.

Eurynomos was at his ear, whispering, "That was very well done, Leo. You've made a friend for life."

"I hope, for his sake, it will be worth it."

They traveled a seemingly endless line toward the hills that did not appear to draw any closer. "Is this, too, an illusion, Eurynomos? That we don't appear to be making any progress?"

"It's possible. But the landscape is ever-changing."

Leopold reached into his coat, drew out the map, and handed it behind him to Eurynomos. He heard the beast say, "It is as I suspected. The topography has changed, extended itself."

"Is that something the archangels can change, Eurynomos?"

"I do not believe so. But I wouldn't put it past their abilities at this point."

"Estimates till we reach the hills? I don't know how much I can push these beasts."

"A few hours at least, Leo."

The lizard beasts seemed to be straining to maintain their pace, and there was foam at their mouths. "I'm going to have to rest them."

"Can you conjure new ones?" asked a distracted Raj, still with his nose in a book.

"I don't know. I'd rather just rest these fellows to be certain."

They got out of the chariot and walked about, stretching their legs. Leopold conjured water for the lizards, and for Mingli and himself. He offered it to Eurynomos but the daemon shook his head. "I don't need water, Leo. I just drink tea and alcohol to be sociable. And I do enjoy the experience."

"Stupid of me for all these years not to have known that."

"Think nothing of it. I drank because you expected me to, and most graciously offered it to me. There's nothing wrong in that."

He sat next to Mingli but kept looking over his shoulder toward the hills.

"Don't worry, Leo. We are close now."

"I want to hurry there…and at the same time, I dread seeing him. Does that make me a coward and a cad?"

She sighed. "I know you feel responsible…"

"I *am* responsible."

"You were a child. You saw your father doing something intriguing and you wanted to emulate that. You made a mistake. People make mistakes. *I* rarely do, but other people do." She seemed gratified that she had urged even a partial smile from him. "Leo, your father would be the last one to ever blame you. I'm certain he blames himself more. And after all, he has no way of knowing that you were safe. He must have been worrying all these years about *you*."

"I never thought of that. Except…when I saw him through the viewer, he was having an invisible tea party."

"That doesn't mean he's lost his mind. It might merely mean he was entertaining himself. I did similar things when I was at my uncle's brothel."

He grasped her hand and held it tight. "You've never really said much about that time. I know you must not wish to speak of it."

She breathed deeply and looked down at her lap before reaching into her neckline and drawing out the jade dragon on its chain tether. "I was sold to the Lotus House when I was ten. I started in the pillow rooms when I was fourteen. The *yuan gui* spoke to me for the first time then. At sixteen, I finally answered them. I thought I was going insane hearing their voices all those years. But I had never answered them before that. And that was when they rescued me. Everyone in the house had to die. I was to leave all of them as a sacrifice. But before I left, I was told to save…this."

He carefully cradled it in his hand. "It wasn't your fault those people died."

"It most certainly was. But I find that—under the circumstances of the time—I don't mind it."

He didn't know what to say to that. Instead, he turned his attention to the jade dragon. "I sense no magic from this."

"At first, I thought that any magic I had came from this pendant, but it doesn't. Of course, being half-daemon, it now makes sense. I had to learn to draw the magic from myself. And still. I think there is more I have yet to learn."

"Madam Hui Ling said you might learn more about your true nature here."

"Yes. I might. I am more concerned with you, in truth."

"I'll be fine."

"And sadder words were never spoken." She tightened her grip on *his* hand. "You and Àkos will be fine because all your friends are around you. We will make certain it is fine. We will rescue Àkos. After all, I will need someone to walk me down the aisle, and who better than my future father-in-law?"

He brought her hand up to his lips to kiss. "What would I have done without you?"

"Your life would have been the poorer for it." She rose, dusted smartly at her skirts, and straightened her hat. "I need to take a walk."

No sooner had she vacated her spot by Leopold than Eurynomos took her place and sat. "I…couldn't help overhearing some of Miss Zhao's words. Did I hear her right? She was *sold* to a brothel at ten years old?"

"Yes. Her parents sold her. I shall never forgive such evil."

"It could be they are here still."

"I hope so," he gritted out. "And that's not even the worst of it. She told me her detestable uncle…Oh Eurynomos. I don't know that I should say."

"You can tell me, old man. You know my lips are sealed."

"Well…" He turned toward the daemon and spoke in quiet tones. "She confessed to me that he gave all the girls their potions and hurt them with surgeries so that they couldn't have children. She almost broke our engagement over it."

"Why?"

"Because…some men would have put such women aside, if they couldn't bear their husbands' children."

"Surely *you* never said…"

"Of course not. I love *her*. It doesn't matter to me."

"But what a shame. With her amazing cleverness, and your skill with magic, what a child you would have had."

"I know. But it isn't the most important thing. *She* is."

He stared at Leopold a long time, cocked his head, and then patted his shoulder. "You're a good man, Leo. For a human."

Mingli was suddenly there again. "I believe we are all rested enough."

Leopold agreed, and they gathered again in and around the chariot when Leopold grabbed up the reins and snapped them upon the lizards' scaly hides.

They grew closer to the hills until their details were distinct. His eyes roved over the crannies and sheer rises with ridges sharp as dragon's teeth, until Eurynomos shot an arm forward, pointing to the canyon.

A chill rippled down Leopold's spine, even in the perpetual heat. He recognized that place, the rip in the sheer cliffs where his father was borne away. He had never wanted to see it in the flesh again.

The canyon appeared unguarded. But Eurynomos was just as suspicious and told them all to stay in the chariot while he disappeared to explore the surrounding hills.

They all stood quietly in the chariot, listening to the constant wind, the fiery eruptions in the distance, the rumbling sky, until Leopold couldn't stand it any longer. He threw the reins down and leapt over the side of the chariot. "I'm going to go look around."

"Perhaps wait until Eurynomos returns?" said Mingli.

"I can't."

She brandished her gun. "Then I will come with you."

"Mingli…"

"You know you can't argue with me, Leo." She raised her skirts and leapt over the side of the chariot as well, landing perfectly on her high-heeled boots.

"I suggest the Inspector go that way," said Raj, climbing out, "and I shall go this way." He gestured toward the leeward side of the canyon and its many outcroppings.

"Sounds like a plan," said Thacker, already floating in the suggested direction.

Leopold set out, looking back at the chariot and its agitated lizards. "What about you, Suchah?"

The imp looked somewhat subdued. "Suchah will stay here. Guard the chariot."

"Don't be silly, Suchah. I can conjure another."

The imp seemed positively frantic. "Suchah no go, Leopold Master."

"Why in heavens not?"

He rubbed his hands one over the other and turned his head away. "Suchah...Suchah did not lie to Leopold Master. Suchah...was not kind to Mister Àkos."

"But you offered before to let him know we were coming."

"Suchah...Suchah forgot some of the things said to Mister Àkos. Then, in the ride here...Suchah remembered again."

"Oh." Yes, Leopold did recall when the imp was an enemy. It was he who told Leopold—*taunted* him, in fact—that his father was still alive and that the imp had tormented him. A wave of rage rose up in him, but it soon cascaded away. Suchah looked miserable. He had realized at last that his actions were unsuitable to his current situation. "I see." Leopold stood for a moment, thinking of the choices they had all made recently, and nodded. "Then...you stay here, if that is your desire."

Suchah sat on the floor of the carriage, hugged his upraised knees, and turned his face away.

Poor sod, Leopold thought. *He probably never had to experience any sort of reckoning for his past behavior. I won't forgive him for what he did, but, for now, I suppose I can dismiss it.*

He and Mingli moved forward into the canyon, peering into the deep shadows and raising their eyes to the rocks above.

"Look for a cavern hewn from the rock," said Leopold, unconsciously lowering his voice. The echoes seemed accentuated within the steep walls, and he had no wish to call attention to himself.

Mingli pointed. "There."

Yes. He remembered this. The slide of rocks converging, leaving an entrance very like...well. The pits of Hell.

"That's it," he whispered. "But beware. It's guarded." Even as he said it, he glanced around the slash of an opening. Nothing was perched above. That meant that the guard might be hiding within.

He nudged Mingli aside—the woman was actually treading in first!—and readied himself to throw enchantments where he could.

And just as he thought how very quiet it was, a huge shadow descended and a hulking figure landed before him, wings opening wide.

CHAPTER SIXTEEN

SOMETHING BUZZED BY his head and one of the widespread wings was abruptly hewn off. The creature screamed.

Leopold turned to Mingli. She had released the clockwork weapon. Yes, there it was embedded in the wall behind the beast.

The demon stumbled forward, crying and growling and holding its shoulder. "You bastard of a human!"

"Now, now," she said. "None of that talk. A lady is present."

The demon raised its face. It had something of a beak with rows of jagged teeth. Its eyes narrowed. "I will tear you apart. Both of you. I will eat your entrails and keep your heads as trophies."

Mingli sniffed. "That sounds very unpleasant. We have no intention of letting that happen."

"You will have no choice, human."

Mingli snapped her fingers and the whirring weapon returned to her. She heaved it again at the beast and took off the arm on the opposite side of the severed wing.

Black blood sprayed the rock walls. The beast screamed an unholy sound again.

"I will *kill* you!"

"Or…" said Mingli, "you can run. Escape. You do have a few more limbs to sever." She snapped her fingers again and the weapon returned to her a second time.

The demon stared at the buzzing mechanism, gazed forlornly at his shuddering arm on the ground, and made up its mind.

It pushed past them both, knocking them to the ground and took off running on the remaining arm and two legs, its only wing flapping uselessly like a torn ship's sail.

Leopold watched the creature go with its trail of black blood. The arm on the ground twitched.

Mingli rose and flipped some secret switch on the clockwork weapon and it ceased buzzing. She dropped it neatly into her jacket pocket.

"I see you've learned how to use that."

"I had some time on my hands."

"Well...jolly good." He brushed off his coat. "But I fear there may be more demons patrolling."

"Of that I have no doubt. Now. Into the cavern?"

Leopold took a step forward. "I wonder where Eurynomos is." He stopped and looked around, searching the crests of the canyon for a sign of him.

Something large landed in front of him, and he startled back.

"Why are you venturing forth alone?" said Eurynomos.

He gave a sigh of relief. "I'm afraid I grew impatient."

"It isn't safe down here. We must go back."

But when they turned, another red shape landed behind him. It was Eurynomos...again! A *second* one?

"Wait," said Leopold.

"That's not me, Leo," said the second daemon.

"Leo, that's an imposter!" said the first.

"No, *he's* the imposter!" accused the second, pointing his finger.

Leopold looked from one to the other. This was decidedly a very bad thing. He considered a spell, but what if it went awry?

"One of you is an Unholy Host," he said, "and one my friend. I'm not going to listen to either of you until I verify which is which. So answer me this: Why are we here?"

The second shook his head. "I can't answer that. I don't want the imposter to know."

"How wily of you," said the first, "since I was about to say the same thing."

"Shut it!" said Leopold, as they continued to argue. "My head is aching." *This isn't working*. He considered. "Very well. What was the first successful spell I ever performed?"

They both thought, both scratching their square chins. The first's face brightened. "I remember now. It was fire in the palm of your hand."

Leopold shook his head. "Yes, I did do that and it might seem like the first...but it wasn't the *actual* first."

The second snapped his fingers. "You're right, Leo. You floated. Not very well, as I recall."

"That's one for you." He turned to the first Eurynomos. "What is the name of my...no. You could have gotten that from my memories when I was first here." He snatched a glance at a very wary Mingli. "I have it. What is the name of the sorceress?"

The daemon chuckled. "You know many of those."

"No, surprisingly, I don't. What is her name?"

The first frowned. And then he seemed to morph into something taller, lumpier, more grotesque until his mangled face changed to a strange configuration of a mouth that looked like a squid's tentacles with heaping shoulders and an overall green visage. The mere sight of him made Leopold sick. "Mortal!" he spat.

Leopold took a step back...into the embrace of his daemon friend, who also sheltered Mingli.

"You are easy to manipulate," said the Unholy Host.

"Not that easy, as it turns out," said Leopold breathlessly.

"Kokabiel," said Eurynomos in hushed tones. "Get out of our way."

He smirked...if that configuration of his mouth-tentacles could be called so. "I don't think so. Kazsmer is ours."

"Not yet he isn't. Get out of our way."

"You cannot hope to defeat me."

"I can but try." He leaned down and hastily whispered to Leopold as he pushed him behind him, "I'll hold him off. You rescue Àkos."

Leopold felt cold all over, even in the heat of the sun-soaked rocks. Eurynomos' words meant that he might *not* defeat the Unholy Host. And then what could they do? How could they hope to escape Gehenna without him? How could he go on in *life* without him?

Nevertheless, he grabbed Mingli's hand and ran with her as Eurynomos guarded the path. Leopold looked back and realized he could not call to his friends so far back in the chariot. *In the chariot? Wait.* As he ran, he pressed a finger to his now painful tattoo. "Suchah!" he stage-whispered.

Immediately, the imp appeared before him, flapping his wings listlessly. "Leopold Master—" Leopold lunged forward to press his hand to the imp's mouth. He dragged him away behind an outcropping. In distant echoes, they heard the fight between the Unholy Host and Eurynomos. It sounded like wild beasts, snarling and screaming. Suchah's eyes went wide.

"Eurynomos is giving us cover to find and rescue my father. Can you fetch Thacker and Raj and bring them here?"

"But…Mister Àkos…"

"Don't worry about the past, Suchah. I need your help now."

The imp nodded. "I will do as Leopold Master wishes." He winked out and immediately returned with his hand on Raj's arm and Thacker floating on his own. They all turned their heads toward the sounds of a raucous fight pinging off the walls of the canyon.

"Eurynomos has given us time to collect my father. Please, let us hurry."

No one questioned him. He almost wished they had. Leaving Eurynomos to his fate with barely a blink of his eye and choosing his father's fate instead? Would they understand? Would Àkos?

He shook the thought loose. If Eurynomos was making a sacrifice, he couldn't allow sentiment to foil his plan. If they couldn't at least save his father, then all of it was for naught.

Leopold searched, each shadow and crevice confounding him. It was Mingli who first saw the turn within the cave and motioned toward it. There was a flicker of firelight within and by this, Leopold was fairly certain that this was the right place. He stopped dead as he heard an old man singing a song he had long forgotten. His throat closed with a warm lump. His eyes burned. *Not now, Leopold,* he told himself. *Gird your courage, man.*

They passed through to the inner cavern and turned a rocky corner to find the old man he had seen in the viewer. His clothes were ragged but still somewhat resembled the brown suit he had worn on that long-ago day. His white hair was long, past his shoulders, and his white beard trailed down his chest. But it was him. And the song he sang—an old Hungarian ballad—something Leopold remembered his father singing many a time, even humming when he read the newspaper.

"Papa..."

The old man stopped. "Who is Papa?" he asked in his faint Hungarian accent. "Wait. This is new. No one talks to me except for stupid imps and demons."

Suchah cringed back into the shadows. Leopold motioned the others to stay back as he took a tentative step forward. He realized that their time was short, but it was impossible to rush his feet. "Papa. It's me. Leopold."

The man jerked back and turned, staring with wild eyes.

"Another imp's trick. You can't be Leopold. Leo is a little boy..."

"But it *is* me, Papa. I'm...I'm all grown up now. It's...been a long time."

The old man blinked, rubbed his knuckles into his eyes, and rose, leaning toward Leopold. "How can that be you? How...how long *has* it been?"

Leopold stepped closer, holding out his arms. "Far too long, Papa. I didn't know. I didn't know you were still alive or I would have fetched you far sooner. I'm so sorry."

"You...you *sound* like my little Leo..."

"Did you think of sheep to calm yourself, Papa? I never forgot to do that."

"*Leo?*" He lurched forward and finally encompassed his son in his arms. "It *is* you, Leo. My boy, my boy!"

"Papa!" he barely choked out. He told himself not to cry, but he couldn't help it. He held Àkos tight. The man seemed so slight, all bones. But Leopold buried his face into his shoulder and simply held him.

"I hate to interrupt," said Mingli, suddenly standing right behind Leopold.

He drew back and wiped his eyes.

"Do forgive me," she said tenderly, "but we *must* go. As quick as we might."

"Papa, she's right. We are going. We're getting you out of here at last."

"Out of…here? But…where is here?"

"Out of *Sitra Achra.* You've been imprisoned here for…for seventeen years. Don't you remember?"

"Good God." He wiped his hand down his beard. "*Sitra Achra,* you say? But…what is *that*?" He pointed at Raj.

"I beg your pardon, Mister Kazsmer," he said with a bow. "I am Raj, a mechanical man. And I am Leo's friend."

"A mechanical man?" He shook his head but his eyes lit with excitement. "I should like to investigate that—" Then he spotted Mingli. "And this Chinese woman…"

He took his father's arm and moved as hastily as he could toward the cave's entrance. "That is Mingli Zhao, a Special Inspector from Scotland Yard and…incidentally, my…my fiancée."

"An inspector…fiancée?"

"Don't worry over it now, Papa. We'll talk about it all later. We must get out of here fast."

"Whatever you say. None of this is real anyway," he muttered.

His words tore at Leopold's heart. He'd set him to rights once they were away. But for now, he had him at last! Now to get him to safety.

They emerged from the shadows of the cavern and crept against the walls. But Àkos reared back when he spied the imp. "Oh ho! This is your doing, you nasty creature. Making me think my son was here."

Suchah's ears wilted, he rubbed his hands, and shuffled his little webbed feet. "Suchah is sorry, Mister Àkos. Sorry for all the times Suchah said dreadful things. But now I am the friend of Leopold Master, and he has come to rescue you."

"This is the worst of all," he ranted, throwing off Leopold's grip. "You trick me with my son as an older man. Have I truly been here seventeen years? No, don't answer that. Your mouth is full of lies."

"It was once, Mister Àkos," said Suchah plaintively. "But no longer. Leopold Master is Suchah's friend and Suchah is sorry for everything now. Suchah never had friends like this."

Àkos cast his glance over all of them...and stopped at Thacker. "And what is this? A ghost? How inventive you are, you little devil."

"He didn't invent me," said Thacker indignantly. "I'm Detective Inspector Despenser Thacker from Scotland Yard. Well...I was. Before I died untimely. But I used to work with your son to solve crimes of an unusual sort. When I was alive, that is."

Àkos turned to Leopold. "You're a policeman?"

"No, Papa. I'm..." He chuckled sheepishly. "I'm...a magician. In London, on the stage. The Great Enchanter..." He gestured grandly before dropping his hand. "As it happens. Obviously, I can perform real magic. Like you taught me. When we used to summon daemons..."

Àkos stared at the ground, apparently trying to process all this new information. "A magician." His fingers worried at his beard. Suddenly, he laughed and clapped his hands. "A magician! Ha! What a miracle! And you summoned daemons to help you?"

"I summon Eurynomos quite often."

"Eurynomos. Now there's a name I haven't heard in a long while." He frowned. "Maybe it *has* been a long time..." he muttered.

"He's still my friend...and he's in danger. He's fighting an Unholy Host even as we speak so that I could rescue you. And now I must save *him*."

Àkos glanced once more at all the various figures surrounding Leopold and shook his head in disbelief. "All right," he murmured. "Why not? Let us go and save Eurynomos."

Leopold's heart warmed at the less clouded look in his father's eyes. "Yes, let's. I hope you remember some magic."

"I don't know if it will work."

"Then stay back behind Miss Zhao."

"Let a woman protect me? I'm not *that* uncivilized."

"I think you will find," said Mingli, "that I am quite adept at protecting those important to Leopold."

He stared into her telescoping eye for the first time and then at the strange gun she held up near her face. "I...maybe I believe you..."

The roars and growls grew louder, and Leopold ran forward, hands raised and already sketching sigils. "To Eurynomos!" he cried.

CHAPTER SEVENTEEN

COLORFUL CLOUDS OF sparking magic surrounded the archangel and the daemon. Eurynomos appeared as Leopold had never seen him. His jaw was suddenly huge and hanging low, and his teeth were long and saber-like. His eyes glowed with a red hue, and his horns had grown enormous. He was all claw and tooth as he harangued the angel—a monstrous figure himself.

The Unholy Host's eyes glowed with a bright white light, like a cluster of suns, piercing the perpetual dull daylight in rays striating outward, blazing the canyon with unnatural illumination. Each threw damaging spells at one another. Eurynomos' breechclout was in rags, and the Unholy Host's robes—if they could be called such—were also in tatters, and each sported their share of bruises. The daemon had a trickle of blood from the side of his mouth. And it wasn't just from spells. Leopold jerked back as they rushed each other again, claws scraping, teeth clamping down on flesh, horns tearing.

...Until the Unholy Host spotted Leopold and his father, and slid to a halt. "What are you doing? Àkos Kazsmer is ours!"

Leopold opened his mouth to speak when Raj stepped forward and pronounced, "That is not entirely true."

Everyone looked at the automaton.

"What is this creature?" said Kokabiel, disgusted. "It has no flesh, but...it...it has a...soul?"

By the lilt of Raj's shoulders, he seemed inordinately pleased by that declaration. "I am the Amazing Raj, the Automated Man. And friend to Leopold Kazsmer...and his father."

"You have no grounds here to even speak to me, you...you *thing*."

"Oh, but I think I do. Call upon your other Unholy Hosts. This has a bearing on them as well."

Leopold turned a terrified glance at Raj. Bring the others? Was he insane? But the seeming look of confidence about his expressionless face gave Leopold pause. He looked to Eurynomos for confirmation, but the daemon seemed just as confounded. He was breathing hard, and Leopold noticed many more scars and bleeding wounds on his scaly skin.

Kokabiel threw back his head and howled an unearthly sound that seemed to crawl under the layers of Leopold's skin. Soon, the earth trembled and, with a blinding flash, two more figures appeared. Radueriel and another.

"Tamiel," whispered Eurynomos.

They were more distinct than Leopold had ever beheld them. Seeing them so clearly roiled his belly, and he bent over and retched. Something about their aura left him sick and weak. They were not holy beings any longer. The opposite was true, and because they had absorbed all that was evil about *Sitra Achra*, it seemed to have penetrated their very beings, made them at one with it, made crooked their souls and suffused their very blood with the essence of malevolence. It couldn't be tolerated by innocent beings. He noticed Mingli holding her stomach too.

Too terrified to speak, Leopold stood frozen to the spot. Their pulsating auras made it impossible for him to think, to plan.

But Raj, calm in deportment and temperament, stepped forward, merely cocking his head, intrigued by their strangeness, the tentacles growing from them at their mouths or backs, the tendrils of what looked like black smoke snaking around their pale, emaciated flesh. Leopold couldn't help but think it was the remnants of the good in their auras that had twisted into some repulsive stench swirling around them at their feet.

"Greetings, Unholy Hosts," said Raj with an abbreviated bow.

"We do not recognize this being," said Tamiel.

"It does not matter whether you recognize me as a being or not," said Raj. "What I have to say is the more important part. Now," he made a sound of clearing his throat which he clearly did not have to do, and began, "my research into this problem has been very interesting. Of course, I am referring to the capture and imprisonment of one Àkos Kazsmer."

"This had nothing to do with—"

"Please," said Raj. "Do not interrupt me, Radueriel. For instance, from my reading—and I'm certain Eurynomos can acknowledge this as well—Archangels such as yourselves, no matter their strength, power, or...status..." he looked them over at their very *un*-angelic selves, "must abide by the laws of Gehenna set down from the beginning. Indeed, they *are* the laws set down by the Great Creator Itself."

Radueriel scowled. "And so?"

"I daresay, even *fallen* Archangels." There was the merest of flinching from the three standing like goliaths before the spindly automaton. "And as the Talmud clearly states—Eurynomos, have you a copy to hand?"

The smallest of smiles curved the daemon's lips. "As it happens, I do." A book appeared in his hands and he flipped the pages. Raj's words had apparently dawned on him at last and he began looking for the proper chapter. "Here is the passage in question, if I have read my mechanical friend correctly. The Talmud states, as pertains to the souls in Gehenna, *after twelve months their bodies are destroyed, their souls are burned, and the wind strews the ashes under the feet of the pious.*"

Raj nodded. "You have not only kept Àkos Kazsmer for well over twelve months, beyond the legal limit, but you have kept a poor and *pious* man. You have kept a LIVING SOUL."

Eurynomos slammed the book shut and it promptly vanished. "Of course! Of *course*! This is clearly against the laws of the Creator!" he cried, his voice triumphant. "You are a miracle, Raj! Why didn't I see this before?"

"You were too close to it, my friend."

"He is ours," spat Kokabiel. "The son is ours—"

"And equally illegal," said Raj.

"We are the Unholy Hosts!" snarled Radueriel. The ground trembled, thunder growled in the distance. "He made a covenant with us."

Eurynomos, now getting into the spirit of the thing, smiled broadly. "Let us look at the Book of Life."

"NO!" the three angels cried at once.

"You must," said Eurynomos, baring his teeth. "I call upon the powers of Gehenna! Bring me the Book of Life!"

An enormous tome appeared with a crack of lightning and thunder. It hovered in the air between them. The three archangels lurched toward it but could not seem to get any closer than a few feet. Eurynomos freely stalked up to it, took the heavy cover, and opened it from left to right. He turned the stiff parchment pages until he found the names he wanted. "Leopold Àkos Kazsmer. Born nearly thirty years ago, planet Earth. He is guilty of the most common of human foibles: occasional pride that is not merited, anger…the eating of pork?" He glanced at Leopold and ticked his head. "But look here. He received a certain tattoo upon his wrist. Not by his own devising, so it does not break the taboos from Leviticus. I see here that it was to keep his soul safe from capture, a noble endeavor. Ah, and I see the receipt of a *second* tattoo done out of pure sacrifice and love." Eurynomos gazed dewy-eyed at Leopold. "It was to save *my* miserable life, in case all and sundry had forgot," he said softly. "For I have not and never will."

Eurynomos, clearly overcome with emotion, wiped at his eyes before he turned more pages. "Let us look at Àkos Helias Kazsmer, born fifty-three years ago, planet Earth."

Trembling, Àkos edged closer. Leopold clutched his father's shoulder in reassurance.

"Again, the occasional foibles, a moment of blaspheming when…when his wife died. Such a thing might be understandable, for it is noted that he did repent of it. He has studied the Torah assiduously, and the Talmud and Kabbalah even more closely. He sacrificed himself so that his son may live. There is nothing on the condemning sides of either of their passages in the Book of Life, and much on their pious sides." He closed the book and glared at the Unholy Hosts. "You must release them both. You have broken the Law."

Radueriel laughed, a horrible sound like a bubbling bog. "Under threat of what consequences, Prince of Death? We are all-powerful. I can even create another life, another demon to strike you down."

"The consequences of breaking the Law do not come from me, Radueriel. But from another, greater than all three of you."

Radueriel's eyes burned bright with the deepest scowl he yet wore, but even in his anger, he was forced to confer with his peers, and they huddled in a tight clutch, murmuring and rasping to one another.

Finally, Radueriel turned back to Eurynomos and the other two fallen angels tightened their stance behind him. "It…it is agreed that Àkos Kazsmer…must be released."

"Papa!" cried Leopold, and enrapt him in his arms.

"But Leopold Kazsmer has made a covenant with us and it cannot be broken. *He* will stay."

Mingli doubled over, clutching her stomach.

"Mingli!" cried Leopold. He broke from his father and moved toward her, but found himself unable to move. And then he was sliding toward the Unholy Hosts.

"Stop!" Eurynomos bellowed.

But the fallen angels merely watched as Leopold slid toward them. Eurynomos lunged to grab him but it was as if an invisible wall kept him at bay. He struggled, and, gritting his teeth, pushed and broke free of the spell, running in great strides toward Leopold and enclosed him in his arms to pull him away.

Radueriel waved his hand, and Eurynomos was cast back.

"He is ours," said the angel.

Raj strode forward. "For all the same reasons I cited, you cannot keep Leopold!"

"Kazsmer came into the covenant of his own free will. I think you will find that he agreed to it, knowing full well the consequences."

Eurynomos turned desperately to Raj, who flipped page after page in the books he retrieved from the Library of the Damned. "I can't…I'm looking… Ah!" He held up the book in triumph. "In such a case," he read, "you must demand a contest. Champions may be chosen on both sides, one each. The culmination of the contest will result in the absolute defeat of one side or the other."

"Then I so demand such a contest," said Radueriel. "I demand it! I shall be our champion. Who shall be yours, Kazsmer?"

Leopold, pushing against the pull of the spell with all his might, thought desperately. He knew that Eurynomos would insist, and he was the only likely candidate. But how could he hope to win? His eyes searched out the daemon's and they surely read each other's doubts. Eurynomos had already been in a fight with Radueriel, and he hadn't been winning. How could he hope to do so now?

Mingli doubled over again, crying out.

"My love!" said Leopold, stretching toward her but unable to break free from the spell.

She stumbled away behind a rock outcropping with a shattering cry of pain. But even as Thacker and Suchah went to help her they were cast back as the ground trembled. Rocks toppled from the canyon walls as the great cry of a beast echoed off the stones.

The sinewy neck of a creature abruptly rose from behind the same outcropping, and all Leopold could think of was saving Mingli, but he couldn't move. He gathered his strength. All he needed to do was free up his fingers to sign some sigils, but he could not even move any of his joints or knuckles. He watched helplessly as the head of the beast climbed and climbed on what seemed like an endless stalk of a neck. The bleary sunlight flickered off the length of dark green scales as the long neck arched toward them, its fearsome head with its hydra-like projections and feelers like some giant catfish. It had horns and a long snout with deadly fangs bared. The eyes were black and focused…on Leopold.

He could not veer away. He could not protect himself. Out of the corner of his eye, he saw Eurynomos try. Even his father tried to remember the skills he used to have to conjure, but nothing seemed to help.

The dragon—for it could be called nothing else with the revelation of its withers and great clawed feet—stepped delicately over the rocky projections. The rest of the body was just as sinewy as its long neck. It roared, forcing the neck forward. Leopold was afraid it would spew fire. But it hadn't. Not yet.

"Suchah!"

The imp fluttered into the air, wings beating madly. His eyes bulged staring at Leopold.

"Save her! Get Mingli away from that beast."

"Suchah will, Leopold Master!" The imp zoomed behind the rock outcropping. Leopold waited. But nothing.

Oh God. Please. Save Suchah and Mingli.

The dragon's neck seemed interminable. Just like the etched dragon markings on that mechanical beetle. But no. It was more like the jade dragon Mingli wore. A *Chinese* dragon. Yes, it was a Chinese dragon in the flesh. What in the world was it doing here?

Mingli, Mingli! I pray you are all right.

As if hearing his cry, the dragon's eyes turned to him once more. The left one was dark as night and blinked, while the right was just as black, but seemed to swirl within with hypnotic speckles like stars or galaxies—

Wait…

"*Mingli?*" he breathed, incredulous. "Is…is that…*you*?"

The dragon's head zoomed down, level with him…but not to snatch him into its jaws. Instead, it settled before him, cocked its head…and winked!

ROBERT CARRASCO 2021

CHAPTER EIGHTEEN

"MY GOD," LEOPOLD murmured. "Mingli." His love, his betrothed…was a dragon. "That's…impossible."

Suchah zoomed out from behind the outcropping holding Mingli's umbrella, and though he flew by Leopold and gave him a worried look, he went directly to Eurynomos and whispered in his ear.

Eurynomos passed a glance over Leopold and then raised his head to look up at the dragon…before he burst into laughter. "*This* is our champion!" he announced.

Leopold tried to shake his head. "No! If that is…if *that* is Miss Zhao then…I refuse to allow it. Miss Zhao, stop this at once!"

The dragon shot a length of steam into the air and rested on its crossed arms, tail lashing from side to side. It glanced at Leopold once before tossing its head back.

"My fiancée is a dragon…" he muttered, raking his gaze over the enormous creature she had become. "Well then…" So *this* was her daemon nature. He couldn't help but release a short burst of hysterical laughter. But of course it was! No one but his own Mingli could be a dragon. A beautiful, marvelous, dangerous dragon the likes the world has never seen.

He felt a prickle of irritation that a woman should be his protector, but it only lasted a moment. She'd been protecting him in a myriad of situations all along. Why not as a…a dragon? His embarrassment fell away. "Very well, Miss Zhao. I accept you as my champion."

The dragon rose up on its haunches and, with a snarl and a certain level of determination, stomped toward the angel.

Radueriel didn't wait for her. He flew at her, and his arms seemed to multiply into spiney limbs like a crab's and attached himself like a fury to her slender neck.

"No!" cried Leopold, and jerked hard, suddenly freeing himself from the enchantment. He planted his feet and began signing in the air, but Eurynomos was upon him, grasping both wrists.

"You mustn't interfere, old chap. It's one champion to a side."

"I don't give a damn. That's my fiancée in danger of her life."

"I know," he said, lowering his hands. "It is her love of you that shall sustain her for whichever way it unfolds. But any interference by any one of us will be disastrous. There are rules."

"To hell with these blasted rules." Reluctantly, he crushed his hands into fists, helpless to do anything for her.

"The rules saved your father. I blame myself for not seeing it sooner. I…I blame myself."

Leopold heard the pain in his friend's voice, but he couldn't fault the daemon. He reached up and clutched his arm. "I know you would have done something had you known."

The angel was still clinging to Mingli's neck and she was screaming. But she angled her head, and blasted the angel with a discharge of water, sustaining the stream until the angel was engulfed and sputtering, drowning. He tore free and spun away, dripping and vomiting water. He bent at the shoulders, breathing hard.

Mingli moved in, opened her jaws, and clamped down on the Unholy Host. She lifted him from the ground and shook him hard like a terrier with a rat, surely trying to snap him in two.

He managed to push his way free and floated before her. "You cannot hope to defeat me," he growled. "Kazsmer will be ours."

Mingli drew back…and suddenly winked out of existence.

"What…what..?" gasped Leopold. "Where is she? What have you done to her?"

Without a sound, she appeared again *behind* the angel, and clamped down on him as she did before, squeezing with her enormous jaws…and then she blasted more water through her teeth.

"Not water, Mingli! Fire!"

She eyed Leopold with such disdain he wasn't certain he hadn't offended her. But she nevertheless closed her eyes, concentrated, and blasted a tongue of fire between her teeth at the archangel.

Radueriel writhed and cried out, clamped as he was in her vice-like grip. She roasted him until he was little more than a withered form. He smoldered and finally burst into flame, a vague figure moving in a ball of fire, slowly being charred to blackness with streaks of glowing red cutting through the blackened skin.

He raised his arms and, with a blast of magic that threw the others to the ground, freed himself. He flew up hundreds of feet, a streaking comet going toward the heavens.

Mingli lashed her tail and paced along the ground, looking up, keeping her eyes on the angel-fireball, even when he was a mere brightly lit speck. She lifted an arm and made a wide arc, slowly creating a circle. As her arm moved faster, the green of her scales was a blur behind it, but now the circle became a green blur on its own, as if it were a portal. And the more Leopold scrutinized it—getting as close as he dared—the more he began to realize that something like a portal *was* being generated by her swiftly moving clawed hand.

What are you doing, my love? How *are you doing it?*

The dot in the sky shot closer, streaking brighter as it aimed toward her, a fiery missile meant to destroy his wife-to-be.

He couldn't breathe. He couldn't watch and turned away…but knew he had to see the outcome for himself, and slowly turned back.

Mingli was spinning the blurry green circle with only a claw now, cocking her head to gauge the speed and the angle at which Radueriel plummeted toward the ground. Like a stage performer twirling a plate on a stick, she moved her hand this way and that to keep the balance, and when the streak-of-light-angel neared, quick as the blink of an eye, she maneuvered the green circle under him. He reached her and abruptly vanished into the circle, whereupon Mingli lifted her hand away, and the circle disappeared.

A deep boom in the ground trembled the rocks around them. Some did loosen and toppled to the depths of the canyon floor, and Leopold and his friends all struggled to keep their footing. But nothing more happened and Radueriel seemed to have effectively disappeared to planes unknown. For good.

Searing pain burned on Leopold's wrist and he fell to one knee, holding his arm with the other. Even as he cried out, he saw the fire dance across the skin of his left arm, saw it shoot out sparks and light. The All-Seeing Eye looked about desperately and finally stared at Leopold, narrowing that gaze that had never stopped staring at him since the beastly tattoo was bestowed upon him. But like the fuse of a bomb, the fizzling marks began disappearing from his skin, burning a path and leaving nothing but smooth flesh behind it, until it was entirely consumed and the eye was last, glaring at Leopold until every speck of it vanished, and with it, the pain.

He caught himself before he fell over with immense relief and ran his fingers over the smooth flesh. Not a trace of it remained, not even the sensation of a texture from the formerly permanent marking.

She'd done it. She'd freed him.

"Mingli!" he cried, showing her the wrist.

She seemed to be smiling with that enormous snout of a mouth as she aimed her enormous eyes at his arm.

Tamiel and Kokabiel took a step forward, their entire beings trembling with anger. "What did you do with Radueriel?" demanded the latter.

Eurynomos looked to the empty skies and smiled. "He has been sent to another plane of existence. He is far from Gehenna now and I have an inkling he always will be. I do believe that Leopold Kazsmer's champion has won him his freedom." He grabbed Leopold's unmarked wrist. "For behold. Your covenant is dissolved."

The two angels, scowling and growling, began to grow to an enormous height. They towered over Leopold's comrades in horrific silhouettes. Kokabiel raised his fist when a lightning bolt met it and crashed a round of thunder over their heads. With that, the two remaining Unholy Hosts vanished.

Mingli scampered toward Leopold and gestured with her head toward her back. Standing this close to her, he realized that she was the length of a train—engine and several cars, not including the length of her tail. She gestured again, tossing her head.

"I...I believe Miss Zhao wishes for us to, er, mount her?"

"That is a most excellent idea," said Raj, climbing up the side of her neck. "I believe we should all hurry. The Unholy Hosts have only disappeared for the moment. But I do not believe that they have entirely given up."

Leopold looked down at his wrist. "But the covenant is dissolved," he said, nearly disbelieving his own eyes.

Raj settled himself and his bag of books comfortably on Mingli's dragon neck. "I don't think they will be good sports about it. Do you?"

Leopold exchanged glances with Eurynomos. "You may be right," said Leopold and as he leapt onto the shiny scales, grabbed hold of them, and pulled himself up, while Eurynomos merely grew tall enough to step over and straddle her neck. The daemon lifted Àkos and set him down in front of him, wrapping a protective arm around him. Suchah fluttered and clutched Mingli's umbrella, while Thacker floated alongside.

"Carry on, Miss Zhao," said Leopold with a wave.

Leopold nearly lost his grip and slammed back when she suddenly lifted from the ground and soared into the sky.

They passed over the changing landscape with ease. Leopold watched as the mountains and hills shifted, the gates sliding to new locations, the rivers parting ways and snaking around new terrain.

Each level of Gehenna passed beneath them, and as he watched their breathless flight, he slowly began to realize that his ordeal was over. He couldn't stop looking at his blank wrist.

He turned to face his father. "Papa! Show me your wrist!" he cried.

Àkos turned back his left sleeve and the familiar tattoo that *he* had was gone as well. His father ran his hand along his own wrist in amazement, just as Leopold was doing

He didn't have to fear the Unholy Hosts anymore. He and his father were truly free.

He suddenly felt the smile on his face and threw back his head in a laugh. He was at his ease now to look around with interest at this unusual locomotion. Smoothing his hand adoringly along his fiancée's neck, he chuckled. "You did it, Mingli."

Even with the wind rushing by their ears, she seemed to have heard him and turned back to give him an equally adoring glance…for a dragon.

Thacker came up beside him and laughed. "That was a hell of a thing, Leo. Your Miss Zhao. Blimey!"

"No one is more surprised than I, Spense," he yelled above the wind.

"I tell you, Leo, I…" He suddenly had a strange look on his face, and glanced over his shoulder.

"Spense, what's wrong?"

Thacker looked down and Leopold followed his gaze. They were over *Sheol* now, and the shadows of row upon row of tombstones covered the landscape.

"Something's wrong, Leo. I…I have to go down there."

"Why?"

"I…I don't know. But I have to…" His voice trailed off as he began to sink toward the ground.

"Spense! *Spense!*"

Thacker grew smaller as he descended. Leopold yelled to Mingli's head. "Miss Zhao! You must land. It's Spense."

She turned her enormous head and began her descent, following the spiraling figure of Thacker. Leopold hated the comparison, but his friend looked like an insect following a candle flame.

Mingli landed and Leopold slid off. Thacker was simply standing among the grave markers, looking up into the sky.

"Spense," said Leopold, cautiously approaching. "What are you looking at?"

Thacker seemed to have to tear his gaze away to face Leopold, and then snapped back again, staring at the blank sky. "Don't you see it?"

"See what? I only see a gray sky."

Thacker pointed. "It's that light. It's…warm, inviting. It's safe."

"Leo," said the deep baritone of his daemon friend who had come up behind him. "The Inspector is talking about the Afterlife. The warm light he sees is the place of his reward. He'll not have to come to *Sheol* again. But…he has lingered too long as a being he was never meant to be."

"Oh." Leopold approached his ghostly friend, frustrated that he could not even take his hand. "Spense..."

"So that's what it is," said Thacker softly. "I wondered. Because... it's calling me, like. Inside me head...and me heart."

"I...I didn't know you'd be leaving us. I thought... I've got so used to having you around."

Thacker smiled, his mustache with it. "Truth to tell, I was worried it would be forever. What if all my friends were gone and I was left alone there?"

"My God, I never even thought of that. Can you ever forgive us for our utter selfishness?"

"I do apologize for summoning you, Inspector." Mingli was suddenly beside Leopold as her old self, telescoping eyepatch in place, dress perfectly arranged with its ruffles and lace. "I never realized the harm it could do to you. I suppose I only saw it as expeditious to our investigations. It was terribly selfish of me."

"No need to apologize, Miss Zhao. I was glad to have the extra time with Leo, here. And he did need my help. It's been a lark. I even got to perform on the stage as Pepper's Ghost. I bet no other Scotland Yard inspector can claim that." More quietly he said, "And...I got to meet Raj and Eurynomos and all."

"And Suchah!" said the imp, madly flapping his little bat-wings and hovering in the air. "You met Suchah."

Thacker laughed. "And you, you little blighter. But...it's time I...move on." His gaze turned again as if beyond his control to the light only he could see.

"Ah, Spense."

"It's all right, Leo, old son. You've already been to me funeral. And you've got Miss Zhao, here. I'll be sorry to miss your wedding, but...if I can...I'll be there in spirit." He wiped a finger under his nose and sniffed. His eyes—though transparent and ghostly—seemed to brim with moisture. "Tell you what, if you have any kids, maybe name one of them Despenser, eh? Maybe as a middle name."

Leopold gazed once sadly at Mingli and grasped her hand, squeezing. Eurynomos wore a hard look.

"I'm...I'm glad we got to have this time together, Spense."

"Likewise. I…" He looked back again into the invisible light, before he turned toward the daemon. "Oi, Eurynomos. It's going to be all right where I'm going, isn't it? I mean, I shouldn't be afraid…should I?"

"No, dear friend. Your time is done. Your Afterlife awaits you. You don't have any more worries."

"Ah, that's good." He turned back to his friends, with a lingering look at Leopold. "I gotta go. That light. Once you've seen it…you have to…go. Strange knowing all that in me head. Well, good-bye, all."

He stepped back even as Leopold reached for him. He turned to them once, then seemed to allow himself to let go of the earth and float upward. He faced them for a while, but then turned and happily rose into the sky until he could be seen no more.

Silence fell. Until Leopold softly observed, "I didn't know he was going to leave."

Hands clasped his shoulders. "It is as it should be," said his father. How had he almost forgotten Papa was with him? "Spirits belong to another place. Someday, we will see them all again."

Leopold looked at his father and nodded. It was good to be certain of it. He would see his mother again. He wiped a tear from his eye and took a deep breath.

"I'm afraid we cannot tarry," said Mingli. "Unfortunately, I cannot return to my dragon form unless I am in distress. You being in mortal danger forced it to the surface, Leo. I simply could not allow the Unholy Hosts to take you."

"And that is the manifestation of your inner daemon?"

"Quite." She pulled the chain with the dragon pendant out of her bodice…and gasped. It was blackened and melted. She took the chain from her neck and stared at the remains of the jade. "How extraordinary. Do you realize that I haven't removed this chain from my person—not once—since receiving it seven years ago?"

"Why Miss Zhao," said Eurynomos. He cradled the charred jade in the palm of his enormous hand. "The both of you have been freed this day. Leopold was freed by your strength of love for him, and you were freed from your *yuan gui* obligations because you used your inheritance to fight for him, the ultimate 'righting of wrongs'."

Breathlessly, she turned to Leopold. "Leo, look down the back of my dress." She turned and bent her head forward.

"I…I…er…"

"Leo! Pull the neck and *look*." He hesitated, licked his lips, and gently grasped the neckline, pulling it away from her skin and peered down her back. He made a sharp inhale. "My love…it's gone." That terrible, beautiful tattoo that snaked down her back from one shoulder to the other hip, was gone.

She turned in his arms and kissed him hard. He was unable to do anything but return that kiss with all the ardor he possessed.

Àkos cleared his throat. "Leopold," he said quietly, "don't embarrass your fiancée."

He drew back and smiled at her beaming face. "She's not embarrassed, Papa. These are things you will soon learn about your new daughter-in-law."

"Ah. So, she is like your mother. This will be interesting."

"But then…" Leopold turned to Mingli once more. "You can't be a dragon unless you are…upset?"

"Perhaps. I have yet to study it further."

"Well…" He moved into her arms again. "Remind me never to make you angry."

She smiled, allowed him to gently kiss her, and then pushed him back. "We must hurry."

"Why?" He walked in a circle opening wide his arms. "We are free, Papa and I. There are no more worries from the Unholy Hosts."

She exchanged worried looks with Eurynomos. "I'm afraid that is not the case, Mr. Kazsmer."

Leopold's relief disappeared, replaced by a creeping anxiety. "What do you mean?"

"What Miss Zhao is trying to explain," said Eurynomos, urging their company toward the gate, "is that they are pursuing us. I suppose they can be considered also-rans. I don't think they mean to let us go unscathed."

A new purpose seized Leopold. *Very well, then. Let them come.* The Earth magic surged inside. He felt its strength buoying him.

Mingli grabbed his arm and yanked. "We can't stay, Leo. We can't fight them here. If we escape to the Library they cannot follow."

"Right." He drew sigils in the air, and their golden glow grew and grew until they formed the very likeness of Mingli as a *gold* dragon.

She moued and looked it up and down. "Not as lovely and green," she said, hand on hip. "But it will do."

Leopold, Mingli, Àkos, Raj, and Eurynomos mounted the slender neck as the dragon lifted into the air and, with Suchah furiously flying beside it, zoomed toward the gates of Gehenna.

PART FOUR
HOME

"Lead, Kindly Light, amid the encircling gloom; Lead thou me on! The night is dark, and I am far from home..." — John Henry Cardinal Newman (1801-1890)

CHAPTER NINETEEN

IT WASN'T LIKE exiting the Library. It wasn't simply there as Gehenna's gates had been when they left the Library the first time. They had to fly to it again through space, through the gases of a galaxy.

The dragon dissipated like smoke once they'd reached the steps of the Library of the Damned. They ran for the entrance. Leopold couldn't be certain if he imagined the feeling of doom coming upon them, but when he looked back over his shoulder into the strange rainbow-cloudy sky, he thought he could see two points of light following them.

He hurried with the others to the entry, yanked the heavy doors open, and slammed them shut once they were all inside.

"I don't wish to alarm anyone, but I'm afraid we have been followed."

"As I suspected," said Mingli.

They moved into the dark rotunda, shafts of strange light angling toward them. The sound of wings drew their attention and they turned.

The raven—or, at least, *a* raven—lighted on the tiled floor and eyed each one. "You have returned. I am surprised."

"You didn't think we'd survive, eh?" said Leopold.

The raven cocked its head. "Frankly…no."

Leopold pulled at his waistcoat to free it of wrinkles. He postured with one hand on his frockcoat's lapel. "I am happy to report that we did complete our journey—successfully, I may add—and we are here to return that which we borrowed."

Raj—reluctantly, it seemed—stepped forward and laid the carpet bag bulging with the books and objects they had taken, onto the ground before the raven. "We thank you for lending us the books and artifacts. They quite did the trick."

Mingli added the little whirring weapon onto the pile, and Leopold took the map of Gehenna from his inside pocket with the intention of laying it there as well, when the raven stopped him.

"The map is very useful, no? I think it's best suited as a permanent loan to your daemon."

Eurynomos stepped forward and bowed. "You don't really mean it, do you? I would be ever so grateful."

"It is yours, Prince of Death. You have the greater need. However, we have the option of calling in the loan at any time."

"Certainly. You have my word." He took the scroll and tucked it into the waistband of his breechclout.

The raven walked up and down the pile of books, stereo-optic viewer, and flying weapon. "It all appears to be here. They seem to be in good condition."

Àkos moved forward and bent toward the raven. "You talk."

The bird raised her head to him. "You're new. You did not leave here with the others. I must then assume that you were the one they wished to rescue. Welcome to the Library of the Damned."

Àkos frowned. "That can't be right."

Leopold stepped forward toward the raven. "May I introduce my father, Àkos Kazsmer? Papa, this is…a librarian."

Àkos raised his gaze to the levels of the library and then back to the raven once more. "Everything is so different than what I have come to expect. Unless this is a very interesting dream. I suspect that is the truth of it."

Worried again, Leopold faced his father. "No, Papa. It truly is happening."

"Pardon me, but you don't sound like my Leo."

"Are you more used to me like this, Papa?" he answered in the Cockney that was his natural speech.

Àkos' eyes clouded, trying to understand.

"I formalized my speech patterns," he said in his gentleman's accent. "For the stage. And…to present myself as an English gentleman. Not a Gypsy thief or…or a Jew from Whitechapel."

"I know life was hard for you," said Àkos vaguely. "You indulged me in my grief. I quite forgot you were grieving too. You…you must have quit school and worked. How else was food put on the table? I was a fool for not noticing."

"What you were doing was important to you."

"It was a mistake. It was wrong. I am your father. I should have been taking proper care of *you*."

"When you…left, I went to live with Uncle Yanko."

He glared. "That barbarian and his barbarian countrymen? Oh, Leopold, Leopold. I am sorry for that."

"It wasn't so bad. I learned some things as a Romani."

"Like to steal! That man. He never liked me. And for good reason. I despised him."

"He tried, Papa. He was alone too."

Àkos looked saddened for a moment before he suddenly grabbed for his pocket watch on its chain. "It's tea time. I must make tea. This illusion has been very entertaining but I must go back to my cave now."

Àkos turned and shuffled toward the door. Everyone cringed back as the door shuddered with a loud bang.

The raven flapped and cast a surprised glare at Leopold. "They followed you here."

"We couldn't help it."

"You must go. Very quickly. We will do our best to hold them off. They must not gain entrance to the Library."

"I thought they couldn't."

"These are unusual visitors. We will hold the gate. You must go."

The others moved to the other door, the one where they had first entered, but Àkos was wandering like a confused old man toward the pounding on the other doors.

Before Leopold could call him back, Mingli was already there.

"Mr. Kazsmer," she said gently, holding his arm with one hand, and with the other, unbuckling her eye patch. "Everything that has happened to you is the truth. This is no dream, no illusion."

When the eye patch fell, she said, "Mr. Kazsmer, look deep into my right eye." Àkos did as bidden and seemed mesmerized, leaning toward her. "Do you see stars and galaxies, Mr. Kazsmer?"

"Yes," he said dreamily. "It's amazing."

"Yes. Keep looking and listen to the sound of my voice" Her soothing tones seemed to have lulled him into a state of submission. "It's been a long time, hasn't it, Mr. Kazsmer. You forgot a lot of things. Your memory has been blurry since you had gone away. While it is true you were trapped in Gehenna, in *Sitra Achra,* for many years, your son's love for you was finally able to release you with the help of Eurynomos and your new friends Raj and Suchah."

"And Inspector Thacker," he said dreamily.

"Ah yes. But remember, Inspector Thacker died nearly a year ago and his soul is finally free. You'd want that for him, wouldn't you?"

"Yes…"

"And you are getting better every hour. I know it's confusing, but for now, trust in us. We are on a strange journey that we must complete. And Leopold is here beside you. *Your* Leopold."

"I'm here, Papa," he said.

"As he's always been," said Mingli. "Now, we must make this journey now. Are you feeling better?"

Àkos stretched and cracked his neck. "Yes, I am feeling better. Stronger."

"Of course, you are. Leo will help you. We are going to be flying. Remember that Leo knows lots of magic now."

"Yes, he does. You know he's a magician? On the stage!"

"Yes, I do." She leaned down to retrieve her eye patch and strapped it in place. "You're going to fully awaken now, feeling more yourself again."

"Yes."

"Good." She snapped her fingers.

Àkos shook out his head and his eyes were clear again. The doors slammed a third time and he shied away from it. "I think we must hurry."

"Yes, Papa. Let's go." Leopold sent a grateful look toward Mingli, who was all business again.

The corvids began to gather. Some were amassing on the floor this time, while the others perched on the railings all around the rotunda. The air was blurry around them as they flapped their wings, aiming toward the besieged doors. The walls, floor, levels seemed to be pulsing with their wing beats. There was some protection magic surrounding them, and Leopold longed to study it…but he also understood how expeditious their exit needed to be. He lifted his topper to the corvids before he ushered his company out through the front doors.

He took the leap of faith and stepped off the edge of the stairs into space…and they were flying on their own again. It didn't seem fast enough to get away from their enemies out of Gehenna, but when he looked back, the Library had shrunk into the distance.

Dear Spense. He gave a wistful thought to his friend as he looked back into the nothingness of space. How he missed him already. At least they had gotten to know one another at last. He'd always regretted not confiding in him when he was alive… He supposed it didn't matter now.

The sky changed again, and soon they felt rain pelting their faces. The clouds were no longer rainbows but the gray skies of England. They passed through a heavy fog and emerged through the hedges and tumbled to the grass of the meadow…right at Ogiel's feet.

CHAPTER TWENTY

THE CHAIR THAT Yanko had been sitting in was cracked and torn to pieces and Yanko was nowhere in sight. Neither was Miklos.

Leopold sprang to his feet, signing sigils in the air. "What have you done with Yanko?"

Ogiel swung his ugly head around and measured each face looking up at him. "Àkos Kazsmer? What are you doing out of your prison?"

Àkos—instead of appearing as the frightened old man he had first been—threw back his shoulders and proudly stepped forward. "I was freed, you beast. By my son…and his fiancée. I am no longer a prisoner. Begone, you ugly creature!"

Ogiel's eyes fell on Suchah. "My friend," he said. "I can free you!"

Suchah fluttered up to Ogiel's face. "Suchah is the friend of the Kazsmers, and in the name of the Cheating Ghost Thacker, I expel you!" Suchah wound back and snapped forward with a blast of magic. Ogiel took several steps back and shook out his head. By the look on Suchah's face, he had expected it to do more, and he suddenly retreated.

Ogiel patted his head, revealing burnt hair, but no more damage than that. "Even you, Suchah?" He scowled. "So be it." He gathered himself to launch forward when he was hit from behind with a barrage of weapons.

Pitchforks, bullets, rocks—anything that can become a missile was hurled at the demon. And Leopold realized, his heart singing with joy, that the entire Romani camp had assembled in the meadow. They had *not* gone after all! They had stayed behind to defend the portal.

It was the first time Leopold felt they had accepted him.

And there, in the midst of them, was Yanko—a little worse for wear with a bandaged head and his arm in a sling, but he, too, was shaking a pitchfork at the demon. And there was Miklos, too, holding a huge log with several other men, using it like a battering ram to rush Ogiel.

It hit Ogiel in the belly when he turned around, and down he went.

"What took you so long, Kazsmer?" asked Miklos. His face was bloodied and bruised as well. It looked as if they had had a violent encounter before Leopold and company had been able to return.

"I got here as soon as I could," he said with a laugh. But he turned swiftly toward Ogiel. He was aware that, though the demon was down, he wouldn't stay there long. He sketched his sigils quickly to bind the beast in glowing magical ropes.

"You are forbidden!" he cried, and wrapped him in more and more layers of magic. "You are sealed with the seven seals and eight ropes. I trap you forever!"

Ogiel gave a cry as he slid into the hedges, shrinking, shrinking, until he was sucked into the earth and trapped properly under the Incantation Bowl.

Everyone fell silent.

...Until the Romani burst into cheers and gathered round Leopold, raising him up into the air. When he was allowed down again, Yanko limped forward and embraced him. "You returned!"

"I'm sorry you were attacked, Uncle Yanko. I thought the wand would keep any demon at bay."

"It worked for a while, but this beast is stubborn..." He trailed off when he caught sight of Leopold's father. "*Àkos*? Is that *you*?"

Àkos stumbled forward. "Yanko? You despicable man. You look old."

"So do you, Kazsmer." They made a stuttering start for each other and finally came face to face. "We thought you were dead."

"I might as well have been."

Yanko looked him up and down. "You're a mess."

He chuckled. "I feel like a mess."

"Why don't we get away from this fighting. I take you back to my caravan and make you tea."

"That awful tea you make."

"It isn't awful. It is good Romani tea. You always complain."

"I always complain about your complaining..." And so it went, their voices drifting into the background as they made their way across the meadow.

Mingli tapped Leopold on the shoulder with her umbrella. "The corvids will not be able to delay the Unholy Hosts for long. We must get to Buckingham Palace. At once!"

"W-what?"

"Come along, Mr. Kazsmer...and company. We must catch a train as soon as we might."

THEY MADE THEIR way down to the Battersea station and took the first train to London. Leopold had glamoured Eurynomos to look like a vicar and Raj as a clerk. Raj was delighted with his studious new appearance, with the high collar and small bowler, and barely sat still in his seat, face pressed to the window, admiring his new reflection.

Suchah, however, didn't at all like his appearance as a schoolboy.

Leopold signed hidden sigils behind the seat, making the train move faster. It roared along the track, not stopping at all for the smaller depots and rattling on toward London. Some of the passengers stood to complain to the conductor that the train had not stopped where they had intended to get off. But the befuddled conductor didn't have any answers and pushed through the crowds of harried people heading for the engineer.

"That poor man," said Eurynomos out of the side of his mouth. "How will you ever compensate him?"

"By saving the world, I suppose. Again."

"I suppose that will have to do."

"We are coming to the station. Be ready," said Mingli, already standing.

Disgruntled passengers were also rising, blocking their way. "This will not do. Mr. Kazsmer, a little help?"

Leopold swished his hand and the people were magically shoved aside, with grunts and squeals of surprise.

He touched the brim of his hat. "Apologies," he said, rushing through them, with Mingli right behind. Mingli tugged on the hand of a recalcitrant Suchah while Eurynomos and Raj followed.

They exited the platform and rushed to the kerb where they hailed two cabs, as they wouldn't all fit into one. But Leopold found himself pushed out of the first cab. "I shall take Eurynomos and Raj. You go in the other cab with Suchah."

"What? Miss Zhao..."

"There's no time to argue, Mr. Kazsmer," she said airily as she slammed the door. "I have things to discuss with Eurynomos." The cab jerked away from the kerb and Leopold decided if he didn't want to miss out, he'd better get going.

"Follow that cab!" he told the driver, and, with the snap of the whip, Leopold fell back against the seat.

"Why does Suchah have to look like a human?" the imp complained.

"Because imps and demons are not the normal fare on the streets of London."

Suchah looked out the window. "Suchah thinks that won't be true very soon. Look!"

Leopold leaned over to look where Suchah was pointing. "*Mindenható Krisztus*!" he swore.

In the sky, the two fallen archangels were in the far distance...followed by a large contingent of winged creatures.

"Driver, hurry! There'll be extra coins in it for you."

The driver did the best he could in the traffic. Leopold hung his head out the window to see if they were still behind Mingli's cab.

When both cabs stopped before the gates of Buckingham Palace at the same time, Leopold threw the man a five-pound note.

"Guv! You must have made a mistake," cried the cabby, flapping the bank note.

Leopold ignored him. If they couldn't stop this Gehenna invasion, little details like money weren't going to matter much anyway.

He met Mingli at the gilded gates. "What's your plan?" he asked breathlessly.

"My plan? I'm going to talk to the queen, of course."

He grabbed her arm as she tried to approach the Queen's Foot Guard with their red tunics and tall bearskin hats. "You can't just waltz into Buckingham Palace and talk to the queen."

She gave him an impatient huff. "Leopold, you claim to know me, and yet you think I do not know the Queen of England?"

He let go of her arm, his mouth dropping open. By God, he did believe it. "Forgive me. Carry on."

She gave him a nod of finality, and stalked up to the sentry box and the foot guard standing before it. He was facing straight ahead, his rifle in his left hand and its butt on the ground against his boot. Only his eyes shifted to look at Mingli.

"Excuse me, corporal. I am Special Inspector Mingli Zhao. And I require an immediate audience with her majesty."

He snapped to attention, stomped one of his booted feet, and swiveled in precise movements. He ducked into his sentry box and moved a lever. They didn't wait long until more grenadiers arrived behind the gate and opened it.

One mustachioed soldier—his eyes nearly disappearing under the fur of his bearskin hat—approached her and snapped his heels together. "Miss Zhao, right this way."

She motioned for Leopold, but all the soldiers lowered their bayoneted rifles at him. "This is Mister Leopold Kazsmer and he has my complete trust to accompany me. The others will wait outside."

The soldiers snapped to as quickly as they had defended, and escorted Leopold and Mingli across the yard at a swift pace. Leopold kept snatching glances at her but dared not ask. Buckingham Palace loomed ahead, and he wondered how much of a fool he would make of himself when he was introduced to the queen.

Before them was a wide arch in the building that led to a great courtyard, the Quadrangle. The shade of the arch was cool—cooler than he expected—and he narrowed his eyes at the crisp gravel beneath their feet. They walked the length of it until they reached the Central Block, with its columns and pediment. When the grenadiers opened the doors, they halted. Before them stood a major-domo in military-style livery and a small, neat mustache. "Miss Zhao," he said with a curt bow. "And…Mr. Kazsmer. Won't you come this way."

How does he know who I am? he wondered.

They crossed the carpeted grand entrance, with its marble columns and polished floors. The major-domo moved steadily to the left where they climbed a staircase that curved in a sharp turn and reached a landing. It let them out onto a gallery whose walls were filled with paintings of royalty from years past. Mingli glanced at Leopold, and mimed a finger under her chin and lifted it to close her mouth.

Leopold hadn't realized his mouth had fallen open and he quickly shut it. He *knew* he'd make a fool of himself.

Mingli, on the other hand, walked as regally as any princess, head held high, posture erect. The rustling of her skirts—a generally pleasing sound—gave him confidence to imitate her bearing, and he cast back his shoulders, imagining himself striding across the stage.

The major-domo stopped before a double door. Leopold took inventory. Was his cravat straight? Was his waistcoat wrinkled? Did his hat sit perfectly? But then he realized how disheveled he and Mingli were. His sleeve was burnt, he only just noticed his coat had lost a button, and grime veiled both of them. He held his breath.

When the doors were cast open, he searched wildly around for the queen, but realized it was only an empty drawing room.

The major-domo said, "You will please wait here while I inform her majesty that you have arrived."

He made another curt bow to them as he closed them in the room.

Leopold exhaled and put a hand to his chest. "Mingli, what in the name of Heaven—"

"There's really no time to explain, Leo. Just remember to only speak when spoken to, and do not touch her majesty. She will not extend her hand to you."

He nodded meekly. "Very well. Whatever you say." He took a moment to throw a cleaning spell over their clothes before the doors opened again, and the major-domo inclined his head. "Please, come with me."

They followed him out and made a right down the picture gallery to another set of wider double doors. The major-domo stepped into the room and announced, "Special Inspector Miss Mingli Zhao. Mister Leopold Kazsmer...magician." He bowed deeply, and stepped aside.

Leopold froze. He could face the most fearsome of demons, but an old woman with a crown seemed quite beyond him. Mingli moved forward first anyway, and he was forced to follow.

He looked and found two thrones, both empty. But when he turned the other way, there stood a rather short, plump woman, her white hair parted in the middle and pulled back to cover her ears. She wore not a crown, but a lace cap. The man standing behind her was much taller, his hair gray, with a mustache that curved up to join his sideburns. He had a wide forehead that receded to a balding pate. The Prince Consort! Several years ago, the country waited with bated breath as he lay suffering with pneumonia, and a grateful nation celebrated when he survived. He was the constant loving companion of the queen and even as she greeted Mingli, the prince's look of indulgence for his diminutive wife shone on his face.

Mingli curtseyed and Leopold was able to master a stately bow.

"Miss Zhao," said the queen. She sounded like any old lady, albeit a noble one with crisp diction and poise. He hadn't expected that. "I have longed to speak with you. I have suspected ever since the dead walked that we were in for a difficult period."

"Indeed, ma'am. The worst of all. Gehenna has let loose. And I am afraid they mean to extinguish us. Mr. Kazsmer here was instructed to destroy the world. Which he refused to do, of course."

The queen turned to Leopold. She wore pearl tear-drop earrings that jostled as she moved her head. "Mr. Kazsmer," she said. "We remember when you repaired St Paul's, and we are ever grateful that you have kept the world intact. Truly, I have heard of your other deeds and England is very grateful."

He blinked, trying to think of words to form on his tongue. *Think of sheep, Leopold.* "Your majesty, I do love this country and the people in it. I see no reason to bow to the evil powers of Gehenna…or any foreign power."

"Quite right." She dismissed him with those words, and walked about the room making plans confidentially with Mingli. As Leopold watched, he felt a presence beside him and looked up into the face of Prince Albert.

"Strong women, eh, Kazsmer?" he murmured in his German accent. "It is hard not to love them."

"Yes, your highness."

"This is your wife?"

"Not yet, sir. We are betrothed."

"Ah! I had the feeling. It was difficult at first, bowing to a woman as the head of our household. Oh, she indulges me that—as a family—*I* am the head, but I am not such a fool. Some men might feel emasculated, but I tell you, Kazsmer, such women are to be adored."

"I know it well."

He slapped Leopold on the back and he stumbled slightly. "Good man! Knowing you are true partners is what makes a marriage work. I have proved the naysayers wrong."

Leopold smiled and looked up to the prince. Not that Leopold had ever felt less than a man with Mingli, but he did wonder…only occasionally…if it made him less in the eyes of other men. But with the endorsement of the Prince Consort himself, Leopold felt worlds better.

"A drink, Kazsmer?" The prince stood before a set of crystal decanters sitting on a silver tray on a side table of careful inlaid designs. "I myself would like a little sherry."

"Thank you, sir. I could certainly use one."

The prince poured a small glass each and handed one to Leopold. "To the queen," said Albert.

"To the queen." They each lifted their glasses and sipped. Leopold licked his lips. It was the best sherry he had ever tasted.

"Ordinarily, I would pour for the queen first," said Albert in confidential tones. "But when her majesty is so occupied, I know better than to interrupt her."

"Miss Zhao is a dragon," Leopold blurted.

"How well I know the feeling," said Albert with a chuckle, taking another sip.

The queen snapped around. "There is no time to waste. We must initiate Protocol Mad Tea Party."

"*Gröss Gott*!" said the prince. He set his glass down. "Then we must get you and the children to the shelter."

"The children, yes. But I must stay and direct."

"Pardon me, madam, but you are the most important personage to the realm. A general can do the commanding."

Albert gave her a particular look and she seemed to accede to it. "Very well." She marched over to a bell rope, but instead of pulling it, she took up a speaking tube hanging right beside it. She blew into it. "Attention. Protocol Mad Tea Party is initiated. The admirals and generals are to meet us in the war room." She turned to Mingli. "You know what to do, Miss Zhao."

Mingli curtseyed again, Leopold bowed, and the prince followed the queen out.

Leopold scrambled to keep up with Mingli. He almost forgot he had the small glass in his hand and set it on the nearest table outside the throne room. The major-domo scooped it up in his gloved hand as he escorted them to the stairs and down again.

"What *do* we do?" asked Leopold out of the side of his mouth.

Mingli turned to him with a wide smile. "Just you wait and see."

CHAPTER TWENTY-ONE

BY THE TIME they reached the gate again, London looked to be on alert. The people on the streets were rushing to their homes. Police were everywhere, blowing their whistles and herding people onward.

With a rush of emotion, he was reminded once again that Thacker was no longer with them. *We might see you sooner than we thought, old chap.* Leopold hurried as they bustled along. This time she allowed him into *her* cab.

"I had to explain the situation to Eurynomos, that's why we shared a cab before. It wasn't out of any disrespect, Leo. Surely you realized that."

"Of course."

They climbed into their cab and Mingli motioned for their companions to take the other waiting by the kerb.

Leopold settled in as the cab jerked away into the street. "What is 'Protocol Mad Tea Party'?"

"I had planned for this contingency for quite some time, and discussed it at length with her majesty. It took some doing to convince her, but after showing her proof, she quite agreed with me that steps must be taken. The prince has been a most helpful patron."

He remembered the letter she carried around when she first arrived at Scotland Yard. Leopold had used the skills he learned as a Romani to pick her pocket in order to read it. It had been a letter of introduction by the Prince Consort himself.

"Hold a moment," said Leopold. "What in blazes do you ever mean that you *planned* for this? How the devil did you know—"

"Leo, there will be plenty of time later to explain. For now, I must strategize."

He thought this meant he would be planning with her, but instead, she sat back in her seat and stared straight ahead as chaos abounded outside their carriage.

Leopold considered what he could do. He had magic in abundance, so that was not at issue. But what *exactly* to do at the right moment was more to the point.

He flicked a glance at her, but she was still deep in thought.

He almost forgot where she'd told the driver to go. They jerked to a halt on Iron Gate Road before the gatehouse to Tower Bridge. They all disembarked as the cabbies sped away.

"Why here, Miss Zhao?" asked Eurynomos' voice out of the old vicar's mouth.

She raised her face to the eastern sky. The two archangels and their swarm of flying creatures—which seemed to be growing in number—were nearer than Leopold liked. And they were obvious now to any onlooker. No wonder people were scattering to safety. If only there *was* safety…

"We must protect the capital. *And* Mr. Kazsmer."

"Thanks for including me," he muttered. "But I have full use of my magic. They can't hope to do damage to me now."

"I am very much afraid that they intend to try. And the ancillary damage to the people and buildings of London may be high."

"Is there anymore point in continuing to glamour Eurynomos, Suchah, and Raj?"

She watched as the streets emptied: Hansom cabs disappeared in a flurry; street vendors left their carts behind in their haste. "No. I suppose not."

He waved his hand and their glamours fell. Raj seemed somewhat disappointed, but he straightened and watched the skies. "What are we to do?"

"We must contact the keeper of the Bridge." She strode forward almost at a trot.

Leopold had watched the Bridge's progress over the years. He naturally continued to use the underground tunnel when necessary, as the Bridge was not yet complete. But already it was a fine-looking piece of architecture. The bascules, or what one might consider a drawbridge that stretched over the Thames, worked efficiently with their steam-powered mechanism, for in England, shipping came first, and street traffic had to wait. The suspension chains, balustrades along the bascules, the upper footbridge, and assorted other parts of the bridge were painted something like a robin's egg blue, while the towers themselves were faced with a sandy stone.

Mingli continued along the bridge's road under the suspenders until she reached the north tower, whereupon she knocked vigorously on a door under the arch. A man with a resplendent beard and mustache answered the door and frowned upon beholding Mingli. It must have frustrated her no end to encounter such indignities time and again. Leopold stepped smartly up to the man, righteously irate for her. But Mingli was as calm as always, and only used the brush of a hand to push Leopold back.

"My good man, I am here to inform you that Protocol Mad Tea Party is instigated. If you don't believe me, I expect you to call Buckingham Palace immediately."

But the man seemed to understand perfectly, and his brusque expression fell away. "Then you are...Miss Zhao?"

"I am, sir."

"Right, miss." He saluted her and opened the door to allow them in. When the man beheld Eurynomos and the others, he fell back against the wall.

"Don't worry about them. They will await us outside."

Leopold desperately wanted to ask, but wisely kept his mouth shut. He remembered the words of the Prince Consort: they were two men who certainly recognized their positions, and—with a glance at Mingli, so confident, so assertive—well...he simply had no complaints.

"I'll wait with them." She gave him a glance but made no protestations. She was all business. He stood with his friends and watched the flight of the angels growing closer. "I feel I should do something."

"I'm thinking," said Eurynomos, "about what exactly could be done."

They all stopped at the sound of an engine firing up, of gears turning, and the sliding of stone on metal.

"Goodness gracious!" said Raj, staring up at the tower, his hand shading his eyes from the sun.

The very top level of the tower—peaks and all—slid back, cantilevering over the bridge. While it moved, a fat-barreled cannon rose forth, and swiveled toward the flying beasts.

"What in Heaven…" gasped Leopold.

Eurynomos chuckled. "Your Miss Zhao certainly *has* prepared for contingencies."

"I don't understand, Leopold Master. What is that?"

Leopold rested his hand on the imp's shoulder. "Suchah, old boy, *that* is a very large weapon."

"Oh. Weapons that kill? Suchah is anxious to see that."

Leopold watched as the enormous cannon moved with mechanical precision, the sound of gears clicking and pistons working…and realized what would happen when it fired. "Everyone, cover your ears!"

He'd only just covered his own when the cannon burst forth with an incredible boom of fire and sound, sending them all to the ground in its wake.

Leopold righted himself so that he could watch its reaction. The missile soared in a fiery streak through the clouded skies straight for the growing number of flying demons. When the missile exploded in their midst, many demons were caught up in the fire and shock, and cascaded—in several parts—to the Thames below.

But many more were still coming.

"Good shot, Miss Zhao!" crowed Leopold.

But now the demons aimed their flight toward the tower and its cannon.

"They're coming towards us," said Raj.

Leopold backed up a few steps. "Er…"

"Maybe we should run?" asked Suchah.

"Maybe that's a good idea," Leopold agreed. But where?

The cannon fired again. He hadn't been ready and the sound was deafening. His ears seemed to be encased in a muffled whine and little else. He saw Suchah's lips moving but he couldn't hear. Eurynomos pointed upward, and suddenly the demons were upon them.

Leopold rolled away from the talons of one while he sketched his sigils. They shot off as explosions, tearing the creatures apart.

A clutch of them fell upon him, and suddenly he was seized with the memory of such beasts falling upon his father and he froze, only able to roll himself into a ball. Talons tore at his clothes, teeth bit through his arms and shoulders, and he must have cried out, for the next moment the side of the tower burst apart and an enormous green dragon emerged with fire in her eyes.

Mingli descended upon the demons, using teeth and tail to swat or toss them away from Leopold. He girded himself and, though his shoulder smarted from teeth marks, he wrote his sigils in the air and created his own beasts to go after the demons.

"Leo!" cried Eurynomos in astonishment. "How did you—"

"Never mind that, Eurynomos. We've got to get out of here. I have an idea and I'll need all your help."

"What of your Miss Zhao?"

Holding his hurt shoulder, he glanced back at his wife-to-be snaking into the air and chomping down on demon flesh whilst shooting alternating jets of fire and water at them.

"I think she'll do fine on her own."

Eurynomos scooped up Leopold and Raj and began running. He moved so swiftly that London's streets were a blur around him. "Where to, Leo?"

"The nearest graveyard. And hurry!"

CHAPTER TWENTY-TWO

HOW EURYNOMOS COULD find a single graveyard at the speed he was traveling would always remain a mystery to Leopold, but he was grateful for the many skills his friend possessed.

"What are we doing here?" asked the daemon as he set them both down at the same graveyard where they had started, St Dunstan-in-the-East Church.

"I need more graveyard clay. A lot of it. I need to make the largest Incantation Bowl I can."

Eurynomos smiled. "How intriguing."

"I fear we will not be able to get enough here."

"We'll get what we can," said Raj, "and go on to the next one."

"Precisely, Raj." Leopold cracked his knuckles and commenced sketching sigils that sparked in the air for a moment before plunging into the ground and began collecting mounds of clay the size of wheelbarrows.

The gate to the graveyard suddenly cast open, and the angry vicar from before came tottering in. "What in Heaven's name are you doing—" He stopped dead when he beheld Eurynomos, grinning like a fool with his wide, red chest, and dark horns spiraling upward from his head.

Eurynomos leaned toward him, and with a flutter of the fingers from one hand, said, "Boo!"

The vicar screamed, lifted the hem of his cassock, and ran—stumbling over the edges of crooked grave markers—until he reached the gate and fell over it.

"That was extremely satisfying," Leopold muttered, remembering the bigoted venom that same vicar had spewed at Mingli.

"Yes," said Eurynomos. "Wasn't it?"

Leopold looked over the amount of clay they had gathered. "We need more. On to the next place, Eurynomos."

And so they went, tugging the growing mound of clay with them on an invisible sledge until they had gathered a wagonload. They went directly to Buckingham Palace, where a contingent of the grenadiers had made a stand with guns and cannon before the gate. They immediately turned their rifles upon Leopold and his companions.

"Hold!" cried Leopold. "I was here earlier with Miss Zhao."

A man in charge stepped forward. He, too, wore the red tunic and black bearskin hat. "I remember you, sir. What is all this?" His eyes scanned the giant, floating mound of clay...as well as Leopold's companions.

"It's the one chance you've got to protect the queen. You must let us through to the east front arch."

He took a deep breath. "I might be able to let *you* in, sir. But not...*these*."

Leopold raised his chin. "These are my friends, corporal. And I absolutely need them to help me in my task. You must let them through."

"I don't know about that, sir."

"Corporal, I might as well tell you that I don't need your permission. I can easily stop all your men with a wave of my hand. I'd prefer if we were all gentlemen about this. As you know, the country is being invaded by supernatural beings." He cocked his head toward Eurynomos and Suchah. "These good fellows are on our side, and you should be glad they are."

Eurynomos clicked his naked heels and saluted with a wide grin.

The corporal's eyes—nearly hidden under the fur of the bearskin hat—rounded. They flicked in turn toward Eurynomos, Raj, and Suchah. Then settled again on Leopold.

"Very well, sir. Open the gates!"

Leopold gave the man a bow and ushered his friends through. He stepped ahead of them to the main arch that led to the Quadrangle. "Here, Eurynomos."

The daemon walked through and felt the air with his hands. "Yes. Yes, I think this will do."

"Then *you* blast the hole, and Suchah, Raj, and I will deal with the bowl."

Leopold settled the great mound of clay on the gravel and, with sigils drawn in the air and the windmilling of his arms, the clay whipped up into the shape of an enormous bowl. Once it took the proper form, Leopold fired it to a red-hot glow until it was solid, and then forced it to cool immediately. He used magic and the help of his friends to lay it on its side in order to paint the Hebrew curses to keep the demons entrapped.

He glanced at Eurynomos merrily carving a hole under the arch. "Is it ready, Eurynomos?"

"Nearly there."

The guards pressed their faces to the gate, watching the proceedings, until the corporal called his men to attention again.

Leopold levitated the bowl—which was as big as any stately fountain—and positioned it over the hole. Then, he twisted his hands and rotated it until it lay upside down. He slowly lowered it to the bottom of the hole, whereupon Eurynomos closed it up again.

"That will hold them if they dare try to breach the palace."

Eurynomos beamed. "Well done, Leo."

"I suppose we should return to see if Miss Zhao could use our assistance."

But when Eurynomos scooped them up again and dashed across Westminster and London, it was evident that the forces employed to stop the demon horde had been to no avail. Buildings were burned and crushed, and countless people were running for their lives, with children and possessions clutched tight to their bosoms.

The Thames was a crowded flotilla, with ferries, skiffs, and barely floating rafts making their way out of London. People were plunging into the water, helping their neighbors, though Leopold feared many would not be rising again from the churning waves.

He looked to the skies, but saw no green dragon. "Mingli. Where is Mingli?" Leopold bolted toward the bridge. The cannon tower had been demolished and the suspenders seemed to be holding on by a thread. Leopold positioned his feet apart, girded himself, and summoned the magical power resting in his chest. His hands moved in a frenzy repairing the tower and securing the suspenders so no more damage would be done.

He exhaled a long breath before he turned his attention to finding his fiancée. "Mingli! Mingli!"

"I'm here!"

He followed the sound of her voice and found her resting on the ground against the side of the tower, back to herself as a woman again.

Leopold skidded to the ground next to her. "My dear!"

"Just a little winded."

"Your shoulder!" He found a bloody gash turning her emerald gown to crimson, and gasped.

A shadow passed over them and Eurynomos was there, gently laying his hands on her arms. Her body glowed with a golden warmth briefly before fading away.

She blinked her one eye and caught her breath.

"How are you feeling now, Miss Zhao?" the daemon asked softly.

"Better than ever." Before anyone could help her to her feet, she'd shot up herself, brushing off her green gown. She made a face at the state of her shoulder seams and the bloodstains, but she seemed to be back to her old self.

"I thought you would be," Eurynomos muttered, and stepped aside so that Leopold could embrace her.

"My dear!"

She stomped her foot suddenly in frustration. "Damn those angels. I nearly had the better of them, but the demon hordes kept coming. There was no stopping them."

"Where are they now?"

"They were heading toward Buckingham Palace."

Leopold postured, shoulders thrown back. "I anticipated that and created a giant Incantation Bowl. The moment they try to breach the precincts they will be trapped."

"Oh, you are very clever, my love."

He stilled and turned toward her. "You…you've never called me that before."

"Haven't I?" She straightened her little hat that she had managed to retain, and picked up her umbrella.

He moved in closer and eased his hands around her tiny waist. "No. You haven't. I like the sound of that. 'My love'. It's most… invigorating."

"Leo, we haven't time."

"Oh yes we do."

He closed the space between them and crushed her lithe body against him, and kissed her leisurely. He felt her resist for only a moment before she fell into the kiss. But, at last, he reckoned what they were all facing, and gently pushed her back. "That was to fortify me," he said softly.

She smiled. "And me. But Leo." Her smile fell away. "What are we to do to stop them? The entire army has been called out, but I fear our mortal weapons will not be able to stop enough of them."

He looked to Eurynomos and Raj. "Gentlemen, any ideas?"

"I can summon the daemons of Gehenna. Suchah! With me!" Both daemon and imp vanished with a loud pop.

"There must be something we can do in the meantime," he said.

"We can keep an eye on them, use our skills to keep them in one location."

"Yes… I suppose so."

He caught sight of possibly the last Hansom cab in London. The driver seemed frozen with fear on his rig when Leopold rushed him. "Take us to Buckingham Palace!"

"I'm sorry, guv. But I ain't going nowhere."

With a grunt of disapproval, Leopold leapt up to the driver's seat. "Then I suggest you get yourself home, my good man. Here." He reached into his coat and pulled out a ten-pound note.

"Gor-blimey!" The driver took the note and jumped off the cab.

"I'll put the rig in a safe place. I promise." Leopold saluted him, waited for Mingli and Raj to climb inside the cab, and snapped the whip over the horse's rump. "Gee-up, there!"

The horse whinnied and pulled away from the kerb, galloping down the paved road with hooves sparking on the cobblestones.

"Where are we going, Leo?" she shouted at him through the trap door.

"Well…I've been thinking," he shouted back. "You once told me that destroying an Alignment Line would annihilate the world. But…I think it's possible to destroy one, suck all the demons of Gehenna into it, and repair it again in time so the world won't go with it."

Suddenly, gloved hands appeared at the edge of the trapdoor and Mingli had pulled herself up, waist-high. "Are you mad?"

"I think I can do it."

"You *think* you can do it?"

"I'm, er, fairly certain. Look, my dear. If the demons and fallen angels get hold of the Earth itself and all the people on it, I'm afraid it won't be a place worth inhabiting. I'm…I'm willing to take the chance."

"That's quite a responsibility, Leo."

"I know. But the idea of you in their clutches… I can't stand the thought."

She raised her chin and looked straight ahead. She could clearly see they were heading toward Piccadilly. That was the closest Alignment Line, a line of power stretching deep into the heart of the Earth. "I see," was all she said. Staying where she was, she and Leopold—and Raj sitting mute in the cab—traveled on in silence.

CHAPTER TWENTY-THREE

LEOPOLD PULLED THE cab up to Piccadilly station. Crowds of Londoners were packed there, trying to get the last train out of town.

"My God," he breathed.

"How will we ever get through?" asked Mingli.

With silent apologies, Leopold stretched out his arms, which magically shoved people aside with oaths and curses on their lips. They raised their fists at him, believing that he was pushing himself forward to get on the train. But nothing could be further from the truth.

His magic pushed the crowds out of his way all through the station. It was wall to wall people, some carrying their belongings, some only carrying the clothes on their backs, all migrating toward the trains. Leopold, too, wanted to get to the platform, but he wasn't going in the direction of the trains. He was heading toward the realm of the goblins, or, at least, where they used to be.

Once the way was clear enough for Mingli, Raj, and Leopold to get to the platform, all the curses shouted at them faded to the background. Leopold led the way to the steps down to where the tracks lay and made quick strides away from the station.

Leopold stayed away from the tracks themselves. The goblins had created their own railway in order to destroy Mankind with their curses. Their rails had exactly followed the lines of power. Leopold strode along in the track ballast, but walking so close to the Alignment Lines made his body hum with the power of it. It was not altogether an unpleasant feeling, but it had the effect of making him feel like an otherworldly being, levitating him into the air. He didn't have time for that.

Mingli was keeping a steady eye on him. "Leopold..." she ventured.

"I'm sorry, my dear. But I must concentrate." He knew this would be the most important conjure of his life...and the planet's, as it came down to it. He *had* to know what he was doing, and how. He pushed away the rest of the world, the sounds, even the view of the endless length of track before him. And so, as his father had taught him years ago, he thought of sheep. Mindless, rounded bodies, one after the other on a wide, green plain. Sheep as far as the eye could see...

He fell into a daze, lids at half-mast, mind elsewhere. He had not known he was going to do it, but he fell into a Hebrew prayer. *O Great Creator, I desperately need Your help and guidance. I want to save the world You created. Help me save the ones I love.*

He didn't expect an answer, but now that he was more acquainted with the workings of Gehenna...he felt it couldn't hurt.

The trick was to manipulate the power from the Alignment Line to engulf the demons and angels and destroy them, and at the same time, stop the release of *all* the power that would annihilate the world. Ironically, it was the one thing the Unholy Hosts had wanted him to do.

A balancing act. A routine. "Much like what I do on the stage," he muttered. Something like he'd been doing all along. A fine balance of prestidigitation...and real magic. "It might work. It *has* to work."

He halted and looked back. They had traveled far into the tunnel caverns of the goblins from whence the tracks derived. It was far enough away from the railway station. Away from endangering the people trying to escape.

"How about here?" he asked his companions.

"Leopold," said Raj, "are you certain about this?"

"As certain as I am about my love for Miss Zhao." He stopped a moment and took her hands in his, simply gazing at her. Even ruffled with a face smeared with soot and that distracting telescoping eye patch, she was truly the loveliest woman he had ever encountered. Confident, strong, and unfazed, she was a creature to reckon with. They had shared the sweetest of intimacies...and he longed to do so again with her. But it couldn't happen again if he failed today.

"I love you. I never knew I could feel this way. I never knew I could ever be unafraid to speak to a beautiful woman. I want my life with you. But if this moment is all we have, then I suppose…it will have to be enough."

"Don't talk like that, Leo. You *must* be successful!"

"I know. But…if I'm not…I just wanted you to know."

She sighed. A smile raised the corners of her mouth, and she cupped his cheek with one hand. "You foolish man. I know all that already."

"I love you, too," said Raj with sincerity, apparently caught up in the moment. Though his expression never changed on his painted face, it seemed to convey a variety of emotions to Leopold's trained eye.

Leopold gazed at him and smiled. "And I you, old friend. Very well, then, you two. I shall begin." He pulled at his waistcoat, straightened his hat, and stepped up onto the tracks.

Instantly, the surge of power nearly overwhelmed him. *Sheep, Leopold. Think of sheep!* The Earth magic that rushed along the Alignment Lines seemed to be attracted to him and converged to fill him, surround him, engulf him. He felt himself rise from the tracks and hover above them, but he used what he had learned of this magic to tether himself to the ground. Oh, the urge to fly away and become one with the magic was strong, but the love in his heart for Mingli seemed stronger, and he knew he must stay and do the job.

Instead of drawing sigils in the air as he was used to doing, he drew them in his mind, and the magic caressed them, swirled around him, seeming to take inventory of this very strange individual who manipulated the strands of magic with his mind. The tendrils gently touched, tenderly whispered into the secret places in his head and found a kinship there. Or so Leopold's feverish thoughts interpreted. *It's almost sentient,* he mused. *I wonder if I just…* He reached gently into the tendrils. *I need your help. Do you understand me?*

He thought he could almost comprehend its communication with him. It was like…music. Like notes plucked on a string. They vibrated with excitement. No creature had ever talked to the magic before! None had ever ventured the notion that the tendrils could appreciate that communication. It was so foreign to Leopold's mind, the sensations, the—dare he call it "thoughts" of the magic.

I…may need to destroy this line of power…

They didn't like the thought of that. He felt it as a strangling hold on him.

But not fully destroy. I need your help to stop my enemy and then to fully restore the line.

The strangulating power around him loosened and instead, cautiously surrounded him again, like a wary cat. Listening.

Use me however you will. But I must stop these demons and malevolence. Will you help me, work with *me?*

Suddenly, he seemed to sense the scent of roses, fields of grass, and the smell of…sheep? *Yes! All of that and all the people I do not wish to destroy in this world. Only those of malice who don't belong.*

He felt the magic's joy, if he could call it that. It seemed to be interested in him and his feelings. It seemed best suited to communicate in that way. He hadn't realized he had closed his eyes, but when he opened them again, he was nearing the roof of the cavern. He glanced down toward Mingli and Raj, both far below.

I will call the angels, then, he said. Or *had* he said it? It seemed that his voice was blended with the sensation of their many voices, or the one voice…or was it his imagination? The sensations were so overwhelming that he couldn't tell one thing from the other.

Mingli looked up worriedly at him. He saw her enrobed in a fluctuating aura of oranges, reds, and yellows. She looked…so beautiful.

And Raj! He was surrounded by purples, blues, and reds all fluctuating like the aurora borealis, shimmering with each of his movements.

No, I mustn't be distracted. He closed his eyes again—at least he thought he had—and sent his message into the ether, searching for the malevolence of the Unholy Hosts…and found them.

Kazzzzzzzsmeeeeer. The oozing voices of the remaining Unholy Hosts. He sensed their change in direction as they headed toward him. He could almost detect their thoughts—how some of the demons were swallowed up at Buckingham Palace by his enchantments; how Mingli as a dragon had devasted still more of them; but how many more there were surging through the rift between the levels of existence that they had kept open.

Had *he* left the gate open by the Gypsy camp? With a slash of his arm, the gate was shut. But the Unholy Hosts had left their own gate open. Leopold allowed the magic—now burning within him—to reach out into the vastness of space and time...and shut the gates.

Eurynomos. Where was he? Had he brought the daemons of Gehenna with him? He reached out again in search of him.

Leopold? Is that you, old man?

It...would appear so.

I'll not ask. But my army is fighting. We can defeat the demons who, in the end, are all cowards, but the Unholy Hosts... I don't know whether we can –

Don't worry, my friend.

Leo...

But he cut off the avenue to his daemon friend. There was too much to control now. Too much to bend to his will while waiting for the Unholy Hosts to arrive.

The magic was like a pet, rolling along his senses, the hairs on his skin, playing as if it were all a game. Would the magic help him? Would it perform as needed?

Mingli, Raj, I must hide the two of you. He didn't know if they heard or sensed him saying it, but he waved his hand and the both of them slid back against the rock wall and blended into it, safe from the perusal of the Unholy Hosts. At least he hoped so...

He felt them. He felt the unadulterated evil approach and he girded himself against it. He knew his eyes were not eyes anymore, but holes of pure light, exuding a brightness that lit the entire cavern from one end to the other. When he turned to face the cavern from the London side, he knew they approached.

Dark spots in the distance grew larger. A ball of malice, of greed and evil, of energy and magic from a distant place. He could observe with a certain amount of dispassion, for the power churning through him took some of his empathy away. But like a precious thing, he knew he had to keep hold of it, and grasped for it, jerked it back into himself. If he had not his passions, then he could not embody humanity itself, and that was somehow important in this battle. But he hadn't the time to think about all that.

"Kazsmer," said the Unholy Hosts, approaching closely. "You play your games, we see."

"Games? I play no games. You are poor losers, is what *I* see." For once in his brief life, Leopold was not affected by the presence of the Unholy Hosts. They had told him they were gods when he had first encountered them. Maybe they believed it. And his body had roiled with the sensation of being in their alien presence, making him sick and anxious. But now…he felt none of that.

Each archangel smiled their strange tusked and tentacled smiles and spoke in unison. "We have lost nothing. We have come to claim *all* of humanity."

Leopold ticked his finger at them…even as it glowed. "But that is very naughty of you. What do you suppose the Creator will say to that?"

"There is no Creator. *We* created *Him*."

Had they? No, no. So much goodness was in the world, in the universe. Nothing good could have come from these creatures. "I don't believe that. Why would you create rules and laws you don't want to follow?"

They scowled in unison. "We no longer need to talk. We merely need to take what we want." They reached for him—their arms elongating to do so—and just as quickly pulled them back.

"Pick a card. Any card," said Leopold, holding in his left hand a set of fanned playing cards facing downward.

"What…what is the purpose of this?"

"You claimed I was playing games. I'm a conjurer. A magician. I am, in fact, the Great Enchanter. Pick a card."

The angels exchanged glances. One reached out tentatively and took one.

"Don't show it to me. Have you looked at it? Excellent. Now return it to the deck."

"Are you mad?"

"It's quite possible. But if I must die, I will die doing what I love. Stage magic. I will wager that you never bothered to see me perform. It was quite thrilling." He urged the deck forward, and, scowling, the angel shoved it back in, nearly where he'd gotten it.

Leopold shuffled the deck one-handed, his fingers doing the business of an oft-performed routine. He removed the top card. "Is *this* your card?"

The confused angels looked at one another again.

"Well? Is it?"

"Yes, you fool! Your stalling tactics do not work on us."

"They don't? I beg to differ. It's called misdirection."

All the time the angels dithered with the cards, Leopold's right hand had been behind his back busily drawing sigils, one after the other. They left a glow, but he was glowing so much he reckoned even the Unholy Hosts wouldn't notice.

The cards disappeared with a flash, and the cavern abruptly exploded into a thousand stars and sparkling beams of white light…

CHAPTER TWENTY-FOUR

THE LIGHT HAD all the intensity of the sun. Leopold couldn't look at it. But he knew that the world was full of this new light and though it illuminated every crevice, every hidden place, it was much too bright to see all that it lit. It was hot, too, and Leopold, suspended as he was in the air, faltered slightly, until he yanked back his concentration. He sweated under his clothes, perspiration trickling down his temple.

The light was only the beginning.

The magic, free from the Alignment Line, was in its purest form, suspended all around them. It seemed to touch everything…from solid objects to breath to the tiniest mote of dust. It stretched outward, extending itself, reaching to the highest peak down to the bottom of seas that had never seen light before. Animals froze. People, plants, birds in the air. Everything stopped, stilled by the enormous energy of magic unleashed.

And even though it had reached the Moon itself, it kept going, reaching for objects no eye on Earth had ever seen, stretching, elongating. It slowed its march, having encompassed everything it wanted. It stopped. As if suspended in amber, everything floated, immobile. Every being, every thought, every breath… *except…* Leopold's. Slowly, so slowly that it could never be detected, his lungs moved, releasing air, inhaling fresh oxygen, filling his lungs with it, but ever so slowly.

He didn't need eyes to see all that transpired. Magic filled his vision and he saw. He saw the moment that the magic began pulling back. Like a tide rushing back out to sea. For he knew that it was going to pull back everything that it had ever touched, pull it down, down into the center of the Earth, build up the pressure, and explode it to irreversible atomized particles in a devastation the solar system had never seen. Every history the world had ever known, every human being, every demon, daemon, angel—fallen or otherwise—would be gone, winked out of existence.

The magic pulled back and Leopold felt the immense pressure of it all, dragging on his very molecules.

Help me, he called to the magic as he strained, using his own power. He had to slow this progression, had to convince the magic to not take it all back into itself as it had always supposed it would, should an Alignment Line be destroyed, as Leopold had destroyed this one.

But the magic had nothing to say. It might have been sentient but it wasn't communicative. It was its own self, never needing others. Perhaps it was amused by him, but not effected.

Please! he tried again. *Please help me to not destroy it all.* He pulled with all his might, pulled with a burning sensation all over him, as if he were on fire. Pulled with the terrible ripping feeling that his skin was tearing off. He used every ounce of magic within him, and more besides, for it kept pouring into him, keeping him uplifted, his eyes glowing bright, otherworldly.

The magic sucked into the line like a drain hole in a bathtub, taking with it the malevolence in swirling energy. Both angels struggled, shooting Gehenna magic at the line, using all their strength and power to remain where they were. But the Earth magic was far too powerful, and the implosion too strong.

For a moment, Leopold thought the struggle was too much, that he couldn't hold it. Briefly, his thoughts toyed with letting go. How peaceful it might be after all, not to have to worry over it anymore. His fight would be done. He could simply fall into the abyss and reach blessed insensibility.

But all he had to do was cast his thoughts to Mingli and his friends, and he girded himself once more. He closed his hands into fists and, by sheer willpower, he gritted his teeth and kept the rest of the world from sinking into the depths.

The angels continued to fight, but they were stretching long and thin, like a child's catapult with its vulcanized band stretching to the breaking point. They shouted their foul curses into the ether, but Leopold ignored them. He concentrated only on rescuing the rest of the world, and plunging the miserable angels into oblivion.

Abruptly, he was aware of another presence. When he opened his bright white eyes, he saw a green dragon pacing in a sinewy line below him. Vaguely, he thought, *Oh. It's Mingli changed to a dragon*. She must have sensed the danger he was in and changed involuntarily. He closed his eyes again. He certainly couldn't bother with that now.

With one hand, he stuffed the angels down, and with the other, he held back the rest of the world.

In the back of his mind—the human part of him—he wondered if this was happening at all, if it weren't some wild imaginings and that perhaps he was floating up to Heaven, or even the Library, for he would have liked to return there to explore at his leisure.

But he pushed those distracting thoughts aside, too. He had to concentrate his whole being in the magic, and once the angels were safely swallowed up, then and only then could he stitch up the line and repair it.

The angels drew closer, and, suddenly, they focused their power and minds on Leopold.

Leopold jerked back, losing the strands of magic. The inward pull accelerated and even as he grasped for them, they slipped through his fingers. *No!* The angels bombarded him with sensations of dread and despair, knowing that this was his weakness. Leopold struggled. The angels slowed their progress to destruction as the rest of the planet sucked into the abyss.

Leopold was falling. Not just his mind, but his physical form descended in the cavern. He saw it happening but was unable to stop it. He felt like a ragdoll, falling, falling, unable to save himself.

All at once, he jerked to a halt, hovering in mid-air. The dread power of the angels cut off abruptly. Leopold awoke and grasped the Earth magic back, decelerated and reversed the world's falling into oblivion. He rose and pulled the rest of the world back up with him. The angels' influence was somehow gone. He glanced for only a moment at them, and to his astonishment, each had been cleaved in half. He looked further and saw Dragon Mingli spitting out their lower halves.

My God! His dragon fiancée had bitten them in two. Their lifeless pieces quickly dove toward the open maw of the broken line of power without any further hinderance. They were swallowed up into the blinding light. Leopold used all his strength to close the rip. He couldn't sketch the sigils with his fingers—he had to keep his hands clenched tight into fists to hold off the world from being sucked down—and instead drew them in his head, one over the other, in a furious course that threatened his very being. His heart beat at too fast a pace, his muscles cramped, his veins felt that they would burst.

And then...all was quiet.

The light faded to nothing.

The earth tremors ceased.

The magic, like fish in a great pond swimming lazily, relaxed and churned around him gently, softly. Until he felt his feet touch the tracks and he opened his eyes—human eyes without the blaze of light emanating from them—once more.

Before him stood a dragon. Her green scales shone like metal in the faded light from deep in the tunnel where London lay. As he took in the sight of her with wonder, she changed, folding in layers and sections, getting smaller, reforming, until, at last, it was a woman again, his indominable wife-to-be. She pushed at her hat to rest it on the top of her piled-up hair again and sniffed. "That is a most uncomfortable experience."

He took a step toward her. "Mingli..."

When she raised her eyes to him, he saw that she was crying.

"My dear." He reached her and fell into her arms. "Are you all right?"

"Am *I* all right? Leo!" She took his face in her hands. "Are *you* all right? You were...so different. That celestial being again. But when the angels attacked you and I saw you fall, I couldn't help but become a dragon."

"And I'm so glad you did. You saved the day."

"*We* saved the day."

She kissed him then. And he decided he needed to think no more.

CHAPTER TWENTY-FIVE

THEY MET UP again with Eurynomos and Suchah.

"You should have seen Leopold!" cried the automaton to the others. "It was an incredible show of power!"

Leopold had an arm around Mingli's waist. The corset under his fingers made them tingle. "We worked together."

Eurynomos sidled toward him and leaned in. "No ill effects?" he said quietly.

"I don't think so. The Alignment Line was repaired. The angels are gone for good."

"Well!" said the daemon, rubbing his hands together. "That is cause for some celebration. And some re-calibration in Gehenna. I will have some work to do, and I'd best get to it. Suchah, my friend, would you like to accompany me to rebuild Gehenna?"

The imp looked up at the tall daemon with some surprise. "You want...Suchah to help?" He put a webbed hand to his chest. "This imp?"

Eurynomos crouched to be at eye level with him. "You have proved yourself a loyal companion. I would be honored to have you join me in this."

Suchah's mouth curved into a smile. He stood straighter. "If Eurynomos wants Suchah, who is Suchah to refuse?"

Leopold stepped toward him. "Then there's one more thing to do." He waved his hand and the Hebrew glyphs carved into the imp's stomach vanished. "You're your own man…er…daemon, now."

The imp rubbed his belly where the carvings had been. "Thank you, Leopold Master," he breathed.

"How about just 'Leopold'?"

"Of course, Leopold Master."

They all laughed until Leopold approached Eurynomos. "And thank you, my friend. We couldn't have managed it without you. All of it."

"Tut, tut. I think there is enough gratitude to go around. I'll be busy, but I have no intention of missing your wedding. Keep me apprised." He grinned with his sharp teeth gleaming. And then he spun in a circle creating a colorful whirlwind that sucked Suchah into it…and then they were gone.

"What's next, Leopold?" asked Raj.

Mingli straightened her hat again and rested the tip of her umbrella on the ground. "I must go to see the queen and report to her majesty of the goings on. Word must be sent to the people who evacuated the city that all is safe again."

"That's a good idea, my dear. Raj and I will fetch my father from my uncle's clutches. It's time I bring him home for good."

In time, they found a Hansom cab with a driver still with his rig. He settled Mingli in and handed her some coins. Once she drove away, he glanced at the automaton. No longer did he fear to have Raj in the streets. Though he garnered stares from those still loitering in and out of buildings—Leopold noticed that the pubs were still full—no one seemed to take offense of him. They appeared to know who Leopold was, and anyone with Leopold Kazsmer was a bit of all right by them.

Nevertheless, he took Raj's arm and magicked them to the meadow by the Gypsy camp. It was empty again, and Leopold feared they had moved on after all, taking his father with them…but he noticed the wheel ruts from their caravans leading out of the meadow and followed them to the place that they had camped before.

All the Romani were still here! Someone noticed Leopold and hailed him, calling out to everyone. Soon Romani were pouring out of their wagons to greet him.

He acknowledged their handshakes and backslaps—and they even greeted Raj with wary cheer. But when Leopold cast a glance toward Yanko's caravan, no one emerged. He stalked across the beaten-down grass, leapt up the short steps, and opened both Dutch doors.

"Papa?"

Yanko and Àkos had arms slung over each other and were both singing an old Hungarian song while quite drunk.

Leopold released a sigh and rested his fists at his hips. "Papa. Uncle Yanko."

"Oh ho! Leopold, my nephew!" Yanko tried to rise, couldn't, until Àkos pushed him to his wobbly feet.

"My son! You must have won. Thank the Lord!"

Leopold widened his arms to encompass both of them. "Yes, I won. Everyone is safe again. Except for the two of you. Getting drunk. For shame."

"It was the end of the world, Leopold," cried his uncle. "I can think of no better way to face it."

Conceding, Leopold took off his hat and set it aside. "I can't argue with that. Pass the bottle."

THIRTY MINUTES LATER there was a knock on the caravan door. "Come in," all three drunken voices called out.

The door opened and Raj stuck his head in. "Leopold?"

"Come in Raj, my brassy friend!"

"Er…Leopold. Mister Kazsmer. Mister…Péntek?"

"Ah!" said Àkos. "Your mechanical friend. Come closer. I would like to examine you."

"Perhaps another time. Leopold, didn't you say you wanted to get your father home?"

"Oh *yes*! Papa, you must come home with me and see my flat."

"So," said Yanko, getting unsteadily to his feet. "You are leaving. Well…I never like you."

Àkos rose and grabbed his coat, pulling it on, though he was having trouble pushing his arm through the sleeve. "And I never liked *you*, you old goat."

"Wait, wait," said Leopold. "You two were getting along just fine an hour ago. Longer."

"Well..." said Yanko. "The gin helped."

Leopold ran his hand through his hair, pushing the long locks back off his forehead. "I seem to be a bit drunk." He waved his hand without even thinking about it, and suddenly he was sober. He blinked and licked his lips.

He hadn't expected the spell to wash over the others, but they were abruptly sober as well.

Yanko shook out his quickly clearing head. "Leopold! What did you do?"

He chuckled. "I'm sorry, Uncle Yanko. I didn't mean for my spell to go so wide. But in the end, it's a good thing, isn't it? No after affects."

"Leopold is right," said Àkos, patting his son's shoulder. "He did us a favor."

"Maybe I wanted to be drunk. Maybe I don't have any more gin."

"Don't be a drunkard, Yanko," growled Àkos and finished donning his coat.

"Who's a drunkard? *You're* a drunkard!"

"I don't want to fight with you, Yanko. We were getting along. And...it was nice for a change of pace."

"Bah. You were just lonely."

Àkos nodded. "Yes," he said quietly. "I have been lonely for seventeen years."

Yanko lowered his face and ran his hand over his beard stubble. "*Hát akkor...*" he muttered, abashed. "No wonder you have so much to say."

Àkos smiled and slung his arm over Yanko's shoulders. "I will be back, old friend. We will talk more. We will talk about...Sárika. We are both old enough now that the past can be put aside, eh?"

"Maybe is true. But we will need more gin."

"That I can bring." Àkos ran his hand over his beard. "I long to bathe properly and give myself a shave. I think I am tired of this beard."

"Come along, Papa."

He walked him out of the caravan and looked back over his shoulder toward Yanko. "Thank you, Uncle," he mouthed.

Yanko waved him off, but he watched them walk across the crushed grass between the caravans. Leopold had a feeling that the Romani might just stay this time. At least for a little while longer.

Raj looked across the plain toward the railway station. "How shall we get to your flat, Leo? I don't know if there are any trains."

"I hadn't thought of that. Look. I can manage it if the both of you are very still." He linked arms with each of them. "Still, now." He closed his eyes and the now familiar and welcoming Earth magic that was already there seemed to fill him from the depths of the ground, melding him and his companions into a mist...

...and then they appeared directly before his lodgings. Leopold paused for a moment to collect himself before he climbed the stairs first and, as he put the key in the lock and dropped the ward with a wave of his hand, he suddenly remembered his *one*-bedroom flat.

Mingli was bound to return. He wanted her to spend the night...

Closing his eyes, he concentrated, signing sigils in the air that flew about the outside of the house and showered down a golden veil around it before it dissipated into the ether. Only then did he push open the door and step into his foyer.

"Papa...let me take you to your room. It's quite private and you will be very comfortable there."

"Leo?" said Raj.

"Not now, Raj. Please, make yourself comfortable in the drawing room."

He walked with his father to a staircase that hadn't been there before, slightly surprised that it actually appeared. He trudged up the carpeted steps and to a door. He closed his hand on the doorknob—solid enough in his hand—and turned it. When he opened it, he was pleased to see a large carved bed, wardrobe, side table and comfortable (and worn) upholstered chair. He sent a spark to the oil lamp on the side table that was covered with a tasseled cloth, and sent another toward the fireplace, lighting the coal. He looked around, pleased with his handiwork. "And through that door, is your bath." At least, he was fairly certain it was there.

"This is very nice, Leo. You have done well. I'm very proud of you, my son."

"Thank you, Papa. There is a razor and all you will need within the bath. Come down when you are ready."

He leaned in and kissed his father's cheek. He made to leave but Àkos pulled him back into a tight embrace. Leopold let his face rest on the man's shoulder and closed his eyes, tears squeezing through as he held his boney father at last. He pulled back and looked at him. "Do get rid of that beard. I barely recognize you." He held his shoulders, feeling the joints under his fingers. "And we will fatten you up again."

"Does your Mingli cook?"

He stopped in the doorway. "You know…I have no idea." He shook his head, wondering, and closed the door after him.

When he returned downstairs, he took up the speaking tube in the foyer and rang the bell. He couldn't hope that Mrs. Granville would have remained…and yet she answered. "Mrs. Granville! You're here."

"I reckoned that your house would be safe enough when demons came a'calling," her tinny voice replied through the tube.

"I'm grateful you're all right. Er…we could use some tea and sandwiches. My…my father is living with me now. In…in the upstairs room?"

"Very good, Mr. Kazsmer."

Smiling, he put the tube back on its stalk. His spell seemed to have worked thoroughly, even to changing *her* memory of what the house looked like. Success indeed!

Doffing his hat and overcoat and hanging them in the foyer, he moved to the drawing room and dropped into a soft chair. Raj was standing and looking at him, until he lifted his glass eyes to the noise on the top floor. "I don't recall you having a top floor, Leo."

"I didn't. But…I do now."

"Your skills have reached an amazing level. You have learned a great deal in a short time."

"Yes, I have. It's…almost overwhelming."

They both heard the rattle of crockery at the back stair and Raj lurched this way and that, trying to find a place to hide.

"No more hiding, Raj. I think you will be welcomed from now on. The people on the street accepted you. Let's try it with Mrs. Granville."

Raj stiffened as she opened the servant's entrance with her tea tray, shuffled across the carpet, and put it down on the table. She straightened and immediately saw Raj. "Oh!" she said uncertainly. "I suppose…that it's to be expected now, Mr. Kazsmer. Strange people and strange…what-have-yous."

Raj placed his porcelain hand on his chest and bowed. "Greetings, Mrs. Granville. I am Raj, Mr. Kazsmer's friend."

"You're…you're a machine, are you? Possessed with demons? I don't know that I care for that."

"Oh no, my dear woman. I am not possessed. I am merely a…a creature with a mechanical body and a soul inside." It was obvious that he took pleasure in the saying of it. "And I must assure you, the only daemons you will be seeing from now on are the good kind."

She swallowed and put a hand to her throat. "There are *good* kinds?"

"Absolutely."

"And *I* can assure you of that, Mrs. Granville," said Leopold, standing, taking her arm, and gently directing her to the stair. "And you'll meet them in time. They helped me to stop the malevolence threatening our city. They are quite good-natured. You'll see. I hope…I hope that this is all right."

"Mr. Kazsmer, the things I seen this day, I reckon I can manage the occasional good…demon…as you say." She looked back at Raj. "Shall I bring another cup?"

"I'm afraid Raj doesn't eat."

"Oh. Er…very well." She gave a brief half-curtsey, and backed out of the room, hurriedly passing through the door and closing it behind her.

"Well…that's that." He sat and took up the tea pot. "Raj, old thing, I wish you could enjoy a cup of tea with me."

"I shouldn't be surprised that you can conjure me a way to do so."

"I'll work on that."

He drank the tea and lay back against the chair with a sigh. He had to admit to himself, that tea was the best salve to his soul. As were the sounds upstairs of his father in his new bath.

IT TOOK AN hour, but Àkos appeared gingerly at the doorway. He had shaved off his beard and mustache and cut his hair as best he could, pomaded it, smoothed it back off his forehead, and parted it in the middle. Leopold gasped. The man looked like his father again.

Leopold met him at the door and led him to the chair. "Sit, Papa. Have some tea."

"Real tea," he breathed. Leopold heated it again with a wave of his hand, poured it the way he liked it with two sugars and a splash of milk and handed him the saucer. Àkos grabbed a sandwich and put it on a plate. "I hope this is no dream. It doesn't feel like one."

"It isn't, Papa. This is real. We are together again at last."

"And Raj. I am glad Leopold has had such a friend."

"I quite enjoyed meeting your son." He nestled into his cushioned chair next to Àkos, but hadn't quite got the knack of crossing his brass legs. "I was with him when he first started his magic act. I am known as the Amazing Raj, the Automated Man. Usually, I sit behind a table reading the cards."

"Fortune-telling? I thought that was all fakery."

"For some, Mister Kazsmer, not for me."

"Oh, please. You must call me Àkos. We are all friends here."

"I shall be very pleased to do so."

Àkos took a bite of his sandwich and instantly a look of ecstasy crossed his features. "A real sandwich."

"Didn't Uncle Yanko feed you."

Àkos swallowed. "Yes. He cooks the same way he always had."

"Oh yes. I forgot."

"But where is your Mingli? I expected to find her here. And our daemon friend."

"Eurynomos had to return to Gehenna and repair the damage the Unholy Hosts had wreaked."

Àkos' eyes darkened. "They are gone?"

"They are gone *forever*, Papa."

"That is good. Very good." He grabbed an egg sandwich and bit into it.

"And Miss Zhao is busy talking to the queen, I imagine."

Àkos coughed and, as Raj was closer, he obliged by leaning forward and slapping Àkos on the back several times.

"I'm all right," he said, waving off Raj. "The…the queen, did you say? Of England?"

"Yes." Leopold smiled proudly over his cuppa. "And I met her too, and talked with Prince Albert."

"The devil you say. Why! My own son, talking with the queen."

"I think you will find that my fiancée is quite an unusual woman and a bit headstrong. But I have it on good authority from the Prince Consort himself that he approves of such women."

"And so do I. Your mother was such a woman."

"I don't remember that. I only remember her sweetness to me."

"Your mother adored you. She would have been proud, too."

"I hope so. So much has happened in the last six months, it's all running together."

The doorbell chimed.

"That should be our Miss Zhao." But as he neared the front door, he saw two figures standing there through the frosted glass.

He opened the door and stood back. "Why…Agnes…Aimee. What are you doing here?"

His twin female assistants exchanged a look. "What'd I tell you, Aimee?" said Agnes in her brassy Cockney. "Didn't I say it was Mister K what saved the day? I said that to Aimee."

Leopold felt his cheeks flush with heat again and opened the door wider. "You'd best come in." He grabbed the speaking tube and asked for more cups and sandwiches.

They were both dressed the same in purple dresses with black lace trim. They weren't supposed to be seen together, but he didn't suppose it much mattered today. He led them into the drawing room. When Àkos saw them, he got to his feet with a smile.

And then Agnes spotted Raj. "Oh, it's Mister Raj. Good day to you." She curtseyed.

"And a good day it is…seeing you, Miss Agnes."

She moved forward and stood directly in front of him, almost too close, but Raj didn't seem to mind. "I'm so glad you and Mister K survived it all. I hope your daemon friend came out of it, too."

Leopold offered an embarrassed smile. "Yes, we all got through it. Eurynomos is busy elsewhere. We won't ever have to be afraid of a repeat of what we just experienced."

"It was Mr. Kazsmer," Raj rushed in to say. "He and Eurynomos and his fiancée drove the villains out. You have him to thank for saving all our lives."

Agnes whirled and stalked up to Leopold. For a dread moment, he thought she might embrace him. Even kiss him.

"Oh Mister K! How can we ever thank you!"

"By calling me 'Mister Kazsmer'?"

She brayed a horse laugh and swatted the air, dismissing him with the gesture. "What'd I tell you, Aimee? It was Mister…*Kazsmer* what done it." She turned back to him with a charming smile. "But what is this about a fiancée?" Her curls whipped about as she looked this way and that.

Mrs. Granville entered again with a tray of cups and saucers, some cake on a tiered plate, and more sandwiches. She seemed relieved that humans were in attendance, and she quickly left the tray.

"Won't you ladies have some tea?" said Leopold, gesturing toward the settee.

"Don't mind if we do." She patted the seat beside her and her sister dutifully sat.

Leopold cleared his throat. "Er…yes. You haven't met her yet, my fiancée. She's a Special Inspector for Scotland Yard."

"Ooooh. Did she work with Inspector Thacker?"

"Well…only after he'd…he'd died."

She elbowed Aimee. "Ain't that a corker! You meet the most interesting people around Mr. Kazsmer."

The usually silent Aimee looked around and quietly asked, "Where *is* Inspector Thacker?"

Leopold sobered. He moved to stand before her and took both her hands in his. "I'm afraid, Aimee, that he has gone on to his final reward.

I know you didn't get to enjoy his company as much as *we* had, but just know this: he is in the best of places. But sadly, he won't be coming back."

She lowered her eyes and nodded.

"Believe me, I miss him, too."

"I keep expecting to see him come through the wall," said Raj softly.

Agnes scooted closer to her sister and rubbed her shoulder. "I'm sorry, Aimee. I know you liked him. But he *was* a ghost, after all."

She nodded, eyes still lowered.

Leopold gestured to the tea. "Why didn't the two of you leave London for safety?"

Agnes shrugged as she poured two cups and handed one to her twin. "Where were we to go? We spent the last few hours huddled in the basement with the rest of the people in the boarding house. Aimee and I sang them songs to keep their spirits up."

"That was nice of you…but you aren't supposed to allow people to see the two of you together."

"Pish tosh, Mister K…I mean Mr. Kazsmer. It was more important to calm people down. And blimey, we knew that you'd be out there seeing to things. We weren't all that scared, were we, Aimee?"

Aimee finally raised her reddened eyes and solemnly shook her head.

"And I reckon with your magic, you can make people forget they ever saw Aimee and me together, right Mr. Kazsmer?"

"I reckon I can. But…I don't know if I'm headlining anymore at the King's Garden Theatre."

"I thought you had a contract with that Barnabas Dawes, the owner."

Leopold straightened his shoulders. "You know something? I do. Why that blackguard. He can't do this to me. We have a contract!"

"Leopold, Leopold," said his father. "Is this the time to worry over contracts? Why don't you introduce me to these lovely ladies first?"

That pulled him up short. No, this wasn't the time to worry over stage shows. London was in a shambles and needed repairing first. And he surely could work on that himself. Afterwards, he'd be in very good stead indeed.

"Forgive me. Ladies, this is…my father, Àkos Kazsmer. And these are the Templeton sisters. That's Agnes, and that's Aimee."

Àkos bowed. "It is lovely to meet you two."

Agnes beamed. "Will you look at that, Aimee? That's where our Mister Kazsmer gets his good manners from. It is a pleasure to meet you, sir."

They chatted amiably with one another for a time. Agnes even jumped up and showed Àkos how she and her sister performed for Leopold and why twins were needed. Àkos was amused by all of it, starved as he was for company. But Leopold recognized when his father, exhausted as he likely was, struggled to stay awake.

He rose and announced, "It was a pleasure, your having come over, Agnes and Aimee. But my father has had a long journey and needs to get to bed."

"Don't be silly, Leopold…"

"Now Papa, don't argue. It's time for bed. Come along now."

"Our boarding house is still intact, so we will be going too. It was a pleasure, Mr. Kazsmer," she said, extending her hand to Àkos. He took it and kissed it, and then kissed Aimee's over her glove.

Agnes tittered while marching to the foyer and the front door, but when she pulled it open, Mingli stood in the doorway.

"My dear," said Leopold. "Er…Agnes, Aimee, this is Miss Zhao…my fiancée."

"Pleased to meet'cha," said Agnes, pumping Mingli's hand. "What'd I tell you, Aimee? The *most* interesting people. Ta, Mister K! I mean, Mr. *Kazsmer*."

They left in a flutter of feathers and lace, with the sound of Agnes' braying laugh and her loud voice still ringing down the street.

"The Templeton twins," said Mingli with a sigh. She allowed Leopold to kiss her on the cheek before she strode into the drawing room.

"Àkos! How well you look. The beard did nothing for you."

"Miss Zhao."

"We really can't have that. I am Mingli to you." She kissed *his* cheek.

"Ah! The advantage of not having a beard. Lovely women give you kisses."

"I was just sending my father up to bed."

She glanced to the ceiling. "Up?"

"Yes. To his ensuite. Upstairs. The, er, new one."

She pulled the hat pin free of her hair and removed her clever millinery. "I see. Well, I'll just put this in our bedroom then, shall I? I could use some tea and sandwiches."

She disappeared through the doorway. Àkos grabbed Leopold's arm and dragged him near the servant's stair. "What does she mean 'our' room?" he rasped. "She's not living here, is she?"

"Well…I…"

"Leopold! For shame!"

"Papa, this is a different day from when you and Mama were our age. This is 1891. There's such a thing as free love, you know."

"Free love. Love is *not* free. You'll see." He stormed in a circle and came back to face Leopold, pointing a finger into his face. "And does she agree with you? Are you forcing her?"

"Papa, no! Of course not!" He certainly didn't want to mention that it was her idea in the first place. "We are two adults who know what we are doing. And we are anxious to seal our mutual affections with marriage vows."

"It's supposed to be the other way around."

"Papa, keep your voice down! She can hear you."

"Never fear, Àkos," said Mingli, striding into the room, divested of her hat and her jacket, revealing a white blouse with a cascade of white lace over her bosom. "Your son is not corrupting me. If anything, it is *I* who am corrupting him."

Leopold dropped his face into his hand. *Oh dear.*

"And he's perfectly right," she continued, threading her arm through Leopold's. "We do have mutual affections and we are more than happy to join our houses in matrimony. All very consensual, I can assure you."

"But…but Miss Zhao. Mingli. Daughter. It isn't seemly—"

"Let me stop you there, Àkos. The life I have led…well. When danger lurked in every corner and each day, each *hour* could be one's last, I have found it more than expeditious to grab life by the throat, to indulge in a few practices that the general public might consider unseemly…and that the upper classes indulged in with frequency. I feel no guilt, nor do I truck with those who would heap their morality upon me. I am who I am, sir. But all *you* need know is that I love your son with all my being. And he—and only he—is who I plan to cleave to for the rest of my life."

It appeared to be Leopold's day for blushing, for he couldn't seem to stop. He glanced at Mingli with all the love in his heart, forgetting completely that his father stood there before them. When he turned to his father, he lowered his eyes. "You see how it is with us, Papa. Please don't scold."

Àkos blew out a breath and threw his hands into the air. "Sárika! See what you have left me with! Ah, me. Yes, I suppose it *is* a different day. You will both be married, in any case." That finger was back into Leopold's face. "Make certain that it is soon!"

Leopold offered a sheepish smile, snaking his arm around her waist and pulling her tightly against him. "Yes, sir."

IN HIS DARKENED room and flushed with love, Leopold kissed his fiancée as they lay under the sheets and blankets, sliding his hands along her smooth skin. He wondered why she ever wore a corset at all. She certainly didn't need one with her dainty waist…but he admitted to a strange attraction to her wearing it…and nothing else.

The kiss had begun heated, but gentled to something softer when he finally drew back. He couldn't help but gaze at her face, then down to her shadowed *décolletage* hidden by her luxurious black locks, free of their coiffure. "I love kissing you," he whispered. His body covered hers from waist to foot. And even though they had just made love, he felt a stirring again.

She reached up and ran a finger along his mustache, as she seemed fond of doing. "I love kissing *you*. Because this mustache makes it so delightfully ticklish."

He waggled his brows. "I noticed very well how you like my mustache…*tickling* you."

"You are quite incorrigible, Mr. Kazsmer."

"I know. But after all, it was you who released me from my inhibitions."

"I do feel a certain satisfaction with that." Her hand had moved to his neck, stroking the hair at the back of his head. The touch sent a shiver down his spine. "I'm sorry I got you in trouble with your father."

"It's not your fault. I just wanted to be with you. And nothing in Heaven, Earth…or Gehenna was going to stop me."

He smiled and leaned in again for another soft kiss that ended up being longer than he expected. His hand below the blanket slid upward, touching things that gave him a little thrill in his belly. He leaned in and kissed her neck and then his finger traced her cheek, down her small nose, and lower to her chin, simply exploring. "I love making love to you. It's ridiculous how happy I am." He gazed at her face. "Your mouth. It's so delectable…" He couldn't help planting his lips to hers again. "For so many things," he whispered, still touching them with his own.

They indulged in this way for a few moments before Leopold drew back again.

"Do you know what I love about you?" she said.

He smiled, letting that smile—and his mustache—do its work on her skin. "Tell me."

"You're extraordinary. You're wise beyond your years. And courageous and funny, and despite all that has happened to you, you love life. It's quite intoxicating."

He drew back to look down on her. "And you? Do *you* love life?"

She cocked her head, gazing at him. "I do now."

He recognized a melancholy underlying her words, and it tore at his heart. "Mingli…if you wanted…if you so desired, I *could* make you forget…"

She never hesitated. "No, I don't think so. Despite some of it, I am grateful to know that I survived it through my own courage and willpower. It's…important to know oneself that way." She suddenly reached up and twined her arms around his neck. And with kisses she whispered to his lips, "But I am more than grateful that you offered."

They indulged in each other's mouths thus for quite some time until Leopold broke away with a sigh. There was no more melancholy in her eyes and his heart was glad.

"I, er, quite forgot to ask you how your visit with the queen went." Another kiss.

She slid out from under him—and he forced himself not to pout—as she sat up against the pillows, pulling the sheet up to cover her bosom. Yet another reason to pout, he mused. "It was very detailed, and very long. I'm afraid I…offered your assistance to repair London as you repaired St Paul's. Forgive me for that. I realize I didn't ask your permission first."

"I'd already decided to do it. You just saved me the trouble."

"Thank you for being so understanding."

"Well, in this case, it's purely selfish on my part. I can't start my shows again until London is up and running."

She smiled, her eyes measuring him as she cocked her head. "Purely selfish. Of course. And…would you like to tell me about this phantom upper floor that your father now inhabits?" She fluttered her lashes.

"Oh." He sat back against his own pillows. "Well…again, purely self-interest. I would have had to give him *our* room. But since I expected to enjoy your company…as we just have..." He grinned. "…it was then necessary for him to have his own accommodations. I should apologize to you for assuming we'd be thus…engaged."

"Did you ever doubt it?"

He couldn't help the blush yet *again* to his cheeks. "I'm afraid I didn't entertain it even once."

She slapped his shoulder. Gently, thank goodness.

"So you see," he explained, "I quickly created him his own floor…and modified the neighborhood inhabitants' memories to remember it the way it is now, rather than in the past."

She leaned toward him. "Leo! How long did this take you?"

"Oh…a few seconds. I didn't have a lot of time to—"

"Leopold Kazsmer! Do you realize the scope of your talents? It's a good bloody thing you're on our side."

"Miss Zhao. Really! Language."

She smirked in a way that made him shiver. "I'll show you language."

She threw the blankets aside, revealing her shapely form. Her eyes roved over him with a certain predatory look as she climbed atop his thighs. "I *expect* to hear some language," she purred, before leaning in and kissing him quite thoroughly.

EPILOGUE

THREE WEEKS LATER—after London's burned buildings had been set to rights, the railway stations repaired, and Queen Victoria herself had knighted Leopold—his father and Uncle Yanko sitting in attendance and both popping the buttons on their waistcoats with pride—Leopold was preparing to wed one Mingli Zhao…or, as she corrected him when they filled in their certificate, "Zhao Mingli," family name first, but, she explained, it was too much trouble in western society to keep reminding the everyday person of this.

Àkos had found an old friend who was a rabbi, one Géza Németh. He was overjoyed to discover that Àkos was alive. It had been a tearful reunion, and, after several conversations, he had agreed to preside over the marriage of a Jew to a Chinese woman who had no discernable faith…at a Gypsy camp.

On the afternoon of the wedding, they all waited in the middle of a circle of Romani caravans, near a smoky fire, and with the presence of dogs wandering about and sniffing the new guests.

A most unusual gathering it was! Àkos, of course, and Uncle Yanko standing together, along with Miklos Antalek, and all the other Romani of the camp, clean and respectful, and keeping a wary eye on a very tall, red daemon with horns, who was grinning from ear to ear and wearing nothing but a long, black breechclout; an imp with bat-wings fluttering around the circle and wearing nothing at all; an automaton in a gold turban wearing a boiled shirt and swallow-tail coat, with long, insect-like brass legs polished to a bright sheen; and two identical twin ladies, one of whom was chatting incessantly to the Romani women around them.

The bride was dressing in the groom's uncle's caravan with the help of Zsófia Antalek, while all and sundry anxiously awaited her arrival.

Finally, the caravan's door opened a crack, and Mrs. Antalek signaled to the musicians. They began to play an old Hungarian wedding song. The violins spun out slow with sweet tones, while the parlor guitar strummed out the melody.

Mrs. Antalek emerged first, opening wide the door. Mingli was suddenly standing in the doorway and gracefully descended the steps. She was all in red silk in some sort of traditional Chinese raiment riotously embroidered with dragons and flowers, with long medieval sleeves that were almost as long as her layered skirts. Her hair was piled-up with elaborate braiding and topped with a gold headdress with red tassels at both ears. She had chosen not to wear her eye patch, and though the galaxy eye was only a little strange if one looked closely, it gave her the overall appearance of any bright-eyed young woman on her wedding day.

"She's beautiful," whispered Leopold to his best man, Eurynomos. Leopold couldn't help his mouth gaping at the splendor of his bride.

The groom was dressed in his finest suit, with a swallow-tail coat, white cravat, white waistcoat, and crowned with a silk top hat. But he simply couldn't compare…to her.

She reached out with one hand to take the arm of her father-in-law, whilst a spray of lilies lay across her other arm. She walked toward Leopold, her face passive, until she gave him the quickest of winks. There was just the touch of pink to her cheeks and a blush of rouge to her lips—as she always prepared herself. But today, in such a dress, with such poise and grace, she seemed like a different person. Like an empress. The person he wished he had known all those years ago before life had hardened her. But no. This was not a day to look back, he told himself as he took her delicate hand in his. Did it tremble ever so slightly? Or was it *his* hand that shook? Very likely. For he could not stop looking at her. "You're beautiful," he breathed to her ear as she joined him under the chuppah, upheld by staffs on each of its four corners by Romani men (Leopold had had to assure them that they must keep their hats *on* to be respectful).

She gave him a secret smile before she turned to face to the rabbi, Àkos' old friend.

"My children," said the rabbi, "I am more than gratified on this joyous occasion to join the son of my old friend—Leopold Àkos Kazsmer to the lovely Zhao Mingli—in wedded bliss. We stand under the sky beneath this canopy in the Jewish tradition. It symbolizes the home they will build together. But you will note, that it is held at each of the four corners by their community. This is no accident. It is because a house does not build itself, nor is a family created out of thin air. Its foundations are created long ago from the traditions of each of their families and friends; of their experiences and of what they build together with all of these tools. Two people make a home. But our family and friends build a community that helps that home thrive. And so, let us now, together, pray to the Creator of all things."

As the rabbi intoned the Hebrew prayers and everyone had lowered their faces, Leopold could not keep himself from gazing at his bride. As if sensing this—of course she did!—Mingli glanced at him. And he could see nothing but love in her gaze.

He completely forgot to listen to the rabbi, for all he could see was her…encased in a cloud of her lilac perfume. Beside him he heard Eurynomos sob, and he repressed a chuckle at it. Mingli pressed her lips together, and they shared that first secret joke between them as the rabbi recited the prayers that would bind them.

He looked up suddenly when the rabbi asked a second time if he "took this woman."

He answered in the affirmative, and replied to all the rabbi's questions, as did Mingli when it was her turn.

A glass wrapped in a cloth was passed to the rabbi. "*By the rivers of Babylon, there we sat, sat and wept, as we thought of Zion.* In our tradition—as it is the tradition of the Romani—we think of the sadness of the past even in a happy moment such as this. And so we break a glass to remember the destruction of the Temple in Jerusalem, our spiritual home." He set the wrapped glass down at Leopold's feet.

Thinking of the past that was no more, the sadness that he and his father both endured, and how it was now truly *in* the past, Leopold stomped hard on it. The glass clinked inside its cloth.

"*Mazel tov*!" cried both Àkos and Eurynomos.

The Romani burst into cheers.

Leopold turned to his bride, edged forward, and kissed her. "Mister and Missus Kazsmer," he murmured to her lips.

"Yes," she said.

IT COULD NOT be said that the Romani did not know how to celebrate. Besides the wedding feast of a roasted lamb on the spit, there was wine aplenty, the musicians played all the traditional music, and dancers danced for the wedding couple at their table.

Leopold poured more wine into Mingli's glass. "Don't worry, my dear," he said with a slight slur. "I know a spell that will sober us up quick as a wink. It really works."

"I have no doubt." She, on the other hand, having drunk just as much as Leopold, didn't sound the least bit drunk.

Suddenly, Eurynomos was standing before their table. "I should very much like to have a dance with the beautiful bride." He bowed. He sounded a little drunk himself. And he hadn't been dry-eyed since the wedding. Even now, he brushed tears of joy from his eyes.

Mingli rose and took his proffered hand—hers appearing so small in his over-large palm. "I would be delighted."

Leopold watched as his daemon friend waltzed with his wife—his *wife*! He shook his head in silent disbelief, took a sip, and decided that his sobering spell would be a good idea about now. He waved his hand and gasped at the sudden sensation of alcohol vanishing from his system. "That's potent," he muttered.

"Leopold!" said his uncle, leaning over to poke at his nephew. "You're going to let a daemon steal your thunder? Whose wedding is it?"

"He's a good friend, Uncle Yanko."

"But you are the groom. Take your bride for a dance."

Everyone joined in with the yelling of "dance with her!" and he knew he could no longer refuse. He rose, pulled his waistcoat taut, and strode out to the center where everyone was dancing. He tapped Eurynomos on the shoulder and the daemon turned.

"You don't mind if I take my bride for a turn on the dance floor, do you?"

Eurynomos burst into another sob and embraced Leopold before he released him and pushed him toward Mingli.

He grasped her hand, gently cupped her waist, and smiled. "You look stunning, my dear."

"You shouldn't keep saying that to me."

"Why not? You're beautiful and I don't care who knows it."

"Well, you're beautiful, too. Did you know?"

"Shouldn't I rather be called 'handsome'."

"If you prefer. But you are a beautiful man…to me."

He leaned in and kissed her. Cheers went up and all took a drink.

"This is going to go long into the night, isn't it?" she said.

"Only until the wine runs out."

"There's no hope of that, is there."

"Why Mrs. Kazsmer, are you trying to get me into bed, by any chance?"

"This *is* our wedding night."

"Come to think of it, I wouldn't mind you seducing me at that."

"You've already been seduced."

"So I have. Well and truly."

"Then perhaps we should begin to say our goodnights."

He whirled her once, bowed, kissed her hand, and led her away from the makeshift wooden plank floor.

Mingli signaled to Mrs. Antalek and they both retreated into Yanko's caravan to help change her into her traveling clothes.

Leopold cast a glance to the dancefloor, where Raj had not stopped dancing all night with Agnes Templeton. He wondered vaguely when and where the perpetually seated automaton had learned to dance before he discovered his legs, when he dismissed the thought.

Suchah fluttered over to Leopold. "Mechanical man Raj tried to explain this to Suchah, but Suchah still doesn't understand. What *is* a wedding?"

"A wedding? Well, Mingli and I are now officially together."

"But were you not together before?"

"Well…yes, but…as the rabbi said, this is our community knowing it with a special ritual."

"Ah, ritual. Who is to be sacrificed then?"

"No, Suchah, we don't kill anyone. We just celebrate with music, food, drink, and dance."

"Hmm. Does not sound as much fun without bloodshed, but Suchah supposes you know best…" Though he didn't quite look convinced.

"I wish Thacker were here," Leopold said wistfully.

Suchah nodded. "Would not have minded if the Cheating Ghost was here. Suchah is fond of your friends."

"They're your friends now too, Suchah. There's no getting around it."

"Strange," he said.

Raj stalked up, locking his knees. "And so, Leo, my friend."

"I'm so glad you were here, Raj. As yourself, and not some display at a table."

"So am I." He turned to glance at Agnes in the distance, wiggling her fingers at him in a wave.

Leopold sidled closer and lowered his voice. "What is between you and Agnes?"

Raj shrugged. "I don't know, Leo. I have never been in this situation before. I was wondering if I couldn't get a little advice from you."

"Oh. Well, surely you realize I haven't had any experience with women before this. But, I suppose, all I know is that I was smitten by Miss Zhao…even when I wasn't certain she was trying to kill me or not."

Raj nodded sagely. "This is certainly a testimonial to the lady's charms."

"Indeed. Look, old man, if Agnes makes you feel as special as you surely are, then I suppose that's all you need." *Except for certain missing anatomical parts*, he mused.

"I suppose all that will come in time. But as for you, my friend, I have it on the best authority that you will be very happy. I read the cards."

"Damn. Why would you do such a thing?"

"It is in my nature, I'm afraid. But it showed only good things ahead, Leo. So don't worry. I never would have mentioned it if it hadn't."

He was actually a bit relieved. He worried over Mingli's many enemies, as she said, but they already decided to look for other lodgings. A house of their own outside the city, where they could ward it properly. That sounded…peaceful. And she was the one to suggest Àkos continue to live with them. They seemed to get along. He had walked in on the two of them more than once when they were having a most spirited discussion of the Kabbalah.

Raj waved his farewells and joined Agnes again.

Eurynomos had been dancing with some of the Gypsy girls and finally came over.

"You seem rather popular," Leopold commented.

"Can I help it if women naturally find me appealing?"

And it has absolutely nothing to do with that breechclout, he said to himself, not ever intending to say so aloud.

"But where is Miss…dear me. I must get used to saying *Mrs.* Kazsmer."

"She's changing. We're getting ready to leave."

"On your honeymoon cruise! I'm so pleased." He wiped his tears again. "Listen, old man." He grabbed Leopold's arm and dragged him away from the others with his apologies. "I didn't want to mention this in front of the others."

"What is it, Eurynomos?"

"Well…it's about your wedding gift."

"Oh that. You don't have to worry about it. You don't owe me anything."

"But that's just it. I already got you a gift weeks ago. A very special gift. You've done an excellent job repairing London, but I'm good at repairing things too, you know, and when you told me that sad tale of our Miss Zhao, well. Just know that this gift will be a little while in coming. I'd say…" He glanced toward Mingli just coming down the stairs of Yanko's caravan, dressed in her usual green satin traveling clothes. Eurynomos leaned in. "I'd say it will arrive in about…nine months? Ta, Leopold. *Bon voyage*!"

Leopold squinted at the daemon quizzically. Eurynomos rushed to Mingli and closed her into a tearful embrace.

And then the other shoe dropped.

With widened eyes, Leopold whipped around towards his wife. *Oh dear*. "Mingli. *Mingli*!"

This concludes the Enchanter Chronicles Trilogy

AUTHOR'S AFTERWORD

LEOPOLD'S ADVENTURES HAVE come to a close at last. I've quite enjoyed writing these Neo-Victorian tales, and got to know and love these characters. Who's to say that we don't revisit them again at some other time with a new set of trilogies?

In fact, I enjoyed the research so much that I am exploring another mystery series set in the *real* Victorian London.

I found researching Jewish mysticism fascinating and eye-opening. Besides different numbers having grave significance, there are also certain colors with their own meanings, and special words (one might even consider these "magic" words, like "Abracadabra". It may have its roots in a corruption of Aramaic, *ab'ra k'dabra,* meaning "I will create according to the word", but this is not proven by linguists) and much more as part of the pantheon that encompasses the Kabbalah and other books of Jewish mysticism.

The Hebrew Scriptures—what most people call the "Old Testament"—are full of such symbolism of numbers, colors, and words. It takes some deep diving into history, languages, and customs to completely appreciate the full meaning of those texts.

I'd always been taught, for instance, that Jews had no Hell, but I suppose that isn't quite true. Gehenna is quite the Dante's Inferno. The levels of Gehenna are as described according to the Talmud and other texts, though I took many liberties with angels and other aspects of Gehenna. It is a paranormal tale, after all. You can find pictures of real incantation bowls on the internet, by the way, and yes, the clay was to be obtained from graveyards. But they were to capture demons, not to keep any portals open. No one certainly would have wanted to do that.

I appreciate your support of my writings. I'd also like to direct you to the very excellent audiobooks where narrator/performer Noah James Butler animates these stories to epic proportion. You will be entertained, I assure you.

I think Mingli Zhao is now my favorite superhero, for surely, she would have attained that status with her verve and chutzpah. Oh what adventures she and Leo will have beyond these pages!

Thanks for reading. You can always find more of my books at JeriWesterson.com. If you enjoy a book, please review it. Cheers.

ABOUT THE AUTHOR

JERI WESTERSON is the author of the critically acclaimed Crispin Guest Medieval Noir mysteries. She also writes historical novels and several paranormal series. An award-winning author, her medieval mysteries were also nominated thirteen times for national mystery awards, from the Agatha to the Shamus. Jeri lives in Menifee, CA, mother to a gray senior cat and a laconic tortoise.

JeriWesterson.com

www.ingramcontent.com/pod-product-compliance
Lightning Source LLC
LaVergne TN
LVHW091042080826
845145LV00002B/592

* 9 7 8 1 7 3 5 6 1 6 0 1 8 *